IN THE

HOUR

OF

CROWS

IN THE HOUR OF CROWS

DANA ELMENDORF

mira

ISBN-13: 978-0-7783-1049-5

In the Hour of Crows

Mira
22 Adelaide St. West, 41st Floor
Toronto, Ontario M5H 4E3, Canada

Printed in U.S.A.

To my daddy and all our mornings of porch sitting

PROLOGUE

I was born in the woods in the hour of crows, when the day is no longer but the night is not yet. Grandmama Agnes brought me into this world with her bare hands. Just as her mother had taught her to do. Just as the mother before her taught. Just as she would teach me. Midwife, herbalist, superstitionist—all the practices of her Appalachian roots passed down for generations.

And a few new tricks picked up along the way.

Before Papaw died, he warned me Grandmama Agnes was wicked. He was wrong. It wasn't just Grandmama who was wicked; so was I.

I knew it was true the night those twin babies died.

"Weatherly." Grandmama's sleep-weary voice woke me that night long ago. "Get your clothes on. Don't forget your drawers."

My Winnie-the-Pooh nightgown, ragged and thin, was something pillaged from the free-clothes bin at church. Laundry was hard to do often when water came from a well and washing powders cost money. So we saved our underwear for the daytime.

My ten-year-old bones ached from the death I talked out of the Bodine sisters earlier that day, the mucus still lodged in my throat. I barked a wet cough to bring it up.

"Here." Grandmama handed me a blue perfume bottle with a stopper that did not match. I spat the death inside the bottle like always. The thick ooze slipped down the curved lip and blobbed at the bottom. A black dollop ready for someone else to swallow.

It smelled of rotting flesh and tasted like fear.

Sin Eater Oil, Grandmama called it, was like a truth serum for the soul. A few drops baked into a pie, you could find out if your neighbor stole your garden vegetables. Mixed with certain herbs, it enhanced their potency and enlivened the superstitious charms from Grandmama's magic recipe box.

On a few occasions—no more than a handful of times—when consumed in full, its power was lethal.

Out in front of our cabin sat a shiny new Corvette with hubcaps that shimmered in the moonlight. Pacing on the porch, a shadow of a man. It wasn't until he stepped into the light did I catch his face. Stone Rutledge. He was taller and thinner and snakier back then.

Bone Layer, a large, hardened man who got his name from digging graves for the cemetery, dropped a pine box no longer than me into the back of our truck. He drove us everywhere we needed to be—seeing how Grandmama couldn't see too good and I was only ten. The three of us followed Stone as his low-slung car dragged and scrapped the dirt road to a farmhouse deep in the woods.

An oil-lit lamp flickered inside. Cries of a woman in labor pushed out into the humid night. Georgia's summer air was always thick. Suffocating, unbearable nights teeming with insects hell-bent on fighting porch lights.

A woman at the edge of panic for being left in charge greeted us at the door. Pearls draped her neck. Polish shined her perfect nails as she pulled and worked the strand. Her heels *click-clacked* as she paced the linoleum floor.

Grandmama didn't bother with pleasantries. She shoved on past with her asphidity bag full of her herbs and midwife supplies and my Sin Eater Oil and went straight for the woman who was screaming. Bone Layer grabbed his shovel and disappeared into the woods.

In the house, I gathered the sheets and the clean towels and boiled the water. I'd never seen this kitchen before, but most things can be found in just about the same place as any other home.

"Why is that child here?" the rich woman, not too good at whispering, asked Stone. Her frightened eyes watched as I tasked out my duties.

"Doing her job. Drink this." Stone shoved a glass of whiskey at her. She knocked it back with a swift tilt of her head, like tossing medicine down her throat, and handed back the glass for another.

Tiptoeing into the bedroom, I quietly poured the steaming water into the washbasin. The drugged moans of the lady spilled to the floor like a sad melody. A breeze snuck in through the inch of open window and licked the gauzy curtain that draped the bed.

When I turned to hand Grandmama the towels, I eyed the slick black blood that dripped down the sheets.

We weren't here for a birthing.

We were called to assist with a misbirth.

Fear iced over me when I looked upon the mother.

Then, I saw on the dresser next to where Grandmama stood, two tiny swaddles, unmoving. A potato box sat on

the floor. Grandmama slowly turned around at the sound of
my sobbing—I hadn't realized I'd started to cry. Her milky
white eyes found mine like always, despite her part-blindness.

Swift and sharp, she snatched me by my elbow. Her fingers dug into my flesh as she ushered me over to the dresser
to see what I had caused.

"You've soured their souls," she said in a low growl. I
looked away, not wanting to see their underdeveloped bodies.
Her bony hand grabbed my face, her grip crushing my jaw
as she forced me to look upon them. Black veins of my Sin
Eater Oil streaked across their gnarled lifeless bodies. "This
is your doing, child. There'll be a price to pay for y'all going
behind my back." For me, and Aunt Violet.

Aunt Violet took some of my Sin Eater Oil weeks ago. I
assumed it was for an ailing grandparent who was ready for
Jesus; she never said who. She said not to tell. She said Grandmama wouldn't even notice it was missing.

So I kept quiet. Told the thing in my gut that knew it
was wrong to shut up. But she gave my Sin Eater Oil to the
woman writhing in pain in front of me, so she could kill her
babies. Shame welled up inside me.

Desperately, I looked up to Grandmama. "Don't let the
Devil take me."

Grandmama beamed, pleased with my fear. "There's only
one way to protect you, child." The glint in her eyes sent a
chill up my spine.

No. I shook my head. Not that—her promise of punishment, if ever I misused my gift. Tears slivered down my
cheeks.

"It wasn't me!" I choked out, but she only shook her head.

"We must cleanse your soul from this sin and free you
from the Devil's grasp. You must atone." Grandmama rum-
maged through her bag and drew out two items: the match
hissed to life as she set fire to a single crow claw. I closed my

eyes and turned away, unable to watch. But that didn't stop me from knowing.

The mother's head lolled over at the sound of my crying. Her red-rimmed eyes gazed my way. "You!" she snarled sloppily at me. Her hair, wild, stuck to the sweat on her face. The black veins of my Sin Eater Oil spiderwebbed across her belly, a permanent tattoo that matched that of her babies. "The Devil's Seed Child," the lady slurred from her vicious mouth. The breeze whipped the curtains in anger. Oh, that hate in her eyes. Hate for me.

Grandmama shoved me into the hall, where I was to stay put. The rich woman pushed in. The door opened once more, and that wooden potato box slid out.

The mother wailed as the rich lady cooed promises that things would be better someday. The door closed tight behind us, cries echoing off the walls.

I shared the dark with the slit of the light and wondered if she'd ever get her someday.

Quick as lightning, my eyes flitted to the box, then back to the ugly wallpaper dating the hallway. My curiosity poked me. It gnawed until I peeked inside.

There on their tiny bodies, the mark of a sinner. A crow's claw burned on their chest. Same as the Death Talker birthmark over my heart. Grandmama branded them so Jesus would know I was to blame.

That woman was right—I was the Devil's Seed Child.

So I ran.

I ran out the door and down the road.

I ran until my feet grew sore and then ran some more.

I ran until the salt dried on my face and the tears stopped coming.

I was rotten, always rotten. As long as my body made the Sin Eater Oil, I'd always be rotten. Exhausted, I fell to my knees. From my pocket, I pulled out the raggedy crow feather

I now kept with me. I curled up on the side of the road between a tree and a stump, praying my wishes onto that feather.

Devil's Seed Child, I whispered, and repeated in my mind.
It was comforting to own it, what I was. The rightful name
for someone who could kill the most innocent among us.

I blew my wish on the feather and set it free in the wind.

A tiny object tumbled in front of my face. Shiny as the hubcaps on Stone's car. A small gold ring with something scrolled
on the flat front. I quirked my head sideways to straighten
my view. A fancy script initial *R*.

"Don't cry," a young voice spoke. Perched on the rotting
stump above, a boy, just a pinch older than I. Shorn dark hair
and clothes of all black.

I smiled up at him, a thank-you for the gift.

"Weatherly!" A loud bark that could scare the night caused
me to jump. Bone Layer had a voice that did that to people,
though he didn't use it often.

Over my head, a black wisp flew toward the star-filled sky,
and the boy was gone. I snatched up the ring and buried it in
my pocket as Bone Layer came to retrieve me. He scooped
me up as easy as a doll. His shirt smelled of sweat and earth
and bad things to come.

Grandmama's punishment was meant to save me; I leaned
into that comfort. Through the Lord's work, she'd keep me
safe. Protect me. If I strayed from her, I might lose my soul.

Grandmama was right; I must atone.

The truck headlights pierced the woods as Bone Layer
walked deeper within them. Grandmama waited at the hole
in the ground with the Bible in her hand and the potato box
at her feet.

Stone and the rich woman watched curiously from the
front porch. The wind howled through the trees. They ex-
changed horrid looks and hurried words, then fled back into
the house, quick as thieves.

Bone Layer gently laid me in the pine box already lowered into the shallow hole he done dug. Deep enough to cover, not enough for forever.

"Will they go to Heaven?" I asked from the coffin, as Grandmama handed me one bundle, then the other. I nestled them into my chest. I had never seen something so little. Light as air in my arms. Tiny things. Things that never had a chance in this world. They smelled sickly sweet; a scent that made me want to retch.

Grandmama tucked my little Bible between my hands. I loved that Bible. Pale blue with crinkles in the spine from so much discovery. On the front, a picture of Jesus, telling a story to two little kids.

"Will they go to Heaven?" I asked again, panicked when she didn't answer. Fear rose up in my throat, and I choked on my tears. Fear I would be held responsible if their souls were not saved.

Grandmama's face was flat as she spoke the heartless truth. "They are born from sin, just like you. They were not wanted. They are not loved." Her words stung like always.

"What if I love them? Will they go to Heaven if I love them?"

Her wrinkled lips tightened across her yellow and cracked teeth, insidious. "You must atone," she answered instead. Then smiled, not with empathy but with pleasure; she was happy to deliver this punishment, glad of the chance to remind me of her power.

"I love them, Grandmama. I love them," I professed with fierceness. I hoped it would be enough. To save their souls. To save my own. "I love them, Grandmama," I proclaimed with all my earnest heart. To prove it, I smothered the tops of their heads with kisses. "I love them, Grandmama." I kept repeating this. Kept kissing them as Bone Layer grabbed the lid to my pine box. He held it in his large hands, waiting for Grand-mama to move out of his way.

"You believe me, don't you?" I asked her. Fear and prayer filled every ounce of my body. If I loved them enough, they'd go to Heaven. If I atoned, maybe I would, too. I squeezed my eyes tight and swore my love over and over and over.

She frowned down on me. "I believe you, child. For sin always enjoys its own company."

She promptly stood. Her black dress swished across the ground as she moved out of the way. Then Bone Layer shut out the light, fastening the lid to my box.

Muffled sounds of dirt scattered across the top as he buried me alive.

ONE

Dog Finger

Fourteen Years Later

Omens come in all manner of ways. Warnings to let you know death is coming. Pretty much everything portends death when Appalachia is deep in your family roots. If a bird flies into your house, somebody in your family is going to die. Same for a broken clock that starts ticking again, or cows you hear mooing after midnight.

Or black ferns that grow where there were none the day before.

Grandmama calls them Devil's Weed, says they're black because they feed off the Devil's soul. Papaw said they were black because of the coal-rich earth they grew on higher in the mountains.

Mrs. Penny Hammer, my eighth-grade biology teacher, said it wasn't nothing to do with coal or evil. It was the anthocyanins pigment that colored them black, a purple-black like blackberries. Except…Mrs. Hammer didn't account for the fact that folklore is stronger than science around here. No amount of biology will convince local folks black ferns are harmless. They eat up the forests, you see. So much so, they gave us our town name.

Black Fern, Georgia, isn't just a town named after its foliage. It's where death shrouds with a heavy hand. Furtive ground for a Death Talker to reside.

The wind chime of trinkets hanging in my bedroom window *clinks* and *twinkles* in the morning wind. Lost or discarded objects that no one would miss. Shiny things. Tiny things. A piece of Christmas tinsel. A broken car key. Cracked crystal droplet from a chandelier. The silver propeller of a toy plane. A shiny copper button with the black corduroy fabric still attached. A cracked mirrored lens from Cindy Higgin's sunglasses.

Barely ten items.

One for every time the crow boy has visited me.

One for every life I have failed.

It's been years since I've seen Rook—a walker of souls; a boy who is sometimes a crow. Years since I failed to save someone. The more time that passes, the more I start to wonder if I made him up. One of those imaginary friends children create to keep themselves from being bored or lonely or sad.

The *ching* of a bike bell rings, yanking me from my thoughts. Tires from my childhood pink pedal bike have long since melted in the dirt. My cousin Adaire, expectant. Hand firmly on her hip. Her expression a clear, *Are you ready? Or are you wasting the morning daydreaming?*

I never will be ready for today.

Besides, daydreaming might be the only gift I get. I glance at the calendar flipped to June. The nineteenth. *Happy Birthday to me.*

I remember what Adaire wore the last time I saw her at

church. Her favorite goldenrod-yellow T-shirt—it was plum ugly by itself and worse with that green-plaid wool miniskirt she cherished. For the love of Jesus, it was hotter than sin that day. Why in God's good name she ever bought that outfit I will never know.

I feel like a fraud dressed like I am. My khaki skirt, pencil straight and too tight, rests sinfully two inches above my knees. My white blouse, with a rounded collar, is thin enough my white bra glows. I pull my long hair forward in hopes it hides my nipples. The brown penny loafers, scuffed to hell, are as restricting as the Bible. It's clear I've outgrown the whole outfit, but it's the most "professional" type clothes I own. And Aunt Violet said that's what I ought to wear in court.

"I'm coming," I whisper to the wind, dreading what's to come.

Grandmama and Bone Layer have already left for the courthouse. I chastise myself for not leaving when they did; now I'll probably be late.

Our four-room house is a modest rectangle deep in the Georgia pines. Sparse belongings that tend to the necessities of life. Nothing more. Nothing less.

Poor folks are people who can't afford what they need. We had food, shelter, and Jesus; we didn't "need" nothing else, but it sure felt like we were poor.

Morning sun filters in the windows of the great room, capturing the dust particles that perpetually float. The haint blue paint on the ceiling makes the room extra bright, cheerful even.

It's a lie. There's nothing cheerful in this house.

The light aqua blue shade goes back to an old Appalachia practice. Blue is the color of water, and spirits can't transverse across water. Healing work tends to bring about things you don't want following you home.

The room is more kitchen than living room as the long

plank table takes up most of the space. It serves as our workstation on days we make the baked goods, jams, and crow dolls we sell at the roadside market.

This table is also where Grandmama embalmed my papaw.

A lone chicken egg waits next to Grandmama's recipe box in the kitchen windowsill. Saved for me. Against the light, the veined red ring and spoiled bloody yolk show through. *Perfect.* Gently, I tuck it into a Styrofoam coffee cup and grab a pouch of rosehip itching powder from the witching box.

Hurrying out the door, I can't help it and glance around for evidence a birthday cake was made or a present has been wrapped. But I know better than to expect a gift from Grandmama, and she's about the only family I got left.

But today isn't about me, or my birth. It's about what the judge decides and the justice our family deserves.

From underneath the porch step, I grab the witching jar I made just for today. A handful of graveyard dirt, nine nails, and a guilty man's name penned three times.

My old white '74 Mustang cowers in the weeds next to the woodshed. A piece of shit, with a hard plastic interior coated in red Krylon spray paint. I scraped my pennies together to buy it, only for it to die four short months later. It had starter issues, so I had to park on hills, roll it into second gear, and pop the clutch to get it going. Now the clutch is wore out, it needs a new starter, and the battery is dead. Two-hundred and fifty dollars to fix it all, Davis said. Half what I paid for it.

Adaire's car door shrieks when I open it. Sunspots burn the Pontiac Grand Prix's silver skin like festering bedsores. Cracked red vinyl pinches the back of my legs when I sit. The fan belt shrills as the engine grumbles a deep gravely sound from being forced awake. The car guzzles gas faster than a drunk at an open bar, but it gets me from A to B and she has no need for it anymore.

Silently, I drive the long road into town. A dark cloud shades the car, and I look up.

Crows, hundreds of them. Low-flying ordinary crows. Their screeching and caws like playful chatter. I sigh and wonder if Rook is among them, watching me. Would he know who I am in that form?

With the windows down, dirt gathers in my teeth from the dusty road and six miles later I roll up on Main Street. A single paved road drawn down the middle of a skeleton town. A hodgepodge of flat-front brick buildings line both sides. Most of the businesses can't make up their mind if they want to stay or close up, about as fickle as the weather. They're all in a state of disrepair except Patsy's Cut and Curl and Mr. Wiggly's, which used to be the five-and-dime back in the day; now it's where you can get your groceries while stocking up on your farming supplies.

Parking spaces are usually a dime a dozen. But today, with the beloved mayor's reputation under legal scrutiny, everybody and their mama is here.

I find a spot behind the old Ritz movie theater, which closed down after its last showing of *Kramer vs. Kramer*—someone has since strategically rearranged the letters to read *ram me*.

The heat and my pantyhose are working together to chafe the insides of my thighs as I hustle down Main Street. Sweat spots weep underneath my armpits. Under my tit-pits. And an angry blister threatens to punch through my heel if I don't ditch these penny loafers soon.

That fragile egg waits patiently in the Styrofoam cup in my hand. Witching jar snug underneath my elbow.

My eyes scan the row of cars until I find Stone Rutledge's Corvette, its red curves like a pair of lips, puckered for an ass-kissing. I duck below the line of sight and crouch next to his car, pulling the witching jar out from under my arm. I crack the lid just enough and slip my words inside.

Do unto you as you have done unto me.

Suffer as I have suffered.

For all the anger you've sewn, shall my rage not relent.

Until truth leave your tongue and your soul repent.

The clock tower *dongs* the eight o'clock hour. *Shit.* I screw the lid back on and stuff the witching jar underneath his back tire and hurry to the hearing.

My words as fervent as a prayer as I tie three knots into the black yarn pulled from my pocket as I rush down the sidewalk.

"With this knot, I seal this hex."

You will not sleep. I tie a knot.

You will not eat. I tie another.

You will not rest until thine is done. I tie the last one.

But then my pace slows as I come upon the courthouse at the end of the street—Holiest House of Ill Repute. Bodies pile up between the double doors like a jammed storm drain. The rest of them spill over and down the fat concrete steps into the street.

I pause, wondering if I really need to go in at all.

I could just stay here.

Watch the people's reaction when the judge makes his decision, then I'd know immediately one way or the other.

Adaire stands there in front of me, silent as the grave. Her eyes pan down to the toes of my shoes. There, twiddling in the light breeze, a black feather. *A wish on a crow feather.*

A sign.

It's enough to push my feet forward. I scoop it up, tucking it away in my bra for later.

A gaggle of farm-fed, thick-bellied men clog the doorway. Even as I try to wedge myself through, I'm elbowed back. Junior Maddox bucks back in surprise. Surprised I'm not already in there? Or that I have the gall to touch him? I'm not certain.

Just when it seems like the human sea will part for me to enter, I realize they're opening the way for my cousin Wyatt's fast exit.

Slurred curses fly from Aunt Violet as Wyatt escorts her out of the door. Snot drivels from her nose. The sickly sweet smell of whiskey tarnishes her breath.

"I've got her!" Wyatt waves a hand for me not to bother helping. He doesn't get Aunt Violet more than three feet from the door when she pops. Whatever liquid diet she's survived on the last couple weeks splatters across the stone steps.

The parted bodies are already melding back together, so I ram through before they seal off the entrance again. Voices hush as I enter. Not for me but for the defendant as they walk him in from the side door.

A smug uncuffed Stone Rutledge walks into the room with a boastful grin slapped across his face and an assured ease about his shoulders.

His navy suit waxed smooth, something straight out of an episode of *Dallas*. Glimmering gold cuff links wink at the end of his starched white sleeves. His sky blue tie, no doubt imported silk, snubs up tight around his neck. His skin Bahamas tan and always flushed red from years of heavy drinking. He's a tall, lean man with a perpetual sternness about him. Like all the emotion has been drained out of him, and all that's left is a block of ice. He sits back in the defendant's chair like a lazy king. Sugar King around these parts, generational wealth he inherited from the sugar plantations, instead of earned. As if that makes him qualified to be the town's mayor.

Court is like a church wedding; you can tell who you're there for by what side you're sitting on. It's a handful on our side and then everybody else. Except the everybody else is too large to occupy one side alone, so unwillingly they've spilled over into ours, though still a few rows back from any actual supporters we might claim. They've all squeezed in here like

Wanda Travis's too-big titties in her tiny bra. Ain't enough room to even breathe.

Just behind Stone is his perfect little family. His wife, Rebecca Rutledge, with her flawless hot-rolled hair and her blush-pink Chanel suit, has her nose stuck high in the air, like she caught a whiff of something unpleasant. She just so happens to be the judge's niece, too—how convenient. Their twin children, Lorelei and Ellis Rutledge, are only a year or so younger than me. Lorelei has that same haughty arrogance as her parents; I guess a fancy Princeton degree will do that to you. Ellis, though, he doesn't seem to have that hard edge like the rest of them. I think he's an artist, which means Mom and Dad pay his bills while he plays with paint. Must be nice.

"All rise!" the bailiff calls for everyone's attention. He announces the honorable Judge Jeb Walker Newsome now presiding. It's about as quiet in here as the preacher's altar call on Sunday nights as he enters.

The judge takes his bench. All the folks sit. I look for my people. Second row on the left, Bone Layer's massive shoulders loom; he's a boulder in a room of rocks. The knotted gray bun on the back of Grandmama's head right next to him. The two seats recently vacated by Wyatt and my aunt are already being filled. Behind them, I see Davis Yancey, his dark tall frame crumpled over. He looks as broken as a sinner finding his way back into church. Mrs. Yancey pats a supportive hand on his back. He ain't family. But he almost was.

It's as if Mrs. Yancey hears me thinking about them. She turns. Her sad brown eyes find me straightaway. Her small smile a patch of sunshine in a cloudy room of stares. My eyes slip to the floor. It's hard to bear her kindness for long. Not when I failed them, too. Failed Mr. Harvey Yancey, who should be sitting there with them, but he died years ago. Because I couldn't save him.

I find a scratch of wall on the left side to wedge myself

against. Protectively holding my red-yolk egg in the cup in my hand.

I had decided not to come. It felt pointless, considering Stone Rutledge and the family were so beloved.

Untouchable.

But then Adaire wouldn't let me alone. Pestered and bugged me that this was important. Whatever bullshit I thought I should deal with was secondary to showing up today. Maybe she's right.

Everybody and their mama is here. The heat of their stares burning up any confidence I brought with me. My head tells me I'm grown, and I don't give a rat's ass what these folk think about me. Then my heart reminds me I was raised here and somehow, in this screwed-up world, their opinion of me matters. Their hateful energy causes me to shrink back into my shallow piece of wall, and I loathe myself for caring.

And I know what they're thinking. The fact our family even pressured the sheriff to arrest Stone Rutledge, the town mayor—we ought to be ashamed. A good man who brought a piece of Georgia tourism our way and saved our last grocery store from closing; it's like he was God or something.

What happened was an "accident."

What anyone has yet to explain to me is how you "accidently" drive over someone *twice*.

"You ready for Sunday's bass tournament?" the judge asks Stone. "'Cause I hear you lost your lucky fishing hat." A murmur of low jovial noise warms the room.

"If the bass you catch Sunday is anything like what you caught last weekend, Jeb, I won't need a lucky hat." The room chuckles right along with Stone.

"Hey now, watch yourself." The judge playfully points at Stone.

Their jesting is a stab in my ribs.

The judge says something to his court reporter, who hands

him the papers he needs. Reading glasses poised at the end of his nose, he takes his sweet time familiarizing himself with the case, as if he doesn't already know the facts. We all quietly wait for him to catch up. The taut silence that's descended is about to spring my last nerve.

"Smithy," the judge calls to the prosecution.

John Delaney Smith—Smithy to his pals—is a well-known drunk. He's a worthless attorney, if you ask me. And in a town where good ole boys can do no wrong, Smithy mysteriously gets assigned to all the "important" cases. I'm pretty sure he was in that same wrinkled black suit last night at the Watering Hole, a honky-tonk off the side of the road that's one foot past the city limits, where it's legal to sell beer in Black Fern County. Except on Sundays.

Hell, this wasn't even a trial. It's just a preliminary hearing to see if Stone might've committed a crime, and should charges be brought against him.

"Yes, sir." Smithy stands, drowning in his too-big suit. Hard drinking will waste you away like that. His shaky hand fidgets with the knot in his sloppy tie. He smooths down his unwashed black hair. There's a sway about him, one you might not notice unless you know a drunk personally. It's like a body forever out to sea, lightly bobbing in the waves.

"Says here," the judge starts, "the family insists the twenty-three-year-old victim was not intoxicated on the day of the event? Even though she lived with a known alcoholic?"

My teeth grind together. Not just *the* family. *My* family.

Judge Newsome shuffles through his papers as if earnestly looking for something. "For the life of me I cannot find the results of the toxicology report to confirm this." He raises a questioning brow to Smithy. There's a tone in his voice. Scripted even. He knows the answer but he's asking it here, out loud, so everyone knows.

My heart crumples.

"Unfortunately, Your Honor, the results were inconclusive. And the hospital was unable to perform a second toxicology test on the body because the family insisted on burial rites. They still practice in some…arcane ways of taking care of their own dead." And he's supposed to be our attorney? Murmurs and whispers scatter around the courtroom. Arcane makes us sound more hillbilly than necessary.

"So we do not have any evidence to substantiate the family's claim?"

"That is correct, Your Honor."

"Your Honor." Stone's lawyer stands. Introduces himself as Attorney John Klein of the Atlanta law firm of Klein, Klein, and Winchester. He's an uppity man with a suit even fancier than his client's. He holds up a set of papers. "Here we have the defendant's own recounting of the events that took place on the night in question." The bailiff comes over to collect the papers and passes them off to the judge. "As you can see, it was well into dusk when my client was driving home."

Dusk. The hour of crows.

"Mr. Rutledge recalls seeing erratic movement in the road ahead. It was not until it was too late did he realize a person was swerving—drunkenly—on a bicycle in the middle of the road. Dark clothing. No proper reflectors. As my client tried tirelessly to resuscitate the victim, he recalls the pungent odor of whiskey on her clothes."

Liar. Liar! LIAR! My teeth grind harder.

"And there is the additional eyewitness testimony…" He hands another set of papers to the bailiff for the judge. "It corroborates that the victim was seen that very afternoon at the Watering Hole. The liquor establishment is not quite two miles down the road from the incident. A place the family is known to frequent."

"Yes." The judge glowers at the document claiming just that. "Not an establishment our Baptist community is too proud of, Mr. Klein. Thank you for this detailed and thorough recounting of events. Smithy, do you have anything else as evidence?"

Smithy fumbles over his words but confirms all accounts of Stone's statement and the eyewitness testimony have been verified and, to the best of his knowledge, there is nothing further to be submitted.

"It is clear to me," the judge begins and my blood starts to simmer, "that without any evidence of negligence or malice, we can assume the defendant is not responsible, and that the victim carried a degree of responsibility as well in the outcome of events. With no clear evidence to be put forward by the prosecution, by the state of Georgia, I hereby accept the defendant's motion to dismiss. Court is adjourned." Judge Newsome slams down his gavel. The finality of the wood cracking like a hammer on the last nail into a coffin.

Voices rise up in the courtroom, the relief and joy enough to feast on.

Doesn't matter how much you expect the outcome; there's still something about hearing it that hits you harder than you're prepared for.

Dismissed, like a teacher who's simply allowing students to leave for the day.

Dismissed, as if Stone's actions were unimportant. Insignificant. Irrelevant.

Dismissed, as if it was no big deal he killed Adaire. Grandmama stands to leave like church is over, the sermon is finished, and there's nothing more to be said or done. Not a stitch of anger—or care—on her face.

"Dismissed?" I scream. It's a mad, startling sound that jars the room quiet.

Everyone stares at me like I've lost my ever-loving mind. Maybe I have. Sheriff Johns regards me like a wild animal that got loose. My blood is boiling now. My feet carry me forward—they tend to do that right before I do something stupid.

I should have brought a knife.

Or Uncle Doug's pistol, if I had known where Aunt Violet hid it.

I take the cursed egg from the cup and grip it tight. The other hand searches for the little pouch in my purse.

"Unto thee what you have done!" The vehement rage and spit fly from my mouth. My dog finger—my cursing finger—fiercely points at Stone. He stumbles back as I climb over the bench.

He's too slow and too late.

My right hand swings out, cracking the egg as I slap his face with it. The other hand slings out the bag of power; tiny rosehip hairs fly, a mist into his eyes.

It's a hard crunch when my cheek smacks the courtroom's wood floor. Sheriff Johns's aftershave and cigarette breath assaults my nose as he pins me down. "Damn it, girl, I told you not to do something you'd regret." A knee pushes into my back as he yanks my arms behind me. Metal cuffs *zip-click* around my wrists.

"You bastard!" I buck and fight against the hands holding me down. "You'll pay for what you did! You'll fucking pay!"

Like a ray of sunshine, I get one small peek at Stone's face as the sheriff yanks me to my feet and shoves me out of the room.

Bloodred from the chicken egg oozes down his cheek and stains that expensive white shirt of his. The rot of it putrefying the air. Stone rubs fiercely at his eyes, screaming from the burn.

May death fall upon your house.

TWO

Bringing in the Sheaves

"Well, aren't you about as dumb as a box of rocks to pull that shit in court," Aunt Violet says to me from the other side of the jail bars.

Sure enough the sheriff let me rot a night in jail before informing me Stone wasn't pressing charges, after all. Egg assault by a woman half your size… Well, you'd look like a straight-up pussy for crying foul. But it was worth every second in this stinking cinder block to see that pained expression on Stone Rutledge's face.

Aunt Violet looks like hell, face puffy and red from crying. Or the alcohol. Or both. That spicy cinnamon Dentyne gum can't hide the smell of cigarettes and vodka still lingering on her breath.

"Stone deserves worse," I say to her and sit up to stretch. My back is killing me from sleeping on the compacted cotton pallet they call a mattress. My jaw aches a bit from when Sheriff Johns introduced my face to the floor.

We both glance down the hall as we hear the sheriff give the order that I'm to be let out. Deputy Rankin, with his belly hanging over his gun belt, grunts as he hoists himself out of his chair. His keys jangle on his hip as he waddles down the dimly lit hall.

"Is Grandmama angry?" I ask Aunt Violet.

"When is Mama not angry," she says to me, then turns to the deputy. "Hey, Dewayne. How's your mama and them?"

Deputy Rankin looks down his nose at her and doesn't answer. "You're free to go," he says dryly, clearly unhappy about having to do any kind of actual work.

"I see you're still eating your mama out of house and home," Aunt Violet says, not happy about getting snubbed.

He frowns back at her. "I see you're still sucking on that vodka bottle."

Aunt Violet makes a *pfft* sound in response, then scratches her cheek with a single middle finger. "Bastard," she mumbles as we walk away. "Don't worry about Mama, Weatherly. She'll find something new to bitch about tomorrow."

The bright morning sun smacks me square in the face as we enter the front office's waiting room. My jaw clamps tight when I find Stone Rutledge, leaning over the intake desk, signing some papers. His wife, Rebecca, hovers off to the side. Her face bunched up in disgust as her eyes scan the room. She clutches her Dooney & Bourke satchel like she's expecting to be mugged.

"No, I'm certain. No charges to file," Stone says to the woman behind the desk. "That family has been through enough." He hands her back the paperwork. In his periphery, he catches sight of me and does a double take.

There's a scratch on his cheek. Good. His eyes are rimmed red and irritated from the rosehip hairs I tossed in his face. Even better.

I give him my best *fuck-you* glare.

A deep sadness washes over his face as he locks eyes with me. The genuineness of it kicks me in the chest and throws me off for a minute. Until I realize he's just playing up the empathetic mayor image for the room full of voters. What an ass.

We're almost to the door when Rebecca makes a tiny grunt of disapproval, giving voice to what everyone else in this room thinks of us…white trash.

"Let it go," Aunt Violet warns, then snags me by the elbow and guides me out the door, making sure I don't do something stupid yet again.

Not two seconds outside, Aunt Violet is fumbling through her purse for her pack of Marlboros. She lights her cigarette with an urgent shaky hand.

We pass Rebecca's sparkling white Cadillac Eldorado—a convertible no less. It's an out-of-place crown jewel compared to the other junkyard relics parked around it. Aunt Violet grumbles when she sees it.

"You know what I heard?" she asks.

"What?"

"I heard Jimmy Smoot hauled the mayor's precious little Corvette to the shop because somebody put a jar of nails behind his tire." Her voice full of mock surprise. "Wonder who could have done that?" She eyes me knowingly, then blows a long plume of smoke out the side of her smiling mouth.

"I have *no* idea." I wrestle back a grin as we get in her car.

"Wyatt's got him a job working at the Lasco factory over in Mercer," she tells me as we pull out of the parking lot and head toward the house. "It's a good job. He'll make lead maintenance technician in no time." She flicks her cigarette ash out the window crack.

"Seriously?" I say, incredulous. "He's not going to stick around and help us figure out how to make Stone pay? He's just moving on? Is that what we're all doing?"

Shame creeps across her face; she won't look at me. "Well,

we gotta keep going somehow. That's how life works, baby girl." From the cup holder, she picks up her Styrofoam drink and swirls it around. Ice shushes inside, mixing the watered-down contents. Then she takes a large swig like it's medicine. I suppose it is.

It's hotter than Hades in the car. I roll down my window to let a breeze in and the cigarette smoke out.

"Have you talked to Davis?" If there's anyone who's going to help me, it's Davis. He loved Adaire fiercely. He's not going to lie down and take this verdict as the final say. "What does he think we should do?"

Aunt Violet lets out an exasperated sigh. "What else we gonna do, Weatherly? Call the governor, tell him we've got a shitty mayor down here? You saw in court how chummy they all are. The Good Ole Boy's Club," she says in a mocking tone. "Rich folk like Stone ain't ever gonna pay. That's how it is. Just something the rest of us have to accept." She flips on her blinker with an angry hand, and we turn down the gravel road.

"I'll never accept it," I say. We ride the rest of the way in silence.

At the house, as soon as she shifts the car into Park, I reach for the door handle—

"Hey." She lays her hand to my arm, and I pause. "I got something in the mail this week," she says with a lilt in her voice, as if whatever this is will make everything better.

From the sun visor, she pulls down a postcard and hands it to me.

Myrtle Beach, South Carolina.

An image of the coastline, blue waters and soft sand, waves across the front. My mama's hurried handwriting scribbled on the back.

Every now and again, I get a postcard from her. Dallas, Texas. Memphis, Tennessee. San Diego, California. Always with a *Wish you were here!* Like it was me who chose not to go with her, and I was missing out. It's a penance for her guilt. If she thinks of me now and again, it absolves her from the feelings of neglect and abandonment. Or so I'm guessing. Really, I'm too grown to give a shit anymore.

"Your mama's sorry she couldn't make it to Adaire's funeral," Aunt Violet says as if that's alright with her, but I see the pinch in her eyes. "Darbee doesn't have enough money to get home right now. But she says she's got herself a promising job at a souvenir shop." Aunt Violet always gives her older sister the benefit of the doubt. I've never understood why.

According to Violet, Mama used to be an honor roll student who loved church. A Goody Two-shoes who never swore. An all-around saint. Then she got pregnant with me, and everything changed. The sister she remembers and the woman I know are two entirely different people.

For years, I let it eat at me that my mama never stuck around. Pawned her newborn off on her parents, like I was a doll she was tired of playing with. Hell, neither of my parents seemed to give a shit about me.

When I was seven, I asked Aunt Violet about my father. "He's a ball-less sack of shit for not stepping up and taking responsibility for his daughter. And your mama wasn't no whore." I should have been relieved, but I cringed. "She wasn't married, but that didn't make her no whore," Aunt Violet went on. "But she wasn't fit to be a mama yet, she had some wild oats to sow—heartache will do that to you. That don't mean she doesn't love you. Just means she loves you enough to do what's right for ya. Now, you go on outside with Adaire and make me some mud pies." She shooed me out the door, half a cigarette flopping from the side of her mouth. I never asked about my father again.

I wanted to believe Aunt Violet, I really did. But seven-year-old me had a hard time understanding how you could leave someone you loved behind.

"She says she'll come home for Christmas, though—if she can save up enough," she adds like it's a consolation prize.

Tell Weatherly I said hi. That's what she wrote on the postcard. Me—an afterthought at the end of her pathetic excuse for a relationship with her family.

"Why bother?" I toss the postcard on the seat and get out of the car. Twenty-two of my twenty-four Christmases I've spent without her. I don't see why that needs to change now.

The smell of fresh cut grass lingers in the air. Bone Layer is busy with the bushhog before the sun cooks everything alive. Laundry hangs on the clothesline strung from the smokehouse to a pole stuck out in the middle of the yard. Wood clothespins clump in a mesh pouch of fabric that looks like it's hanging on for dear life. I hate the way my clothes smell after drying on the line—thick with the outdoors and baked stiff from the sun.

Grandmama stoops over in the vegetable garden, picking tomatoes. Her long-sleeve blouse, brown floral and faded from the years, keeps the fine hairs of the tomato vine from itching her arms. It's eighty-plus degrees and she's got on nylons, too. I'm burning up just looking at her.

Agnes Wilder reminds me of a shriveled up apple that fell on the ground and rotted; what's left barely resembles the sweet fruit it once was. She loves her some Jesus, but she don't act like she's learned much from him.

I imagine she was born into this world bawling and squalling, and that permanent scowl just never left her face. If she's ever smiled, I've never seen it. I don't know what happened to her, but it made her foul-tempered and damn near impossible to live with. I loved my papaw something fierce, but I can't imagine what he ever saw in Grandmama that made him fall in love. Or so I'm guessing, because otherwise I can't square how the two of them ever married.

"It's gonna be a scorcher," Aunt Violet says to her, following me across the yard.

Grandmama props the bushel basket on her hip, then casts a scornful glare that lands right on Aunt Violet.

And just like that, her spunky confidence shrivels, her eyes cast down, looking at her shoes like they have the answers.

Aunt Violet has never lived up to the standards of what Agnes Wilder thought her daughters should be. My mama fit that mold for a time, until she did the unthinkable and got pregnant out of wedlock. It's almost like Grandmama blames the daughter that stayed for the one that ran away. Aunt Violet has that wild and free spirit, too, though. Being pinned under a religious thumb just didn't suit her. The tighter those reins got, the more Aunt Violet bucked. Until eventually she didn't give a shit anymore and lived how she wanted to—going through men like they were handkerchiefs, drinking like a fish, and finding trouble with the law every chance she got.

"Your squash looks good," Aunt Violet says, trying to seem unfazed by her mother's coldness.

Grandmama responds with a grunt, then turns to me. "You acted like a fool yesterday."

"Well, that bastard deserved it." Aunt Violet quickly comes to my defense.

Grandmama's hand flies out, faster than thought possible, and slaps Aunt Violet across the face with a wicked smack.

"Grandmama!"

"Don't you cuss at me." Grandmama pushes herself right up in Aunt Violet's face.

Tears glass over my aunt's eyes as she cradles her stung cheek. A ghost of the feeling mirrors my own, something I've felt a time or two myself.

"I just meant he was no good for what he'd done." Her gaze slips back to the ground.

Secondhand embarrassment lingers thick in the air.

"That ain't right," I say cautiously. Even as Grandmama wields those hazy white eyes on me, I bolster up my confidence, ordering it to not back down. It cowers, anyway. Years of fear and habit are hard to break.

"Get inside," she snaps at me. "We have work to do." She gives Aunt Violet a *get-gone* look, one Aunt Violet doesn't have to see twice.

As I follow Grandmama up the porch steps, she tells me about some new salve she wants to try out today. I turn back to see Aunt Violet pull a pint of vodka from underneath her car seat and pour the last of it into her Styrofoam cup.

For a moment, I'm struck by a glimpse at an all too likely future, slipping vodka into my soda, just so I can deal with Grandmama. I should have moved out years ago. But this house and these four walls are all I've ever known. Opportunities are rare around here.

In the kitchen, the cobalt blue perfume bottle that usually carries my Sin Eater Oil sits empty on the counter next to Grandmama's secret recipe box.

Recipes in that box go back generations. Every Granny Witch has one, a grimoire of sorts. Filled with old-world traditions passed down from our Scottish roots, mixed with indigenous rituals our ancestors were taught when they immigrated here. Diverse in their practices, some Granny Witches are gifted naturally in herbalism and midwifery. Others in realms such as magic. Grandmama wasn't born with witchery in her blood, so she uses me—and my Sin Eater Oil—to bring her charms and hexes to life.

Like rashes for cheaters. Misfortune for thieves. Insomnia for liars.

On the box, the thin script reads RECIPES in a faded charcoal black. The painted red rooster on the front is all but worn away. It's a simple box with dovetailed corners made from soft wood. Grandmama keeps it locked with a bone-tooth key that lives on a brass chain around her neck. Carved from dark wenge wood with teeth for the bits. Animal or human, I do not know; both, I imagine.

I've never seen inside the box for more than a second or two at a time. She holds those recipes and their secrets close, for her eyes only. Over the years she's shown me how to mix herbs to make medicinal cures for common ails. Taught me how to birth babies. Shared a few minor spells that don't cause too much of a fuss. But anything more than that, any of her Granny Witch magic, that's a secret she's not willing to part with. Not yet, at least.

The tipped-open lid reveals the recipe she's been working on this morning. I stretch my neck to see what it is—

"Load the visiting basket," Grandmama says and slams the lid shut.

That long-handled basket can mean only one thing: it's harvesting day. Like that old hymnal "Bringing in the Sheaves," but instead of harvesting grain, we're harvesting Sin Eater Oil.

Every few months, when the bottle runs dry, we make our rounds to the nursing homes in the neighboring counties. If we don't find a soul that's soon to be parting from this world, Grandmama will find one that's just about ready and help it along, so I can swoop in and save them before dying. It works—most of the time.

Harvesting is God's work, Grandmama says.

I say it's awfully damn convenient how God's work always coincides with our supply running low and our pockets empty.

The Pleasant Hill Nursing Home is a redbrick facility with a dirt-brown shingle roof. It sits on a soft rug of green Bermuda grass. Misshapen boxwood shrubs scatter along its base. Two cheerful crape myrtle trees flag each side of the long covered walkway, their fluted forms fan heavy with pink blossoms. This place reminds me of my old elementary school, but instead of children, it's full of the elderly.

Bone Layer parks the truck near the back, so it's a bit of a walk to the front doors. Ms. Claudette, the attendant at the front desk, nods a hello as we enter.

Inside, we're greeted by the perpetual smell of antiseptic and vanilla air freshener. An uncomfortable silence haunts the halls, only broken by the occasional moan of someone distinctively old and mentally declined. As a child, I thought this place was filled with sadness and sickness. And I suppose it might feel that way to a kid. But I also discovered the magic a young person has on the aged.

"How are you, Miss Martha?" I say to the tall sweet woman sitting crooked in her wheelchair, always parked near the front door. I kneel to get on her level. "I see you've got a pretty yellow dress on today." I smooth flat her hem that was hung on the brake lever. Not once has she ever spoken; the result of a stroke some years back. But her left foot starts tapping as soon as you speak to her, she's still very much there.

We visit often enough, trying to sell our baked goods, tinctures, and salves so that harvesting day doesn't look any different than the other times. But we try not to visit the same home twice in a row, just in case the harvesting doesn't go as planned. Or should anyone start asking questions. But still, we've done this enough that I know the patients well—their names, their stories.

Grandmama raises her brow in question. I shake my head no. As old as Miss Martha is—their longest resident to date—I don't pick up a hint of death around her. Grandmama sharply waves for Bone Layer to come along as she shuffles up to the front desk. He dutifully carries the basket of "goodies," following behind her.

"Claudette," Grandmama says to the attendant. "I have the perfect new salve for that stubborn arthritis of yours."

Grandmama pulls from the basket a small baby food jar she's mixed: dried nettle leaves, almond oil, and beeswax. It's tinged a slight purple for the tiny drop of Sin Eater Oil she's added to it. Something that will make it extra potent and effective.

I begin my rounds in the opposite direction, taking a light stroll down the hallways. I check in on each resident, letting my extra senses sift through the souls filling the facility. I'm searching for that soft whisper of a soul's song. That tonal sound we all carry, but that's different for each of us. For one, it was a tinkling piano. Another, the coo of a dove. And on one particular occasion, the purring rev of a car's engine.

It's not something I hear with my ears, but an echo inside my head. It calls to my own soul, which always answers back.

I'm rounding the third hallway at the back of the building, when I catch it. A delicate sound. I glide the back of my hand along the cool wall, following the growing sound, leading me to the person who doesn't have long to live.

I stop in front of Miss Evelyn's room, and my heart sinks. She's one of my favorite residents. A tender-hearted petite woman with a sunshine personality that makes you feel special just by being in her presence.

But there's no denying it. It's here, the song of her soul. A light shushing, like the rustling of fabric from a breeze drifting through an open curtained window.

Faint still. A little ways off but soon enough death will arrive and take Miss Evelyn.

"Here." Grandmama startles me and shoves something in my hands. I'm about to tell her no, there's no death here. But she already knows I've locked on to something, probably followed me down the hall to see what I'd find.

I look down at the Saran-wrapped package I'm holding. A black picot ribbon tied around it with a black fern frond tucked underneath. Zebra bread. Dark veins marble through the spongy slice, made of sweet molasses and spicy cinnamon. Two ingredients that can hide the rancid taste of Sin Eater Oil.

"Well, hello, sweet girl." Miss Evelyn looks up from her book. *Romeo and Juliet*, of course, her favorite. "You bring me some of that delicious cake I love?" She eyes the gift in my hand.

Quickly, I glance toward Grandmama, who's already moved on down the hall. Then back to Miss Evelyn who waits patiently with a bright smile.

She looks so tiny as she approaches death. For a minute, I panic—what if Grandmama miscalculated and put in too much Sin Eater Oil? It could kill her straightaway. Then again, her husband passed a few months back, and she's been so lonely without him.

We've done this harvesting ritual for years, but today something doesn't feel right.

A chill prickles the hairs on my arms. It's only Miss Evelyn and me in the room, but I could swear we're not alone. Maybe it's something my heart wants to believe, but I feel like Adaire is here with us. Reminding me how precious life is.

Miss Evelyn only has the one daughter. Maybe she doesn't have much time left in this world, but it's not for me to decide. Not when loved ones are still here to spend that time with.

I look at the bread in my hand and do something I've never done before.

"Oh, this?" I say, holding it up. "No, ma'am. This is a soggy batch of banana bread that got mixed in with the good stuff." I toss the poisoned zebra bread into the wastebasket.

THREE

Language of the Dying

I am the Death Talker. I don't heal. I don't cure folks of whatever ails them. I talk to death. Whisper what it wants to hear. Tell it why it should love me more than the person it wants to take. Death longs to be desired, just like the rest of us. I convince death I love it most, then I invite it in.

It's funny how I couldn't tell you what I was wearing last week, much less seven years ago, but somehow I remember what Adaire and I wore the day I tried to save a dog.

Adaire Sorrell was a nasty scar of a girl with brows as stern as lectures. Her brown hair was chicken-scratched, short and always confused about what direction it should go. The abundant freckles on her face made her look perpetually dirty—the curse of our Scottish genes. If clothes were saving graces, well, let's just say Adaire would have none. She had more flair in her wardrobe than Elton John. That day, she wore Kelly green shorts with a purple tie-dye halter top she made from two doilies. Thank Jesus she lined it with fabric, or you would've seen her breast buds straight through it.

I kept it simple: striped T-shirt, white trimmed blue shorts, and plain white sneakers. It suited me just fine. I blended in. Looked like any other kid in America. That was the way I liked it. It was bad enough folks knew my mama had abandoned me, then to have a Granny Witch grandmother didn't help none. I didn't need my clothing to speak up any louder.

It was one of those usual hot summer days, the kind Georgia likes to smother you in until you're damn near certain you'll melt into the asphalt. We were on the cusp of discovering boys, that in-between stage where you're barely a teenager, but you start acting the part because you know something new and exciting is coming.

Adaire and I walked two miles down Law Road (not counting the two cotton fields we crossed) to get to Quickies, a hole in the wall convenience store for country folk to stop in on their way someplace else. Papaw had brought us down there more times that we could count, when we were little. It always coincided when Grandmama was chewing him an earful for one thing or another, and then he would suddenly declare he had a hankering for bologna, saving Adaire and I from her ire by taking us with him.

Quickies hasn't changed much over the years. A square wood building with a dirt parking lot that's been there for forty years, at least. Once a small church, it now sold a handful of groceries—a row of candy and chips, a wall of sodas, fresh produce in the summer, and a deli in the back. Sometimes on Saturdays and Sundays, Slim Jim (who wasn't slim) would set up his smoker and make ribs and pulled pork that he sold by the paper plate.

Rowdy and Pops, two old men who seemed like permanent fixtures to the building, always sat out front in wood chairs watching the cars go by—the handful that passed through.

The front door creaked when you opened it, old and tired from doing its job so long. But inside was an arctic oasis.

Bubba Dunn, who owned Quickies, was three-hundred pounds and wore a long-sleeve shirt and Dickie overalls 365 days a year. A stout air conditioner mounted in the wall worked harder than a ditch digger to keep that place icebox-cold. You weren't allowed to loiter, but Adaire and I took our time, wandering through the rickety shelves, as if struggling over what to pick, knowing good and well we would order the same thing we always did: a hunk of bologna, sliced cheese, saltine crackers, and one of those ice-cold Coca-Colas. Summer thirst demanded the refreshing sweet burn only a frosty bottle of soda can give.

We weren't crazy about having to eat our lunch outside on the picnic table, but it was shaded under a hundred-year-old oak, and there was a pretty good breeze. After we were through, we counted up our collective change to see if we had enough to buy a pack of soft and chewy Hubba Bubba.

We rarely did.

We were halfway down the road after lunch, Adaire was telling me about the latest rerun of *Dukes of Hazard* I had missed because we didn't own a TV, when I shushed her quiet.

"Listen," I said, pointing to the ditch.

I had heard a whimper, but that wasn't what called to me. It was the sound just underneath it that only my ears could here.

A soul-song.

It warbled and stretched out to me like a yawn.

Then a painful cry crooned from among the foot-tall grasses.

A sound that could only come from a wounded animal.

The ditch was clogged with weeds. I was bound to get eaten up by chiggers or covered in poison oak. Or both. But I didn't care and neither did Adaire.

He was just a puppy, with fur the color of a dull nickel. His back leg was definitely broken. The asphalt had chewed up one of his shoulders. His jaw didn't look right.

"Fix him, Weatherly." The fear in Adaire's voice wasn't something I'd heard before.

I knelt down beside him and hovered my hands over his body. The twinkling of his soul was dwindling.

Tears were slipping down my cheeks so bad it blurred my vision.

"It'll be alright," Adaire said. I wasn't sure if she was talking to me or the dog, Blue—that's what his name tag read.

I took a deep breath to steady myself, then I bent closer to him and carefully cradled his paw in my hands.

I caressed the back of my finger over the rough pad of his front paw. My soft touch to let death know I was there. Then I pushed my mouth closer and whispered the secret scriptures, low enough so only death could hear. Words my papaw taught me to say that death cannot ignore.

The air around me grew colder, a sign that death was pulling on the energy to manifest itself. That slight shift as Blue's soul-song grew stronger, slipping from death's hold, told me so. I hummed my own soul-song—a nameless hymnal sung by the grave, but it has played in my head now for years. It invited the dog's soul to join mine out here, to dance in my palm.

I readied my hands open, so I could clap our two souls together, so we could push death out—

A brash truck horn honked. It caused me to jump and Blue to flinch. Bubba Dunn, in his old Chevy, came to a screeching halt on the roadside next to us.

"Come on, Weatherly. They told me to fetch you and hurry," he hollered out the passenger window. His oldest son hopped out of the truck and nodded for me to get in.

But I didn't want to go. I wanted to save Blue.

"You hear me, girl!" Bubba yelled. "Leave that damn animal alone and get in!"

His son wrenched me up by my elbow and shoved me in the truck like I was a petulant child that needed handling.

From behind, I heard Adaire cursing as she hurriedly jumped in the truck bed before we took off.

"Did it work?" I screamed through the back glass to Adaire who was kneeling at the tailgate, stretching her neck, watching to see if the dog moved.

After we made it down the road a piece—too far for her to see anymore—she turned around and shrugged, then sank down in the truck bed, her heart just as heavy as mine, tears threatening to spill down her cheeks.

My chest tightened as an awful burn lit up my lungs. I coughed once, then a second time. Quickly, I grabbed the dirty grease rag from the floorboard and hawked up a small wad of black ooze. Sin Eater Oil. Wasn't much but I hoped it meant I had saved Blue.

When we made it to the house, Grandmama stood there in the driveway. Scowl-faced and angry, she turned away at the sight of us pulling up to the house, tossing a dismissive hand toward Bone Layer.

I didn't have to ask what we were doing. I knew. Somebody was dying and needed me. From the looks of it, whoever it was, Grandmama didn't approve.

Silently, I got in the truck as Bone Layer held the door open for me, and watched in the side mirror as Adaire stood there, arms smarted across her chest and anger scrunching up her face.

Bone Layer, in his yellow-plaid farm shirt and plowing khakis, drove with a furrowed brow, like his only mission was the road. He didn't say word. An expressionless and emotionless rock like always.

"If it's Mrs. Coburn, I won't do it," I told him after a long silence. "That old hag spat on me and called me devil child." Of course, it was because Adaire and I had toilet-papered and egged her house, but we only did it because she tattled to the preacher after she caught us smoking behind the church shed.

As we approached the center of town, instead of heading out to the country to visit one of the church folk, Bone Layer turned north, up the mountain.

"Why we going up here?" A lick of fear rose in my chest. We lived on Appalachia's edge, not in the thick of the trees. We're not hill-folk, but we're not flatlanders, either.

And we weren't allowed north.

Well, Agnes Wilder wasn't allowed.

Papaw never told me what Grandmama had done to get kicked out of the hills, cast down to the bottom with a good riddance. But there was no going back for her, it seemed. I'd only been up here once before myself.

We drove high, where the roads wound and narrowed. Pines stretched tall and thickened. Homes, sparse and toothpick-frail, looked as if they'd slide right off the mountain if given the chance.

The narrow dirt road led to a small square house. An older home with faded gray lap-jointed wood siding with the prettiest pale pink painted on the shutters. In the yard stood a bottle tree taller than Bone Layer. It crooked to the side, its branches weighed down by the colorful glass bottles, all shades of blue, to trap the spirits that tried to get inside.

A big-boned elderly woman in a floral cooking dress stepped out onto the front porch to greet us. Just from the looks of her, I imagined she smelled like home cooking and Jesus.

Worry lines etched deep on her face, but then relief relaxed her shoulders at the sight of us. I didn't know this woman from Adam, but I could tell in the assured steps Bone Layer took to get to her and the careful way he cupped her hands in his own, she was someone important to him. I'd never met Bone Layer's friends, wasn't aware he had any. But the heavy murmur of his words comforted her in a way that only people who went way back could.

I smelled death before I even stepped on the porch. A stagnate smell. Like the rotted stump water mosquito larvae thrived in.

"Are you sure?" she asked Bone Layer after sizing me up. "She looks awfully young."

He nodded. "She got it from Augustus," he told her. My papaw's name, though tainted by his marriage to my grandmother, was all she needed to let me inside.

"She looks like her mama," she said, admiring my face. "Cleodora," she introduced herself as she opened the rickety screen door for me to enter. "But you can call me Miss Dora."

Inside was pristine; it smelled like Pine-Sol and fresh biscuits. Curio cabinets were tucked in all the corners of the room with every kind of religious figurine you could imagine. Angels and crosses. Little mini churches. Baby Jesus and crucified Jesus. They lined the walls and down the halls.

I swallowed hard, my unholiness stuck out like a cowlick in such a religious home.

"This here's my grandson, Lucky." She stepped to the side so I could see the pitiful man lying on the couch underneath a crocheted blanket. Maybe late twenties. His eyes were sunken, rimmed with dark circles. His lips were bone-dry and shriveled. There was a familiar frailness to him, one I'd seen a time or two before. Cancer.

Not sure what kind. It didn't matter.

Death was creeping in on him, like a shadow, slowly inching over his body a little bit every day. His death probably wouldn't be for weeks yet, but it was coming.

I thought at first, what I had heard when I walked in, was the muffled sound of a church choir on the AM radio. But that murmured harmonic music was coming from the man.

His soul-song was a sweet, mournful sound. Whoever this man was, he was worth saving.

"Doctors said there's nothing more to do with him. Just take him home until the Good Lord calls," she said to us, but looked down on her grandson like he was a most precious gift. "But I told them, the Good Lord set people on the earth that can do things better than them. That's why I called you, Jonesy," she said. He'd been called Bone Layer so long I'd forgotten he had a Christian name.

A weak smile pushed up the corners of Lucky's mouth as he looked at me. "If I'm seeing a sweet angel, Big Mama, I *must* be dying," he said and gave me his best effort at a wink.

"Hush now." Miss Dora fanned that nonsense away with her hand as if shooing flies. "I don't want to hear none of that talk. You let this girl do what she does. You'll be up and about in no time." Her worried eyes weren't so sure, though. Then she turned to me. "Jonesy and me will be out on the front porch if you need us." She patted her grandson's leg one more time with an *everything's-gonna-be-alright* kind of pat, but the tears welled at the edge of her eyes.

I waited until they both stepped outside before I slipped off my sneakers and knelt on the braided rag rug beside the couch.

He opened his mouth to speak, but it took him a second. "I knows your kind of people before," he managed. Then he took a ragged breath like those few words had already worn him out.

His right hand gripped mine, the back side scarred over from a bad burn. I felt the echo of someone else. Someone like me. A Fire Talker, I guessed. I'd heard of them in the stories Grandmama told. Stories of magic and witchery that still went on up in the hills, hidden from the modern day, clinging still to the traditions and ways of old. But I never knew they existed for certain.

I rid my head of the thought, and focused again on the task in front of me.

And then I began.

I rubbed my hands together to awaken my soul's energy, letting that sweet hum of my soul-song rise. Cupping my hands, I ran them over my face, then pushed that energy onto him. Then I scooped up the energy from his soul-song, that powerful gospel choir that lived inside him, and dumped it back onto myself. Back and forth, I did this, until the outlines of our souls blurred and death could not tell us apart.

Hot as it was in the house, a chill set upon us.

Into the palm of his hand, I whispered to death the secret Bible verses. I rocked on my knees as the words drifted over his skin.

Our soul-songs hummed in harmony. Tempting death.

Two for the price of one.

Eyes closed, I rose up on my knees. Fingers rubbing his palms where our souls danced.

Lucky's in my left hand.

Mine in my right.

I opened my mouth for death—then I clapped. A loud smashing that made no sound but popped your ears from the stark silence of it.

Lucky gasped, a grand and powerful wheeze that lifted him upright as death unsheathed itself from his body. The black smoke of death, now with no home, barreled itself inside me, looking for its prize. The force of it knocked me to the floor.

It pushed inside every corner of my body, searching for my soul. Under my skin. Over marrow and bone.

But I waited, curled against the floor while my insides were pillaged. The death flu began to rack my body, eating me up with sickness. I kept my clasped hands gripped tight together. Not allowing our souls to return just yet. Holding them outside our bodies a moment longer. My arms quivered from the effort.

Then there it was—death began to slow, finding nothing inside me to feast upon. Nowhere to gain purchase within my body. Without a soul, it thickened into a useless sludge, that slipped helplessly back into my lungs.

My eyes scanned the room for something, anything to spit in.

"Here." Miss Dora had come back into the room and thrust a blue Mason jar into my hands and pulled my long hair out of the way for me to puke. Black bile gurgled up in my throat and dribbled out of my mouth in tarry clumps of phlegm. Sin Eater Oil.

The coppery tinge of Lucky's cancer coated my tongue. I purged once more, then spat to clear the last out of my mouth.

"You poor girl." Miss Dora used a wet rag to clean my mouth. The cold compress felt like heaven to my forehead. "Is it always this bad?" she asked Bone Layer as I wilted onto the floor into a limp pile.

"Only once before." Bone Layer's eyes narrowed on me a moment. His deep voice might have sounded concerned if it didn't come off so brusque.

"Agnes will want it as payment." Miss Dora tried to hand Bone Layer the blue jar filled with my Sin Eater Oil.

He eyed the jar, then her again. "Burn it."

Bone Layer scooped me up like I weighed nothing and carried my limp body to the truck.

Later that night, I found the strength to leave my bed—or maybe delirium fueled my willpower. But I walked across the scant field of trees, from my house to Adaire's. Weak as a kitten, I climbed that familiar old oak tree, the one that led to her bedroom upstairs. Through her window, I crawled, the one she left open for me, like always. Fever burned up my brow. My bones ached from the flu my body would go through until it purged out the last of the death I'd talked out of that young man...and hopefully Blue.

Adaire pulled back the covers, and I curled up in the bed next to her, shivering so hard I thought I'd crack my teeth.

Three days I lay in her bed, fighting for my life. She never left my side.

FOUR

Fetch the Death Talker

Whoever said "Time heals all wounds" is a liar. It's been five weeks since we lost Adaire, and that hole in my chest has only grown.

Angry dust clouds huff around the car as I pull into the church parking lot. Greenwillow Baptist is a simple lap-joint-sided white building. Picturesque and quaint, it sits off the side of a country road nestled in a cluster of oak trees. A moat of wild tiger lilies surrounds it, clawing their way out of the ditch.

Adaire's presence feels so strong. The end of a joint still sits in the car's ashtray, something she rolled one Sunday two months ago while the preacher reminded us hell was just a breath away.

Though not for Stone Rutledge, apparently.

The car door rips a shriek through the quiet country air as I get out. I cut across the grass toward the garden shed where they house the mower and other tools that keep the church's property looking respectable.

Every day these past few weeks, I've been meeting my stress-release right here.

Waiting inside the shed, smelling like a pack of smokes, is Ricky Scarborough. He's a scrubby fellow with a too-tight muscle tee for those dumpy muscles. Baggy jeans hug his barreled waist. His camouflage baseball cap is permanently glued to his head. He isn't ugly, by any means, but he ain't nothing to look at, either. He and his group of redneck friends sit around drinking beers, talking cars, and smoking cigarettes all day. They're each just a slightly altered version of one another. Like a pack of coyotes, you can't really tell them apart.

Ricky doesn't even go to church here. Heck, I'm not even sure he goes to church at all. But he works at the gas station off the main highway down the road. He's close and convenient.

I kick the door shut behind me. Words aren't even spoken. Just hands and tongues and raw aggression. He cocks up my dress and grabs the back of my legs, lifting me on top of the plywood worktable. One of my flip-flops drops onto the floor. A splinter stabs the back of my thigh and digs in. I ignore it.

I ignore the gasoline-stained fingers that run through my hair. I ignore the sandpaper-rough hands as they paw at my breasts. I ignore the fact that Ricky forgot the rubbers, again.

Six minutes. That's all it takes to go from tension-twisted to sagging.

"So, hey," Ricky starts in, buttoning his jeans.

"I've gotta go," I say, not wanting to hear whatever nonsense he's suddenly so serious about.

"Wait, what? Right now? But you just got here."

"I'm meeting my friends at the quarry pond," I say. Weeks I've kept to myself in my room, my own prison; that is, when I'm not working the roadside market—or my hookups with Ricky. If I don't meet my friends today, Wyatt says he's going to stage an intervention. "So…later." I slide off the workbench; I can't get out of here fast enough. I shimmy my dress back down and retrieve my lost flip-flop.

"Okay. Later, as in tonight?" His shaky confidence weakens his voice. "Because some guys are taking their girlfriends down to the bottoms to drink some beers and—"

"I'm busy," I say before he can ask me to do something more involved like date.

"Well, I was thinking maybe this time—"

"What did I tell you about thinking?" I stop smoothing my hair and give him that look. The one that says we made a deal to do this discreetly and keep it uncomplicated. No dating. No labels. No couples stuff. Just me and him and…this, whatever this was.

"Look, I've been doing some thinking myself," I start, and Ricky's shoulders collapse, knowing what's coming. "I think this has run its course. Maybe we should just cool it for now." And by *for now*, I meant forever.

He yanks off his baseball cap and runs a frustrated hand over those spiky hairs of his, then snugs it back on. No point in him arguing because I've made up my mind, but that won't stop him from trying. God, this shed is muggy and hot. I'm about to suffocate.

"Weatherly, you know I like—"

"I gotta go." I cut him off in the middle of his attempt to rationalize. I grab the door latch to the shed to leave. "It was good talking to you."

"Weatherly," he pleads one last time. I pause, giving him a half second of false hope. Not intentionally, though, I'm peeping through the door crack to make sure the coast is clear.

"Wait five minutes before you leave," I remind him. Then I slip out of the shed.

Adaire used to wait for me at the top of the path that leads to a hideaway pond, that church-rolled joint having been put to good use, her eyes heavy slits. Her brows would be a little looser, like a pair of chilled-out caterpillars.

Now, it's Davis who's waiting for me at the edge of the path.

"Ricky Scarborough? Really?" he says, watching past my shoulder as Ricky sneaks out of the shed.

I groan a *mind-your-own-business* sort of sound.

"I don't want to talk about it." We haven't shared more than a handful of words lately. He keeps trying; that's what friends do, I guess. It's like he needs me—and our connection to Adaire— to get through it all. Drowning himself in work and EMT-training school only does so much.

People heal their hearts in different ways.

Me, I plan to ignore the pain in my life until it numbs me from the inside out. I offer him the last hit of Adaire's joint. He declines.

"Picking up her habits now?"

"Don't start," I snap back.

We walk down the rear path. Overgrown weeds poke at my bare legs. An errant grasshopper flees out of the way as we enter the woods.

Ethereal. That's the word that comes to mind when I walk into the woods. Adaire told me about that word after reading it in one of her fantasy books years ago. It sounded airy and magical and soulful. That's what these woods feel like when I enter them. Like where I'm going is a secret place that only my heart knows.

"I got a package from her." Davis says this as if it's the most normal thing in the world to receive mail from the dead.

"Recently?" I perk up at what he's telling me. There's a stupid flash in my brain that says, *Maybe she's alive!* A fleeting thought as I recall the burial.

"No. I found it in one of the bottom drawers of the tool cabinet. I think it's been sitting there since my birthday back in February. She's probably having a good laugh that it took me so long to find it."

I smile at that. "What was in it?"

Davis shrugs. "I don't know. I haven't opened it." He pauses, letting the emotion that's risen to the surface simmer back down. "If I open it, then that's it. It's over. The last piece of her will be gone."

This kicks me hard in the chest. I'd do anything to have one last piece of Adaire.

I touch him softly on the arm. "You open it when you're ready" is all I say.

It's a good ten-minute trek to the hidden pond. A circular valley surrounded by stretching Georgia pines. A rock quarry once, so many years ago, that eventually filled up with rainwater. Voices from the others sneak through the trees until we reach the small clearing.

This is supposed to be a celebration of life in remembrance of Adaire. Enjoying a few beers, reminiscing on the good times. I don't want to think about it, much less talk about it.

Raelean Campbell stretches out on a sunning rock, waving an arm hello. Wyatt, Adaire's older brother, clings to a rope swing like it's the only thing holding him up. He tosses off his baseball cap, ready to dive—when a gunshot cracks within the depths of the forest, causing us all to jump and hush quiet.

A murder of crows scatter over tree canopy where the shot rang out.

It sounded close.

"What the hell?" I scan the woods from the direction it came.

There's not much hunting that goes on in the summer. The acres of land beyond the pond are privately owned by the Latham family. They don't allow anyone to hunt there, but it's not unheard of for folks to shoot guns on their own property.

A quiet moment passes as we wait to see if there's anything more. After a few seconds of nothing happening and the eeriness of it already fading, everyone slowly winds back up to normal.

Wyatt, with a slippery beer-grin and the rope still in his hand, swings out over the water, releasing at the highest peak. The water erupts around him, causing a wake throughout the small pond.

He's got Aunt Violet's and Adaire's dark hair, minus the galaxy of freckles the rest of us inherited. I'm the oddball in the family with my strawberry blond.

Davis joins the others. After a quick hello, I duck behind a holly berry bush, slink out of my sundress and into my bikini. Dark movement to my right snags my attention, but by the time I turn my head, the black shadow is disappearing into the branches.

Cautiously watching the woods, I stuff my clothes into my bag, then make my way back.

If Adaire were here, she'd be sporting her silver one-piece that looked like a blanket from the Space Shuttle. I never understood where she got the ideas for her bizarre clothing. But they helped get her into an art institute for fashion design, so what do I know?

I climb over the cragged rocks to get to the larger flat boulder people lie out on. The muted gray surface burns the bottoms of my feet after I kick off my flip-flops.

"You doing alright, Weatherly?" Raelean asks, handing me a beer.

I shrug, then take the beer and gulp down a good swig of it, surveying the motley crew of twentysomethings I'm proud to call friends.

Wyatt's a country boy through and through. From his John Deere baseball cap to his plaid button-ups down to his boots. He's an oak tree, physically and at heart. Wyatt became man of the house after Uncle Doug died years ago.

Raelean's a head shorter than me but she's feisty, with an *I'm-gonna-kick-your-ass-if-I-don't-like-the-way-you're-looking-at-me* attitude. Willowy is what she calls me. Makes me think about the willow switches Grandmama used to whoop my ass if I didn't mind her just right. She waitresses down at the Watering Hole most evenings and every weekend.

Davis is tall and dark and lean. He and Adaire made an oddly perfect pair. Now that she's gone and with his EMT training almost finished, I doubt he'll hang around here much longer.

So it's only me that doesn't have it all figured out just yet. I wasn't the college-going type, never seemed to get much out of high school. I was waiting—for what, I'm not sure, something, anything to happen, to call to me, besides a soul-song. Adaire used to ask how long I was willing to wait to start my life. I never gave her an answer.

Wyatt pulls Davis to the side, offering a few secret words. Brothers, despite their skin colors, bonded through Adaire. Davis chokes back his emotions. Something men tend to do, no matter how much they hurt.

"See any more of Stone Rutledge lately?" Raelean asks.

"No, ma'am," I reply as I shake my head. "One run-in with the law this summer was enough for me, thank you very much."

"That may be, but what are we going to do about Stone? He can't just get away with this. It's been over a month and I'm still mad as hell, can't imagine how you must be feeling."

I appreciate Raelean wants to take this on with me. We've become friends over the last year since she's moved here. But this isn't her burden. It's personal. A family problem.

"He *did* get away with it, though, didn't he?" I take another chug of my beer before setting it and my drawstring bag down next to her. I stand at the edge of the diving rock and tug my highlighter-yellow bikini from Walmart out of my ass crack. "Besides, *we* aren't going to do anything. If anyone's going to handle Stone, it'll be me" is all I say before I plunge into the water to wash off the gasoline paw prints still ghosting on my skin.

Water trickles down my face after I come up for air. Far off behind me, I hear Raelean talking to Wyatt and Davis about a barbecue she's having at her house on Sunday; they both nod in agreement, like it sounds like a nice idea. Davis moves on to ask what we think that gunshot was all about. I hum an *I don't know*, not sure if he hears me, but I don't engage further and stop swimming as something in the woods catches my attention.

I watch. And wait.

Their murmuring conversation is a buzzing gnat in the background. I slink deeper into the water and glide smoothly away. Eyes skimming the woods for another glimpse.

There it is again. I catch a darkness moving in the depths of the woods.

Not low and stalking like a coyote. Nor cautious and gentle like a deer. No, this is something in the tree canopy that scatters and compacts, then scatters and compacts again and again.

Curious, I swim closer to the other side, farther from the group, their voices now a distant mumble, tracking the erratic movement. The waves of the water rock the horizon line along the shore, blurring the edge of the woods. Eventually, the darkness stays tight together until a shape forms just beyond the tree line.

I squint to make out the shape—a man emerges in the shadowed space. I rear back, taken by surprise.

He isn't coming from the direction of the church. Nor in the direction of the gunshot.

Shade and small breaks of sunlight through the trees camouflage him; I can't quite make out who it is. Just a blur of dark hair and pale skin dressed in all black. Or maybe that's the shadows?

From behind, I hear the others hollering at me, their voices growing louder as I return to my surroundings.

"He's calling for you, Weatherly!" Wyatt yells out over the pond, and I turn, confused.

Wyatt jabs a finger in the air in the direction of the church; so I look that way to see what he's getting all worked up over.

On the other side of the pond, Ricky is waving for me to come over to him.

Good lord. What now? I swim back to the rock to see what the fuss is all about.

"What do you think he wants?" Wyatt asks as he pulls me out of the water. No towel, so I stand there, dripping.

"Who knows? He probably just doesn't understand what 'it's over' means," I mumble, but then I realize there's a panic to Ricky's stride. Everyone stands, catching on to the sense of urgency.

I glance back over to the trees where the shadowy figure was, but there's nothing there now.

Ricky cups his hands around his mouth and calls my name. Contrary to my good sense, I head over, picking up on a *something-ain't-right* vibe.

"Hey." Ricky labors to catch his breath—courtesy of years of smoking. "We got a call at the gas station. From the Latham family. About the boys. They said—" More labored breathing. "They said…fetch the Death Talker."

FIVE

Once Is All You Get

Zeke and Worth Latham are two brothers who roll around in the dirt, beating the hell out of each other more often than I care to count. Hearty, hefty boys who work like dogs on their father's farm. At fourteen and sixteen, they can do the work of any man.

It's faster for me to run up through the forest the half mile than go back to the church and drive the winding four miles of road. But I can't help the feeling I'm not alone in these woods as I make my way there.

I don't know which Latham boy is hurt, but I hope it's not Worth. I've already talked the death out of him once before. He was barely four at the time. A bad fever stiffened his neck and worked its way to his brain. Meningitis, they said. Fourteen-year-old me crawled up in the bed, we snuggled close, and I talked the death out of him.

Once is all you get. I've never tried to talk the death out of somebody twice.

I'm out of breath by the time I make it there. A white clap-board farmhouse with a fresh metal roof. Clumps of moss hang from old hearty oak trees anchoring the property. The home goes back generations, but the Lathams have taken great care of it.

"She's here." Zeke hops up off the porch at the sight of me. Dread washes over me. It must be Worth that needs me. Zeke's a burly kid with strawberry blond hair that looks more like a man at sixteen than most do grown. He rushes over, blood staining his shirt.

"What happened?" I ask, still trying to catch my breath.

"We were looking for a place to build a deer stand when we saw…" His eyes scan my face. There's a petrified fear shrouded in those gray eyes of his, like whatever he saw will forever haunt him.

"Saw what, Zeke?" A knot thrums in my throat where my heart got stuck.

"You'll just have to see for yourself." He shakes his head, like he's pushing away the horror. "Worth found him first," he says. "He tripped, his foot sunk into a hole—almost like a grave or something."

"He who?" I ask as he opens the front porch door for me to go in.

"Ellis Rutledge."

I freeze. A half-second hesitation, really. A Rutledge is dying—Stone Rutledge's son. How I feel about it tests my good nature.

Between a crack in the porch boards, the tiniest of a black frond peeks through. The coil of its foliage unfurls like an open palm.

"Praise Him." Miss Caroline Latham greets us from the living room. Her fair skin and apricot hair, just like her boys', makes her look frailer in this situation. Worth looks seasick, green as celery, as he waits on the couch, wringing his hands. Miss Caroline drags toward the rear of the house.

The smell of Ellis's death trails down the hallway. Not the traditional smell one might think of, like an animal rotting on the side of the road. No, this is the curdled smell of soured milk; reminds me of the bibs and burping cloths at the church nursery.

"We called his family, they're on the way. He's too bad to transport." Her voice cracks. "We called Dr. York, but he's all the way in Mercer at a family reunion. So we called you." She pushes into the bedroom. Facedown on the bed is Ellis Rutledge, shirtless. A towel soaked in blood covers the upper part of his back and shoulder. Closest hospital is almost an hour away. With that much blood, he wouldn't last the trip. I should have brought Davis.

"She's here, honey. She's here." Miss Caroline's voice is shaky but full of relief. She kneels on the floor to look Ellis in the face. I nod a hello to Mr. Latham who stands in the corner, trying to keep it together, but looking like he's going to vomit.

"Um…hey, Ellis." I kneel beside Miss Caroline, feeling very conflicted about helping someone whose family caused mine so much pain. Ellis's brown eyes find me, and he attempts to smile, but his mouth barely twitches. He's much slimmer than the chubby cheeked boy I met as a child. His curls longer and fluffier than back then.

Miss Caroline lightly lifts the bloody towels at his neck to show me. A punctured hole, where the neck meets the shoulder, weeps with blood. She quickly covers it. "Boys say they found him with a branch pierced through his neck. He must have fell back and speared himself." Just hearing this makes me queasy.

Ellis's head wobbles and a spittle of blood splatters on the pillow when he tries to speak.

"Don't try to talk," I tell him.

Death is so thick I can barely hear his soul-song—the soft sweet sound of a violin. A weeping sound that tugs at your heart and makes you feel sorry for it.

"I'm gonna see what I can do for you, okay?" I say to him. "At least until the doc comes." I stand and look at Mr. Latham. "We need to get him on his back. It'll work better if we can." I glance up to Zeke and Mr. Latham, expectant.

They exchange looks, as if checking with the other whether they think they can or even should move him.

"Hurry!" I urge, getting them to snap to it. Mr. Latham and Zeke jump into motion. They fold the covers from the opposite side of the bed over his body, sandwiching Ellis in between, readying to flip him.

"Miss Caroline, I need a mug. Some kind of coffee or tea-cup," I instruct her. She nods, leaving to go fetch one. "One that's never had whiskey in it," I add.

She glances over at Mr. Latham, who promptly looks away, unable to attest that such a cup exists in their house.

"I'll find something." Miss Caroline disappears into the hall.

On the count of three, they flip Ellis over. He makes a god-awful garbled scream, one that'll surely be in my brain for the rest of my days.

Miss Caroline returns with an old tin cup with *BABY* engraved on the outside, a common heirloom around these parts.

"I use this for cutting biscuits." She passes it to me, her hand shaky. "Should be safe from whiskey." She cuts a glare to Mr. Latham. He nods a confirmation.

"Y'all know how this goes. Let me do my work."

Hurriedly, everyone leaves the room.

Miss Caroline pauses at the doorway, her blue eyes pinning me. "It's a good thing what you're doing. Helping this young man, despite…all that's happened." Then she shuts the door, leaving me alone with Ellis.

And death.

I wonder if the Lathams weren't here, would I still do this? If no one would know, would I just walk away and let him die? But no, he didn't kill Adaire; he shouldn't be made to pay.

Bubbles of blood foam around Ellis's mouth; he sputters a cough. I use the wet washcloth to wipe clean his chin.

"She's—" Ellis tries to speak, but it comes out more like a hiss.

"Don't worry about Miss Caroline," I try to reassure him. "She wants to help."

He gasps for air to speak again, a wet breath. "She's here." His words a garbled slur from the blood. His eyes loll to the window.

Hairs on my neck prickle. I don't think he's talking about Miss Caroline anymore.

"You've lost too much blood. It's got your thoughts all jumbled up. Just focus on me."

Ellis tries to speak again, but when he does, he chokes on more blood.

The pungency of death clings tight to him. It's now or never. I drag a wooden chair over to his bedside; it's a wicked scrape across the floor. I pull his arm out from underneath the blanket and gently open his hand. Smoothly, I brush my hands over his shoulders and down the length of his arms. Caressing over him and then over me a few times, mixing the sounds of our souls, letting death know something more desirable is here, wanting it.

Ellis's breathing is shallow now as he struggles. I do my best to tune it out and focus on the task.

I lean forward and poise my mouth over his open palm. The secret scriptures slip between my lips and over his skin. Talking to death. Luring it to me.

The gift my papaw passed on to me before he died. A gift to be passed to the opposite sex before I die, or it will be lost forever.

The temperature in the room drops to the icy cold of a winter's night as death answers my call. Clouds of my breath puff as the words begin to draw death out of him. The frigid air burns my throat like taking a long drag off a harsh cigarette. It dries my words into a thin rasp.

The soft violin of Ellis's soul grows stronger as it frees from death's grasp. I hum my own soul-song, and it invites Ellis's soul to join mine, so together we can expel death.

Our soul-songs dance alongside each other, his in my one hand, mine in the other.

Ready.

Then I clap, combining our two souls into one and boot death right out of him, then—a zinger of a vibration hits my teeth. Sharp and unexpected. It sends an electrical jolt through my entire body and knocks me out of my chair.

The sound of my soul-song and his crash, forming a disharmonious chaos, like two violins choking each other. I clamp my hands over my ears as it pierces my hearing. The squelching grates down my spine like nails on a chalkboard.

"What the hell?" The ringing in my ears slowly fades as the connection of souls is broken. As soon as they touched, it was like a static zap to my nervous system. That's not how it's supposed to go at all.

My throat clinches tight and starts to close up. I gag. With a harsh cough, I hack to clear it. A wad of phlegm clogs my throat. Up it comes and I spit into the tin cup. A translucent wad oozes down the side.

Not the black death-ooze my body usually makes.

What in the hell is going on?

Oh, shit! The weed. The beer. Could that be it? My gaze slips to the tin cup. Whiskey—or any alcohol—can't be in the cup or ever before, but does that mean alcohol can't be in me, either? This isn't a situation I've ever been in.

I catch Ellis watching me with troubled eyes, so I fumble a smile. "It's okay. Just a bad connection. We'll try it again." I ease back over to the bed.

Ellis's eyes are barely slits as he struggles to keep them open. I push aside my worries and try harder. Seek deeper. Hum my hymnal more smoothly.

I trail my hands over my head, my face. Then over his head, his face. Then again over me. Over him. And again. Back and forth. As I reach out my soul to grasp ahold of his, a lightning bolt of electricity rips up my arms and jars my body into a paralytic freeze.

The ice of death causes the room to shrink, vacuuming itself back into Ellis's body. His chest bucks up at the suddenness of it. His eyes widen with fear.

"Weatherly," he croaks, my name a desperate plea. He grabs at my hands. He gasps once. Twice. A cragged noise that comes from his throat, then his eyes soften as they lose focus. His body relaxes into the bed.

"No! No, no, no. Wait." I pull at Ellis's limp shoulders; his head wobbles loosely.

A cold clammy hand grips my elbow and yanks me off him.

"You satanic whore!" Dr. York shoves me out of the way, mumbling something about the Devil's work. He immediately starts to administer CPR.

The cold wash of his words lands home. I shrink into the corner so the doctor can attempt to perform the impossible. The frigid look on Miss Caroline's face sends shame flaming up my cheeks.

Desperately, I offer, "I'm sorry. I'm sorry. I'm sorry." To each one of them. To Ellis. To the room.

Clumsily, I back away and collide into Grandmama. When she arrived, I don't know. Her surly form blocks the doorway. Disgust, that's what I read in that leathery, wrinkled face of hers. Her wiry gray hair cinched in a bun as rigid as her hate. Her foggy eyes search the room through sounds and movement, seeing only blurs of color and light, but assessing everything. She bares an open palm to me, and I place the tin cup in her hand. One sniff of the contents and her loathing deepens, nothing but worthless ooze that wouldn't even sicken a child.

If drinking that beer kept me from saving Ellis, and Grandmama finds out, I'll never hear the end of it.

Grandmama grips my arm tight and ushers me from the bedroom as the doctor confirms what we all already know. Her fingers dig into my elbow from her angry grasp as she pushes me down the hall. My feet shuffle and stumble. I feel ten again. That childhood fear prickles the hairs on my skin.

With a quick shove out onto the front porch, she simply says, "Go home." The battered screen door slaps against its frame, cracking the silence of the woods.

Bone Layer, who waits there, spares a glance long enough to realize Grandmama wasn't speaking to him. He returns his focus on the stick he's whittling.

Dr. York—a bony fellow with pale skin and arms covered in a carpet of dark hair—walks over to talk with Sheriff Johns, who is the very opposite in stature, as he's getting out of his patrol car. The bloody towel the doc wrings between his fingers, as he cleans his hands, feels like damning evidence. He glares my way.

Satanic Whore, my mind whispers. It revels in repeating this.

Some believe my death-talking is a gift from God. Though nothing about me, or what I do, feels holy. Others deem it the work of the Devil. Yet, I never asked Satan for this burden.

It's neither good nor evil. Taking the death from one and leaving it for another day is more like shuffling the cards and re-dealing them.

Except instead of God, Grandmama is the dealer.

At the sound of skidding gravel, we all turn. Stone Rutledge's bright red Corvette whips into the yard. My footing stutters at the sight of it.

Lorelei Rutledge, Ellis's twin sister, jumps out of the passenger side of the car. Stone eases himself out as well, terror leaching the color out of his face.

"Where is he?" Her frantic cries cause the sheriff to step into action and hold her back. He's doing his best to calm her. But it's the doctor's solemn confirmation that breaks Lorelei.

Stone stumbles backward at the news, as if he's going to pass out. He catches himself on the hood of his car and sits, looking stunned and lost. His shaky hand worries over his face, his life shattered by the loss of his only son. I might have felt sorry for the bastard if I didn't hate him so much.

"We should go," Bone Layer whispers next to me, pulling me toward the truck. I couldn't agree more.

"Somebody killed him!" Lorelei screams in a panic.

Inside the truck, I keep watching as we pull away.

We're not too far down the road before a deputy flies past us, lights ablaze. Urgently headed to the house.

"Do you think he was murdered?"

Bone Layer shrugs, then he flicks on the windshield wipers as the rain begins to pour.

SIX

Unto the Otherworld

It's well past midnight when I decide to sneak out of the house. That zinger death jolted me with still has my nerves frazzled. A single beer—is that all it took to keep me from saving Ellis? I push the guilt out of my head. Nothing a little bit of whiskey can't fix. I take another long slug of the warm liquor from the flask I have with me, then tuck it away into my back pocket.

Carefully, I remove the screen to my bedroom window and crawl through. Something scratches my stomach as I do. A tiny clatter hits the porch at my feet. Kneeling, I search the darkness for whatever tumbled from the windowsill. Heat lightning rips through the sky. A glimmer of something shiny on the worn wood catches my eye.

A trinket.

A gold square with a toggle on the back. Reminds me of the clip-on earrings the old ladies wear at church. I tell the hope that quickens in my chest to stop lying to me. Trinkets have been left on my windowsill before, but it hasn't happened in some time. Then again, I haven't failed in some time, either.

I remember the chilly autumn we found Cindy Higgins in the woods. She didn't come home the night before, and her mama reported her missing the next morning. Her car was left abandoned out by the highway, and the sheriff put together a search party, mostly locals. I was twelve at the time, Cindy was sixteen, but for some reason when you're that young, teenagers seem infinitely older. I wandered off from the search team, zeroing in on the carousel music I was hearing—Cindy Higgins's soul-song.

She sat unconscious, slumped at the base of the tree, badly beat up and half-dressed. I knew even then someone evil had wronged her. She was probably too far gone to save, but I wonder if my fear and shock of what had happened didn't play a part.

Then I heard a caw from the tree branch above me. It echoed out into the vastness of the woods, reminding me how alone I was, away from the fold of the others.

One minute Rook was a crow in the tree, the next he was a boy on the ground next to me. He knelt down, reassuring me that everything would be okay. That he would take care of her now. I don't remember if I called for the other searchers or if they just found me, but I didn't let go of Cindy's lifeless hand until they came.

There have only been ten or so souls I could not save. Every time they brought Rook back to me. Usually only for a few days. It always depended on how quickly he could move their soul over.

The whisper of flapping wings shushes across the lawn. I jump off the porch and run after the sound as it disappears into the woods.

A hundred yards in and I've lost the patch of dark I was chasing. Whatever I thought I saw has disappeared into the night.

Leftover rain drips from the branches in sporadic *plops* around me. The leaves beneath my feet a *shushing* rustle. Filtered moonlight sneaks through the canopy, offering glimpses of my surroundings. As my eyes adjust to the stillness of the night, I scan for some inclination as to where it might have gone, if I saw anything at all. Whiskey haze already muddying my thoughts.

It's the sound of a sweet violin that turns me toward the north. Whisper-soft. A light kiss. Then it's over before I can be sure I heard it at all. Maybe it's just remnants of Ellis's soul-song still playing in my memory.

I'm just about ready to tell my imagination to take a hike, when off in the distance a faint white orb floats. It dissipates into the darkness, only to reappear a few feet farther on. Then again. Luminous before fading, it bobs and sways through the trees like the blinking glow of a lightning bug.

There are tales of the dead who lure you into the woods. Some are helpful, sending you a warning. Then there are the others, the ones who stand the hairs on your neck and have intentions that could only please the Devil.

This soul…seems lost. A sad sight to see. I follow it.

It floats down an invisible river through the waist of the forest. To the backside of our property where a creek bends toward the quarry pond.

The orb winks out as if spooked. I wait to see if it returns. After a long silent nothing, I turn back around to head home—

Then I hear it again, the soft imploring of a violin.

Out of the corner of my eye, I see a ghostly figure standing at the edge of the trickling water. Wisp-thin, like smoke you could easily blow away. His lean frame and lazy curls immediately recognizable.

Ellis Rutledge.

He waits there, seemingly stopped by an invisible force. Haints can't cross water, I realize, as he stands in front of the creek bed. Wherever he's intending to go, that trail of water keeps him from it.

The last thing I want to do is invest any more effort in someone whose family has done so much harm to mine. But I can't help but feel like he's called me here. Whether it makes sense or not, I'm inclined to help him.

"You're with me now," a voice from nowhere speaks. I dip back behind the tree, stealing just a peek.

A dark figure holds in the shadows of the night on the other side of the narrow creek. The moonlight alights on a single inviting palm offered to Ellis. My pulse quickens. I study the dark, trying to catch sight of what my heart tells me is Rook.

Ellis's spirit steps back, wary of the man. There's half a breath where I wonder if Ellis's fearful hesitation might have some validity.

"What's your name?" the man says, his tone soft. I roll the sound of his voice around in my head, assessing it for any sign of familiarity. That deep thump in my chest says, *Yes, yes, it's him.* But I have nothing to compare it to, only the memory of a boy who I haven't spoken to in years.

He steps slightly farther into the light. Shadows and dark still mask his face.

Ellis's gaze drops to his chest where the orb I followed here starts to reform. His body thins, growing more translucent as his soul brightens. That sweet violin rises in tune, a weeping sound that softens the heart.

"You're with me now," the man says again, desperation lining his words. The pulsing glow of Ellis's soul quivers, unsure about staying or leaving.

That's when I know it's him, for Rook is a Soul Walker, trying to cross Ellis into the otherworld.

I dare to lean forward an inch, but my weight shifts and my foot presses on a branch with a soft *crack*.

Ellis sharply turns my way. A swear passes over my tongue. In the vacuum of a second, Ellis appears inches from my face.

I skitter backward at the sight of him. Blood weeps from the death-wound on his neck and dribbles down his chin. That gentle violin a charged voluminous sound that stretches to the stars, begging. His gentle eyes plead as the orb in his chest radiates out.

Liar, he whispers. The word, not spoken, but a violent echo in my head, and I run.

Through the woods and down the path toward our little barn. The dead have never come at me like that before. So fierce, so intense. I make it all the way across the open field to the oak tree in our yard and stop.

Nothing followed me.

Not so much of a hint of anything lingering here in the dark. Only my panting breaths to fill the silence.

Dots of rain drip on my face. Another crack of heat lightning rips through the sky.

Off in the distance, a cloud of black smoke forms above the trees. My first instinct says to keep running, but I pause. Curious. It's moving fast, expanding, then contracting. Expanding, then contracting.

Not smoke. Crows.

In unison, they drop, barreling my way, starting to meld into one another.

My body tightens, understanding what I'm watching but not sure what the hell to expect.

But I keep my eyes open. I want to see him do it.

The cluster of crows ascends from the sky, spiraling downward. The force at which it comes is enough to make me throw my arms up, cover my face. I peek through the narrow space between my fingers.

A flock of crows converges into a single black mass feet from me until…*swoop*, Rook appears, stepping onto the ground as if he descended from a set of invisible stairs.

Long and lean. Pale as the moon. And no longer a boy.

He's as real and alive as the blood racing through me.

And he's beautiful.

You don't expect to call a man beautiful. But he is. His dark hair has grown out since I last saw him. Solid black with jagged edges that dust his shoulders, tattered and wavy. Creamy skin like maybe he's from Seattle or Forks, Washington, or some other place that doesn't get a lot of sun. His nose is perfect and straight. And those lips, CoverGirl pretty. Cousin Wyatt would slug me if I said that about him.

The silly part, I didn't expect him to be so grown. So mature. It's like he's aged right along with me.

At the creaking of the smokehouse door, I scramble backward under the cover of the fat oak tree.

"Who's there?" Bone Layer's deep voice calls out into the dark. The distinct *shift-crunch* as he cocks his shotgun, audible over the rain. The tiny smokehouse porch creaks as he paces, searching the yard.

Crows erupt from the space where Rook just stood. I duck to the ground and cover my head as hundreds of them swoop down and swirl around me. A cocoon of wings. They break away and flood the sky.

My breathing a heavy huff in the deafening silence left behind. My heart thunders in my chest.

Against the sky—much like that first night all those years ago—the crows swoop into a spiral until they condense into a single black bird that I'm left to watch as it flies off.

SEVEN

A Wish on a Crow Feather

"Shit!"

My whispered curse is sharp against the night as I watch my sneaker tumble through the wet branches to the ground below. You'd think, as many times as I've climbed up this tree, I'd have the proper skills to keep my shoes on. One swift kick in the air and I send the other one flying. It bounces on the rain-soaked lawn with slurpy *thwaps*.

My head is still reeling from the sight of Rook—or maybe it's the alcohol. But he's here. Back. I have to tell someone, even if it's a ghost.

Crusty paint bites my palms as I press against the window frame and sloppily push. The old wood stutters a *welcome* as I shimmy up it. A far-off storm rumbles as it draws nearer. I straddle the window so as not to knock over Adaire's bookcase and duck my head—*son of a bitch!* I press a hand to my throbbing temple where I whacked it against the windowpane.

As kids, Adaire and I would escape to a cave in the woods near the quarry pond to hide from Grandmama and Adaire's father, a real asshole, God rest his soul. A place only birds could reach, maybe a mouse. Or two curious little girls with a rope and a bagful of courage. We stole a few of the pastor's albums, records of Loretta Lynn and Johnny Cash, and would play them on an old windup Victrola Adaire found in an abandoned farmhouse.

That cave was a hell of a lot less drab than her room. Gray walls, tan bedding, and bland brown-speckled carpet. Even the furniture was sad, dinky remnants left over from church bazaars and yard sales. Child-sized, so that you have to bend down just to get your clothes out of the top drawer of her dresser. Her room still smells of Dr Pepper and incense. I let the familiar odor envelope me as I lower myself onto the bed.

So many nights, Adaire and I have lain here together. Our bodies always huddled close in the narrow twin bed. Many times after I talked the death out of someone, or at least tried. Sometimes just so I could prattle on about whatever my heart felt full with that week.

For a time, she didn't believe my wild stories about a boy who was sometimes a crow. We were kids. She thought he was my imagination gone wild. Hell, I thought it, too.

But hadn't I made a wish on a crow feather once, to save a little boy's life?

Barely nine at the time, I saw it lying there in the dirt. The setting sun captured its blue-black sheen. The wind tickled it. Grabbed my attention by my collar. I thought it was a sign. I could have sworn I heard that boy asking for my help.

Adaire saw him long before he went missing. I'll never forget the blank, lost look in her eyes as she stared off into the oil pan Bone Layer used for the truck.

Gazing is what we call it. Others call it scrying. It's when you see something that hasn't quite happened yet in a dark reflective surface.

Gazing is in Adaire's blood like death-talking is in mine. Aunt Violet used to gaze, before she gave herself over to drinking. Wyatt never quite got the hang of it. But Adaire could do more than either of them—she even had visions.

She showed Papaw on a map right where to find the boy. She'd seen him, said he was stuck in between coming and going but wouldn't be there for a few days yet.

Sure enough, a couple days later a boy fell in the river up at Blackbeak Falls in Tennessee. Rapids were fierce that winter with all the ice storms and flooding that hit us. They combed the woods from Tennessee all the way to down Georgia where our borders kissed, hoping he'd got free from the waters and was wandering in the forest simply lost.

Papaw and Bone Layer found him right where Adaire said he'd be. Washed up five miles south down the Savannah River here in Black Fern's Creek. They said he was laid on a stretch of slate rock, eyes wide-open to the sun, looking like a waterlogged raccoon with his heavy dark corduroy coat that probably weighed him down below the surface.

The boy was stuck between coming and going but not in the living and dying kind of way. He was dead, but stuck between this world and the next. That's what happens when an innocent life is snatched too soon.

Papaw's ancestors say it's the crow's job to take those ill-fated souls to the other side. Guide them safely into the afterlife. That's why I made the wish that day.

I figured, at the time, if you could talk the death out of dying, then maybe, if a Death Talker worked the prayer just right, they could convince death to leap out of the dead just the same.

But death-talking doesn't work that way, Papaw said. We shouldn't try talking the death out of the dead.

Shouldn't.

Late in the night, he and Bone Layer finally returned home

with the boy's body wrapped up in one of my great-granny's quilts. They left him in Bone Layer's one-room smokehouse until the sheriff could come the next day to collect the child and return him to his family.

I wanted to see the boy. So I snuck into the smokehouse and pulled back the quilt—about jumped out of my skin to see him looking back at me. His eyes were wide-open, cloudy white, but you could tell they were once blue. His dark hair was shorn tight to his head. His skin pale as moonlight. He was beautiful, even then. So beautiful I kissed him. Coldest kiss my lips ever felt. And there was a terrible ache in my chest, seeing him lie there, lifeless. So I bent my head next to him and whispered a little prayer, something from Psalms that drifted comfortably into my thoughts.

And then I talked the death out of the dead.

I twiddle a crow feather between my fingers in the moonlight that's streaming through Adaire's bedroom window. Rain drizzles down the glass pane, casting wormy shadows on the wall.

"You think Rook will stay this time?" I ask aloud, my voice cutting through the darkness of her room. My whiskey-filled head begins to think maybe I didn't see Rook at all. That he was just a dream. Or an omen.

Pathetic how I let my emotions get here. Wanting him to come. Trying to hold on to something in this lonely world. Makes me wonder what's broken in my head—or maybe my heart—that dreams about a man who can't stay. But this time might be different, I tell myself.

A cold breeze pushes through the room. My breath a frosty cloud. I turn toward Adaire. Our noses a finger's width apart.

You gotta let me go, she whispers. I close my eyes and choke back my feelings and let the liquor and exhaustion drag me off to sleep.

EIGHT

Violent Delights

A thundering fist pounds my head. An angry sun rages against my eyelids.

Then the pounding comes again, only this time I realize the fist is on Aunt Violet's front door and not just in my head. There's a murmur of voices as she curses whoever is racking on the door at the damn crack of dawn. I glance at the alarm clock that reads after nine. *Oh, shit, I've gotta go.*

Shielding my eyes from the sun, I peer out the window and spy a police car about the same time I hear Deputy Rankin announce himself. My first thought: *What in the hell has Aunt Violet done now? Car in the ditch again?* As the fuzz starts to clear from my head, though, I remember Ellis is dead, and I am a satanic whore. *Damn it.* The last thing I want is to talk with the sheriff. So I tumble out the window and into woods behind their house that lead to mine.

On the front porch, Bone Layer slathers on a layer of blue paint around the doorway; same bright aqua color as our ceiling inside the house. Extra precautions since I couldn't save Ellis.

I head inside, straight to our herbal cabinet and take a piece of willow bark to chew on, though I doubt it will be enough to get rid of this hangover. A cup of black coffee is what I need. With the bark between my teeth, I set about making some.

From my pocket, I pull out the trinket I found on my windowsill. In the light of day, I can tell it's not a clip-on earring but some kind of toggle button. A cuff link, I realize. Looks like brass; surely it isn't real gold. I set my coffee cup down and start to scratch at the speck of black on its flat surface—

"Where have you been?" The cragged sound of Grandmama's voice jabs at my back. I startle at the sound, then shove the cuff link into my pocket. Her eyes drop to my muddy feet. She walks over to her recipe box that had been left open and slaps the lid shut, locks the box, and returns it to the square niche above the kitchen window. When she turns back around, I cast my gaze to my coffee cup, attempting to tamp down any curiosity she might detect.

"Out" is all I offer, yet I know it won't be enough. The roadside market opens at ten, and I need to shower, so I head to my room.

"Here, now!" The words, sharp claws that hook into my back and command I stop. "Don't you walk away when I'm talking to you. Answer me."

My teeth grind together. I am not a child and have not been one for some time now, but sometimes it's easier to lie. One slithers from my tongue like a slippery snake. "Wyatt and I were—"

"Devil's eyes, don't tell no lies." Grandmama sings each word slow and clear. The hairs on my neck stand. "He sees the secrets you try to hide."

It's the same rhyme she sang to Adaire and me as kids before she'd switch us for hiding the truth. She always knew when we were lying or when we'd done wrong. She said the chickens told her. Whispered it on the wind.

I believed her.

Chickens are the Devil's birds. He chains them to the ground to keep them close. That's why they can't fly.

Grandmama always gave us a choice. Truth or the switch. I always told the truth.

Adaire, even if the truth would set her free, always took the switch. Never made any sense to me. Not until I realized there was power in not giving in. Where I was last night and what I was doing is none of her damn business. I exhale my last ounce of patience and turn around.

Grandmama stands there, hands locked in front of her with the poise and patience of a nun. Frail, slender arms covered in a sheer black long-sleeve blouse. A mini ruffle trims the collar and down the button flap, hinting to a sweetness or softness—but there isn't anything about my grandmother that is sweet or soft. Her long khaki skirt stiff from the durable cotton material. Saggy thick stockings cover her broomstick legs that hide inside heavy orthopedic shoes.

Those eyes—unseeing, yet all-knowing. They zero in on me like a snake that senses the heat of its prey. "Where were you last night?" she asks again.

Why do I stay in a world that's growing harder and harder to live within? When I was little, I thought church and Grandmama were everything. I've come to realize for some time now I was raised up on the wrong side of right.

"Out," I say crisp and clear in case she didn't hear me the first time and head to my room.

Clementine's, the local family-owned restaurant, sits off the main highway, and up behind the diner is what all the bus tours come here for. The Sugar Hill Plantation. Named after the sugar cane once grown there. At some point, sugar was no longer needed and cotton took its place. A dark history that brings tour buses through Black Fern for an education. An important reminder of the scars we set upon this land, its people.

The roadside market with homemade goods from locals helps occupy the tourists on their way to and from.

It's past five when I get a break between tour buses. Adaire used to help us at the market until she started waitressing at Clementine's to save up for school. I'd sometimes find her leaning against the brick wall behind the diner, taking smoke breaks by the trash bins.

I'm half looking over my shoulder as I toss the garbage in the dumpster; my gaze snags on the plantation at the top of the hill.

It's a perfect dollhouse from this distance. You'd think the fresh white paint and the towering columns of a gorgeous mansion wouldn't jostle your nerves. But Sugar Hill comes with too much weight for me to ignore.

Clementine's rear kitchen door shrieks open. The manager, Mr. Pruitt, steps out. His short-sleeve white business shirt and thin black tie a decade behind. He glares at me through chunky black-framed glasses. His eyes dip to my Led Zeppelin T-shirt disapprovingly. Bastard wouldn't give me a job when I asked.

My fingertips pinch the cherry off the joint I've been smoking, and I tuck the leftover roach in the tiny pocket of Adaire's high-waisted brown shorts I borrowed this morning. They look like they're made from a vinyl snake. I'm pretty sure I've seen the same fabric on a bar stool before.

I spit a fleck of the bud off the tip of my tongue and meander back to the front.

At our booth, a small crowd of tourists have gathered around Bone Layer. He brings his taxidermy birds to sell at the market—he finds them out by the Dillard's abandoned barn, the ones who didn't have enough sense to stay away from the cats who have run of the place. It's how he makes the eyes that fascinates people. Incredibly realistic, tiny bead-like things, perfected by dipping and re-dipping liquid acrylic and painting layers in between. The artistic act so beautiful, you could almost believe Bone Layer was a good man. Kind, even.

The caw of a crow yanks my attention upward. On a tele-phone wire, a black bird perches, surveying the land.

Folks at church say crows are foretellers of death, that they portend bad things to come. Deemed "unclean" because they're scavengers.

I think it's a crock of shit.

I watch the bird, wondering if I would know it was Rook or not.

Black birds are everywhere. Especially when you're look-ing for a particular one.

"Are these angels?" a Christian lady with a Bellevue Baptist T-shirt asks me. She points to the simple folk dolls I sewed from vintage fabric, adding feathers for wings.

"Forgetting Dolls are what we call them." I take one down to show her. "They're for forgetting things you don't want to remember anymore. Grieving, your worries, heartache, or whatever weighs you down. There's a little pouch inside the chest." I open its arms to show her the ribbon that closes off the pocket. "You write down your worries or a person's name and stuff it inside. Then you bury the doll and say a little prayer. Let your grief, your worries, your…whatever fly into the heavens." I flitter my fingers upward, my standard sales maneuver. Then I catch sight of Rook in my periphery and freeze.

It's him. I'd know those dark eyes anywhere. My heartbeat punches in my throat and hammers in my ears. I'm terrified to move, for fear he'll disappear.

Quickly, my eyes dart around for Grandmama.

"That sounds like voodoo," the woman says, yanking back my attention. She assesses the doll with judging eyes. "Only Jesus can heal our grief and broken hearts."

I fumble some apology, trying to explain it's just a silly notion and Jesus does all the heart healing in our house, too. But she's no longer interested and wanders over to Myrtle's stand, who's selling crosses made out of grapevines and pussy willow.

Rook has stepped away. I eye his shadowy figure through the chicken wire of our display wall and make my way around.

I bite the inside of my cheek to keep myself from smiling like a fool. His eyes meet mine. They trail over my face, my mouth, and back to my eyes again.

I've changed equally as much as him these last few years.

A black T-shirt hugs him tight, something he's grown too large for. He points to one of the dolls. "Crow feathers?" The depth of his voice is sin to my ears.

I swallow hard, suddenly feeling awful that I have to say yes. Grandmama sets out pokeweed berries soaked with my Sin Eater Oil for the crows that try to nest in our barn. She claims they're a nuisance (though it's said it's a bad omen to kill them). I always wondered if there was another reason— I dump them out when I find them, in case Rook were to wander inside.

Then Bone Layer showed me how to make Forgetting Dolls. But I don't tell Rook any of this.

"They are." I quietly follow him to the backside of our booth, farther away from my grandmother's ears. "I stitch them with little crystal beads," I say, as if this makes up for the fact that they died.

Quietly, he observes each doll. I cringe with an unspoken apology. His silence makes my skin itch. He trails his fingers over each set of wings, the slight bend from his fingertips causing the blue iridescence to flex—the same color captured in his dark hair.

"They're beautiful." There's a Mona Lisa quality to him. Like he's hiding something. I quirk my head ever so slightly, as if just by doing so I could tune into his thoughts. That hidden smile of his grows a fraction. It quickens my pulse.

His hand moves near mine. His eyes land on the gold initial ring on my pinky, pleased to see it there. Of course, I still wear it.

Now I'm looking at him more freely. He's taller, and no longer the lanky boy I once knew. I'm surprised when I see the tattooed crow on his forearm. The ink is a rich black color, and it's amazingly detailed: inside the torso of the crow's body the face of a woman. Her eyes—*my eyes*—stare hauntingly back at me. How could a tattoo artist capture them so well? Unless they were described by someone who knew, really knew them, could convey their depth and color so accurately as if they'd been studying that one pair of eyes their whole life. That's what I tell myself. That I might mean as much to him as he does to me.

"When did you get this?" I trace a finger across the tattoo. He shakes his head. "I don't remember."

I draw back, confused. He can't remember?

"Excuse me, honey," says a new customer holding three dolls, disrupting the electricity of the moment. "Can I pay with a check or are y'all cash only?"

"Cash only," I say, giving Rook a quick apology. The lady calls her husband over for some money. I have to return to the front, where Bone Layer guards the cash box, to fetch her change.

As soon as I'm done with the transaction, I work my way back to Rook when Grandmama grabs me by the elbow, bone-crushing tight.

Fear spikes up my spine. I glance past her shoulder, but Rook is nowhere in sight.

"Sheriff Johns would like to speak to you." Her head nods toward the parking lot where the sheriff's vehicle waits.

A sinking feeling bottoms out my stomach.

My eyes skim to the hill behind her until they find the plantation. I can see it now: a frenzy of cars, not to mention reporters, and more sheriff vehicles.

Something is definitely wrong.

NINE

Bone-Tooth Key

Black Fern's county jail is nothing like what you see in movies. They don't have the thick glass with telephones on either side. No interrogation room with a two-way mirror. Instead, it's a bunch of fold-up tables I'm pretty sure they got when the Aberdeen Baptist Church closed its doors.

Stapled to the faux wood paneling is a sign that reads Appropriate Attire with the visitor rules: No sleepwear, no tank tops, shorts can't show your buttocks, no sexually explicit T-shirts, and undergarments are required. How they know if you're wearing underwear is beyond me.

Deputy Rankin sits at the intake desk. His big greasy self is gnawing on a pickled pig's foot like it's a fried chicken leg. Disgusting. You'd think his exposed ass crack would conflict with the "can't show your buttocks," but apparently the rules don't apply to him.

A fat fly lands on a dried sticky stain on the table. A lone ceiling fan pushes hot air around the stifling room. The only other sound is the *tick-tick-tick* of the fan's pull-chain tapping the light globe as it wobbles in rotation.

Sweat trickles down the back of my legs. June in Georgia can burn you up if you don't watch it.

I'm about to ask what the hell is taking so long when the jailer door opens and out walks my ex-boyfriend Oscar Torres, along with the memories of us during my last summer of high school.

Being with Oscar made you dream of white picket fences and raising babies. He deserved something better than a soulless Death Talker. Besides, a nineteen-year-old joining the sheriff's department shouldn't be having sex with a kid still in high school. I did what he couldn't and broke us up.

Right behind him comes the sheriff. I stand like I'm readying for the national anthem.

Sheriff Thomas Johns is a burly man with an *I'll-kick-you-in-the-teeth* horseshoe mustache. He might be gray-haired, but his biceps are meaty as a steer. He's ex-military; army, I think.

And he's damn fast when he needs to tackle you. I should know.

"Have a seat, young lady." He nods.

I sit. He fires himself up a Camel, nonfilter cigarette.

"We have a few questions regarding yesterday." Sheriff takes a stiff drag.

I knew it. I knew that damn doctor told him I was doing something witchy. Maybe I could get Miss Caroline or Mr. Latham to attest to the contrary, since I saved Worth that one time.

"Of course, you know Darbee May Wilder," the sheriff states more than asks, throwing me for a loop.

I stare blankly at him. Obviously, this is a joke. I look to Oscar, trying to read what on earth this is about. Black Fern is small enough you know just about everybody even if you don't want to. I know I'm a bastard child, but what's *she* got to do with Ellis's death?

"Yes," I say through gritted teeth. "I know who my mother is." Her name, yes. Her personally, only a handful of times. A day or two here. A week there.

Haven't seen her since I was thirteen.

"We believe your mother was a squatter on this property." The sheriff slides something across the table for me to look at. "Can you tell me when the last time you visited this house was?"

It's a vintage-colored photo of my mother, a sultry young woman, wild as a fox, all slunk down in a regal chair fit for a queen—had it not been ragged and worn-out. Clad in a long gauzy bohemian dress with boots meant for a cowboy on her feet. One leg is cocked over the large wooden arm of the chair with her legs spread, but nothing is revealed, except her wickedness.

Chunky rings adorn every finger, even her thumbs. Her long blond hair dyed black, pitch as night and frightful with rage for how untamed and free it looks. It makes you fear her and want to be her all at the same time. Part of my mother's face hides behind her curled hand that shields a wry smile. Her smoke-rimmed eyes full of sin. I know because they're the same eyes I see in the mirror every morning.

Behind the chair, a bold ugly wallpaper with giant roses— a note of familiarity tickles my thoughts.

"I've never been there." But something inside me says, *Yeah, you have.*

A thin ribbon of smoke trails off the tip of Sheriff Johns's forgotten cigarette. The ash on the end grows long as the silence stretches. That *tick-tick-tick* of the fan's pull-chain racks at my nerves.

"I guess you also wouldn't know how this got buried on the

property now, would you?" The sheriff's dark hand pushes a plastic evidence bag across the table.

The thumping in my chest ramps up.

It's a child's Bible. Pale blue with crinkles worn in its spine. Jesus reads a story to some children on the cover. Gold lettering in all caps spell out my name, WEATHERLY OPAL WILDER.

My childhood Bible.

The one buried with me…and those twin babies.

Fear flushes over my body. How'd they find the grave?

Zeke Latham's words flash back to me. Ellis's foot had sunk into *some kind of hole*.

My heartbeat is overwhelming now, and the only sound in my head is the muffled *thud-thump, thud-thump, thud-thump*.

"I said…when was the last time you were at this house? Do you recall ever being there with your mother?" Sheriff Johns knocks on the table next to the picture

I blink myself out of a trance and shake my head no.

"Are you sure? Take another look." The sheriff's voice firms up as he senses there's something I'm not telling him.

I study the photo once more, pretending to give it an earnest consideration. My mind riffles through my past, trying to force my brain to give up something it's hiding. The whisper of a feeling that maybe I do know this house starts to form.

Dirt. The dank smell of earth bubbles up like it's trying to remind me. A little red suitcase sits on a dirt floor. Lightly worn from use, but it's mine. I'm going on vacation to see the ocean with my mother. I can almost recall the excitement from the anticipation.

I've never seen the ocean, then or now.

The ocean, the ocean, the ocean. I squeeze my brain to unearth more nuggets from my past. Then I catch sight of what's dangling from my mother's hand. I pull the photo closer and lean in. I've seen a necklace similar to this one, pretty much every day of my life. It's a wooden bone-tooth key. Bigger than the one that Grandmama wears around her neck that opens her secret recipe box, but they're fashioned the same way.

My eyes dart back to the wooden chest propped underneath one of my mother's boots. Bigger than a shoebox, smaller than a cedar chest. A jagged keyhole, fit for such a key cut in the front.

I school my face and confidently slide the photo back to the sheriff. "Nope, never been there." I force my eyes to not flit to Oscar and give myself away. "What does this house or my mother have to do with anything?"

They haven't mentioned the babies' bodies, the ones Grandmama buried with me and that Bible all those years ago. Maybe wildlife carried them off?

"Deeper in the woods, a hundred or so yards past a grave we found this Bible in, a body was hung in a tree. I guess you wouldn't know about that, either?"

He places another photo in front of me. The image so gruesome I gasp.

A slack-jawed mouth hangs open with black veins of Sin Eater Oil streaking out and down the throat, staining the fine wool suit. The haunting, distant eyes of Stone Rutledge as he dangles from a tree branch. Dead.

I swallow hard. My gut sours. "God, no!" I shove the photo away. "What in the hell happened to him?"

"No?" Sheriff Johns quirks his head. "Nothing about Stone's death familiar to you? Those black lines of poison. Awfully similar to your grandfather's."

"Papaw died from sepsis, the medical examiner said," I say a bit sharply and remind him what he already knows. But it doesn't take away the suspicion.

A man who spent his entire life talking the death out of folks, it's bound to catch up with you. Only so much mucus you can expel after the fact. The toxic black ooze built up and ate through his body. Seeped inside his bones and rotted him from the inside.

Augustus Hamish Wilder was a sunny old man full of imaginative stories with a voracious appetite for poking fun at Grandmama's moodiness. He gave me his death-talking gift when I was only nine. Papaw told me what he could do, then he told me how to use the secret Bible verses to do it. The gift jumped out of him and into me.

There are only a few rules for death-talking. If you tell someone the secret scriptures, your gift is gone. You can only pass it to someone of the opposite sex. If you die with your gift, it disappears forever. And you can't talk the death out of someone twice.

What Papaw didn't tell me is how you shoulder a lifetime of guilt for all the souls you can't save. That I'll spend the rest of my life trying to make up for it.

Papaw must have known he was leaving this world, giving the death-talking to me so young. Had I realized he was dying, I would have turned around and used it right back on him.

Clear as day, I can still see his dead body stretched long down the length of our kitchen table, while Grandmama prepped him for the afterlife. I sat cross-legged on top of the thick pine box Bone Layer had made for him and watched her.

Grandmama's people came from Appalachia a long way back. Taking care of the dead was the way of things. She tied him down with twine on our family's heirloom laying board— heirloom, like a death board is something you hope your kinfolks pass down to you.

Tarnished Scottish burial coins kept Papaw's eyes shut, a wedding gift from a dear friend. Three things Grandmama stuffed inside his mouth: Tobacco blossoms with the seeds intact, so he'd have something for his pipe. Coffee grounds mixed with bacon fat, to keep him from ever going hungry.

And a single chicken's foot, so he'd always know she was watching him, even when he was six feet under.

Traditionally, a handkerchief tied around the head kept the corpse's mouth closed. But Grandmama used four wild plum thorns and pinned Papaw's lips shut. Sealed tight with needling thread dipped in dove's blood and crisscrossed around the thorns like bootlaces.

That was to keep him from telling the dead—or the Devil— her secrets.

When she took out his innards, she made me go outside and play. It took two burlap sacksful of dried rosebuds and lavender she collected back in the summer to fill him. She said it wasn't no different than some of the animals we taxidermied. It was the only way to keep him fresh until the hard winter ground softened enough for a grave to be dug.

On the first night of sitting up with the dead, he laid in front of the fireplace inside his pine box. Red flames licked the wall behind it. The dim glow of embers backdropped Grandmama's silhouette as she sewed in her rocking chair next to him.

It was the cracking noise in the middle of the night that woke me.

Sounded like the *crackle-pops* of kindling wood being added to a blazing fire except with a hollowness only bones can carry. I woke up from my pallet on the floor and watched as Grandmama paused her work for a breath to listen, then went back to rocking and sewing like bone-cracking was an ordinary thing. I didn't understand until I was older that it was rigor mortis setting in, which would cause Papaw to sit upright as he stiffened. Hence why he was tied down.

Funny thing about that pine box they buried Papaw in, not ten minutes after I found him dead Bone Layer brought it in from the farm shed. Exactly my grandpa's size.

Grandmama said she knew Papaw was to leave this world.

Claims the chickens told her evil was coming. Their eggs turned bloodred on the inside, another sign of death.

"Because what I see here is a possible murder," Sherriff Johns says, jarring me back from my memories.

"Or a man so ragged with grief after losing his son he hung himself," I say rather poignantly.

"There wasn't a suicide note," the sheriff says.

"So?"

"So we're investigating all our options."

Suffer as I have suffered. My own hexing words come back to haunt me. I cursed Stone that day at court. *Do unto you as you have done unto me.* I wanted him to hurt the same way I hurt after Adaire died. I got my wish, and his son, Ellis, died. He felt that pain, as equal as mine I'd imagine. Did I do this?

"Tell me about these ritual bones." Sheriff Johns slaps down more pictures—damn happy photographer. The rotting skeleton of a large crow lies on the ground below Stone, sitting on what looks like a small burn pile.

"Early this morning, when my men went to investigate this scene where the Rutledge boy incident occurred—"

"Incident. Don't you mean accident?" I ask him. He stares at me a long hard moment.

"No," he replied. "As I was saying, next to the location of the boy's *incident*, we found Stone's body," the sheriff finishes. "We need to know your whereabouts last night."

"My whereabouts? What the heck is going on?"

I snuck out my bedroom window and got drunk is where I was. Not before I followed a ghost into the woods—and found that little gold cuff link on my windowsill. Something only the rich would wear. *Shit*—I've got to get rid of that as soon as I get home.

"A group of kids were playing in the woods yesterday morning," Sheriff Johns says, snapping my thoughts. "Said they saw a woman, hiding behind the trees, chanting some weird prayer, then chased them down. They all seem to think it was you."

If there's anything I know, it's where I have and have not been. And I have not been skulking around the woods following some chicken-ass kids, chanting spells.

"Liars." I firm up in my seat, getting tired of being prodded with all these questions. "I was running up the hill from the quarry pond to save Ellis."

"Mmm, huh." His judgment thick in the air. "Surely I don't need to remind you of the public threat you made against Stone Rutledge at the courthouse." Sheriff Johns's tone as flat as his face and equally as accusing.

"Are y'all arresting me or something?" I look pointedly to the sheriff, then to Oscar, who knows I'm done with all this free questioning. "Because if not, I ain't gotta be here, right?"

They exchange a brief look, and the sheriff sits back to let Oscar speak. "His body was found on the same property as your Bible. These kids say they saw you. You threatened him in front of dozens of witnesses, officers of the law included. It doesn't look good, to be honest. There's a lot of questions we don't have the answers to. For now, we appreciate your cooperation."

"Last night I was at Aunt Violet's, you can ask her." Though I snuck in, so I'm not sure if she knows I was even there. "That Bible…" I nod to it. "We donated it to the church years ago, when Grandmama bought me a new one," I lie. "Could have been anyone who put it there. Besides, what does my mama and that house got to do with Stone?"

Oscar cracks open his mouth like he's about to speak when the sheriff cuts him off.

"I think we've got what we need for today." Sheriff Johns stands, ending our little chat. "If we have any more questions, we know where to find you."

"That you do." I nod and take my leave. My feet carry me out of there faster than I intend, guiltily fast.

It's dark out now, and a long ass walk to my house. I'll have to call Bone Layer to pick me up. I mutter a swear to myself.

"Weatherly," Oscar calls. I about jump out of my skin. He jogs out the door after me. "Let me give you a ride home, since it's so late."

I park my hand on my hip and square him with a look. "Sheriff send you out here on official duty? Or you offering as a friend?"

He thumbs his gun belt and returns the same hard glare. "You want a ride or what?"

Silently, I get in the passenger's seat of the sheriff's Bronco.

"You need to know they're going to be watching you," he says, as if I didn't already suspect this. The gravel *pop-cracks* under his tires as he backs out of the station parking lot.

"I figured." I smart my arms over my chest and turn my gaze out the window. The night, a gorgeous black-blue, reminds me of Rook's hair. My eyes instinctually scan the sky, looking for a speck of black. I'm scared he's already gone again.

The headlights split the dark as we turn down the long country road toward my house.

"You don't understand," Oscar says earnestly. "Sheriff knows you're hiding something."

I sharpen my eyes on him. "Hiding what?"

"Something about that Bible. Or your grandfather. The burned crow. The evidence of poison. Hell, everything, maybe."

I puff a disagreeing sound and roll down the window, suddenly feeling hot.

Oscar goes on. "I shouldn't be telling you this." He rakes a shaky hand over the spikes of his hair. "They are getting a toxicology report on Stone, but the medical examiner seems to think the poison is organic in nature—he was the same ex-

IN THE HOUR OF CROWS

aminer when your grandfather died, he remembers. He's rec-
ommended they exhume your grandfather's body. He thinks
whatever killed him killed Stone."

"Shit."

"Exactly." Oscar chews the inside of his lip. I'm sure his Boy
Scout morals are already reprimanding him for telling me.

I told Oscar about my Sin Eater Oil and its confessional
properties, and the few times it was used for mercy killings.
In hindsight that seems pretty stupid, but his do-gooder heart
had a way of making you fess up to stuff like confessional to
a priest. And he's no dummy. The oil could be used in non-
mercy situations as well. I can't count on him to keep this
bit of information to himself forever. I think the only reason
he's kept it quiet this long is because how do you explain to
a practical man like Sheriff Johns my body makes a mucus
that can kill people?

"They're looking for any reason to arrest you."

Awesome.

Oscar slows down to turn into my driveway, but stops
short. From the nearby fray of woods, crickets fill the silence.
I turn to him, not sure why he's not heading up to the house.

"Weatherly." He sets his hand on mine. I know where he's
going with this conversation even before his words get there.
"I know you're hurting. It can't be easy losing someone you
were so close to."

I slip my hand out from underneath his. His great-
grandparents are still alive. What does he know about death?

I turn my gaze out the window so I don't have to see the
pity in those beautiful brown eyes of his. I shove down the
emotion wanting to bubble up. "I don't want to have this conversation right now." I hop out of the truck, but he calls my
name, and I stop.

His demeanor shifts as he switches from friend back to deputy. "What happened was a tragedy. But if you or anyone in

your family has done something or knows something, you need to tell me. I've got your back in there, but if I find one piece of evidence that says otherwise, I'll arrest you myself. Stone's death will not bring Adaire back."

A knife of truth that stabs me in the heart.

"But damn if it don't feel good that motherfucker is dead, though," I say and shut the Bronco door in his face.

TEN

Scrying Skillet

At the house, a lone porch light waits for me to come home. But I've got to check on something first. I need to be sure my mind isn't misremembering.

Underneath the back porch steps, I reach for a tin tobacco box my papaw gave me before he died. About the only place I could hide something Grandmama wouldn't think to look. A little bigger than a pack of smokes and rusted around the edges, but I'm able to open the lid. I pull out the browned wad of cotton to get what's underneath.

The few things I hold dear. A Scottish coin my great-great-grandmother did her witchery with. A seashell I've held on to for as long as I can remember, a promise from my mother. Something I treasured but couldn't recall why until now, just a foggy memory that slipped loose and didn't return until the sheriff showed me that picture.

It's the bone-tooth key that hung from my mother's hand.

A tattered ribbon, a piece of thin flowered cloth tied in a

bow, attaches the key to the brass chain. The jagged teeth cut into my palm as I squeeze it. Trying to extract those precious drops of memory from that last Tuesday night I spent with Adaire, four days before she died. I was too stupid to listen to her then. I squeeze my eyes shut, that key tight in my grip, and I try to recall.

Like many nights before, I tumbled through Adaire's bedroom window with a terrible crash. "When the hell did you put that bookshelf there?" I asked her, incredulous.

"Are you drunk?" Adaire snapped at me—unconcerned I almost broke my neck. She sat on the floor at the end of her twin bed with a fantasy novel in one hand and a Dr Pepper in the other. She grumbled something about people abusing family privileges and how breaking into a house through a bedroom window was considered a felony.

"Maybe. But Aunt V is shotgunning beers in the driveway with Joe Lucky Sr., and I didn't feel like being chatty." I inspected the wounds on my legs. Angry red scrapes marred my shins, threatening to bleed, but they didn't.

"Aren't you too old to be climbing in through the window?"

"Aren't you too old to be reading fairy tales?"

"Fantasy, not fairy."

"Does it have a fairy in it?"

She glared at me. My point had been made. "I need a favor." I lowered myself to sit next to her.

"I ain't in the business of doing favors," she said without taking her eyes off the page.

"Scoot over." I shoved my way next to her when she refused to budge. She swore under her breath, knowing I wouldn't leave her be until she agreed.

"What?" She stowed a luna moth conjuring card between the pages of her book to hold her place.

"I need you to scry for me."

She stared at me for a long moment. I knew this was something she wasn't fond of doing, but I wouldn't have asked her if I weren't desperate. Aunt Violet was no good at it anymore, and Wyatt could only see in a fire, not glassy surfaces.

"Get out." She reopened her book, back to reading.

Oh, okay. It was going to be like that, was it?

"Seriously, Adaire, I need your help. I was thinking—"

"That's never a good idea."

I made a smirking sound. "You don't even know what I need you to scry for, if you'd just—"

"Not. Doing. It." She turned the page—I swatted the book out of her hand. She fumbled to catch it, spilling her soda. "What the hell?" She used a random T-shirt from the floor to absorb the mess.

"You've gotta help me, Adaire. I'm in trouble!"

"Are you dying?"

"Wait—what?"

"Going to prison?"

"No!"

"Then you aren't in trouble." She stuck her nose back in the book.

I swear to Jesus she was the most stubborn, useless, unconcerned friend I'd ever had the displeasure of knowing.

"If you were in trouble, I'd help you." I huffed and crossed my arms. I had no idea how I was going to get out of this pickle if Adaire didn't help.

She scowled at me long and hard. Long enough I felt squirmy. Interpreting her scowls was a talent that came with years of practice. That particular one wasn't hate or anger or annoyance. Heck, it wasn't even her pretend face she used when she acted like we weren't best friends. No, this was concern. "Define trouble."

I perked up, surprised she might change her mind. "Okay,

here's the deal. Dickie Meldrum is paying me two-hundred dollars to be at the drag race on Saturday night, in case he wrecks and needs me...again."

"But you've already talked the death out of him once before."

"I know."

"You can't talk the death out of somebody twice!"

"I know! That's why I'm in trouble. I just need you to peek into this Saturday and see if he wrecks—or how bad." Because Dickie didn't have the best track record when it came to racing.

"Just don't go. It's not like you have to be there, you can say no."

"See, I kind of already took the money."

A slew of curses flew free, followed by a lecture on how death-talking wasn't a business—says her, but it earns me some favors and makes me some money here and there.

Then she reminded me how our papaw died younger than he should have from a lifetime of death-talking. That hit home. Every gift has a price.

"I'm just insurance really," I tried to explain to her. "A confidence booster. He thinks if he has me as a backup, then he won't worry about the risk and go all in. It's a head game for him. Truly."

"Give him the money back and tell him no. I'm not scrying for you."

"I already spent the money." I winced. A second round of swears were flung at me. Even after Adaire gave me an earful, she still didn't seem like she was going to budge, so I added, "I thought we were going to the ocean." It was a mumble, really, but I was doing my best to ply some feeling out of that cold dead heart of hers.

By summer's end, I was supposed to have enough money saved up to fix my car's clutch and replace the starter...*and* get a new battery. Adaire asked me to road-trip with her from ocean to ocean, before she left for that fancy art institute in Charleston she'd got into, where she'd be able to design all the clothes her heart desired. I said it sounded like a plan.

Her plan, not mine.

There were responsibilities that came with death-talking. A town full of people we'd grown up with that depended on me—when they weren't fearing and hating me. How could I leave knowing someone back home needed me? Enough deaths slipped through my grasp as it was. I couldn't live with myself knowing I could have saved one more.

"So you're just gonna stay here until Grandmama dies?" Adaire had asked when I didn't commit to leaving. "Just keep kowtowing to the church folk. Trying to keep in their good graces. For what? A one-way ticket to Heaven?" The echo of her words still made me wince.

Adaire leaving at the end of summer felt a little bit like that, too. But she and Davis had plans, and I wasn't interested in being a third wheel.

Adaire screwed a side-glance my way. "So you used Dickie's money to repair your car? Davis didn't tell me you paid him."

"It was a...surprise?" I lied. Instead, I mailed a check to that fancy art institute to help out with her tuition and student loans. It was a *forgive-me-for-not-going-with-you* goodbye gift.

Adaire stood abruptly, then stared down at me like I needed to be throttled and she was volunteering to do so. "The shit I do for you," she said.

I popped up on my feet and followed her out the door. "Does this mean you'll help me?"

She growled in response. Like her facial expressions, I had perfected interpretation there as well. She would help me, but she wouldn't like it.

"I'm going to need to borrow your car Saturday night, too," I hollered behind her. She grumbled something rude, but it wasn't a no. "The race is all the way in Mercer. You can ride your bike to work *one* time." Though it was the third time that month; my car was busy growing a grass beard until I could afford to repair it. But she worked the late shift at Clementine's; it wasn't like she needed the car Saturday night, and I'd be back in time to take her home.

Downstairs, the kitchen was sadder than Adaire's room, if that was possible. The cabinets splintery thin pine veneer seemed thirsty they looked so dry. The flimsy faded curtains hadn't seen a good washing in years. Twangy old country music from the radio drifted in through the window—Aunt Violet and Joe had moved the party to the porch, it seemed.

Adaire dug out a cast-iron skillet from under the harvest-gold stove that had somehow always been missing its bottom drawer. The faucet sputtered awake as she filled the pan. The familiar smell of boiled eggs that always accompanied well water permeated the air.

Some folks used mirrors or water in a bowl for gazing. Any shiny surface would do for most. One time, Adaire said she saw a doorway to another world in the reflection of a crystal candy dish. She wouldn't even so much as look at a candy dish after that, said she might cross over and never come back. That was why she was fickle about scrying.

Carefully, she sat the pan on the table, the surface a black mirror. Her scrying skillet. A single bare bulb hung over their mismatched kitchen table and chairs, reflecting in the dark water—the cheap glass shade broke years ago when Wyatt had thrown a football across the kitchen.

Adaire held out her hand, expectant. When I didn't clue in, she said, "You want me to scry or what?" Now she was really annoyed. "You know how this works, I need something of Dickie's."

"I don't have anything. Can't you just do it by thinking about him or his car or the race?" Having something tangible to hold on to when you were scrying helped. But a memory would serve in a pinch.

Her face soured at this minor setback. "It isn't much to go on."

Adaire sat in the chair and released a long exhale, readying herself. Then she stared into the black glassy water. Her eyes softened as she started to zone out. Unfocusing, that blurry vision where one minute you're staring at something clear as day, but as you relax, your eyes lose focus. Then your mind opens up to seeing what you want to know. I tried it once before, but gazing isn't in my blood.

I watched her as she slipped into that other place. *Looking over* is what she called it. Even though she was physically here, her mind was looking over into the elsewhere for the right answer—though it's not always clear what they mean.

Out on the front porch I heard a crack, then a burst of laughter from Aunt Violet and Joe. Adaire didn't flinch. I leaned back and snuck a peek out the window. The porch swing hung cockeyed to one side, its chain broken.

After a few long quiet minutes, Adaire gasped, as if jarred awake, but her eyes were open the whole time.

"It went black" was the first thing out of her mouth. A troubled look shuffled across her face.

"Black? You mean like lights out for Dickie?" This was not good.

Adaire dumped the water out into the sink, her thoughts chugging over what she saw—or didn't see. "No, not that. When I try to look at Saturday, it's just black." She dried the skillet with a dish towel in slow circles.

"What does that mean?" It sounded like a load of crap. "Are you messing with me? You were thinking about Dickie and the race when you were scrying, right?"

At the sound of Aunt Violet's and Joe's voices shuffling closer, Adaire glanced in their direction.

"I know how to scry, Weatherly," she said in a sharp whisper.

"I didn't say you didn't, I just mean—did you see Dickie? Does he wreck his car and die?" I followed her over to the couch.

"No, I didn't see Dickie die. But I couldn't see anything on Saturday. Like, at all. But there's a key."

"A key? Like a car key? If Dickie loses his car keys, he's going to want his money back."

"It's not that. Help me with this." She shouldered up against the brown-striped couch, wanting to move it.

For the love of God, that sucker was heavier than a Mack truck. But we managed to scoot it over enough for Adaire to find what she was looking for.

"Mama used to hide her liquor here when Daddy was alive." She pried up a loose floorboard. Aunt Violet wasn't a closet drinker. She just didn't want Uncle Doug to steal her booze for himself.

"The race is only a few days away, so I thought I would try forward-looking," Adaire says. "It's where you comb through today, tomorrow, the next day until you get to the day you want. It works sometimes, if it's happening soon." She felt around in the hole. "Except every time I tried to push past Saturday, the visions got murky, like they were shrouded in this fog. Didn't make no sense. Then it would flip me back to my house. To a vision of this."

Adaire pulled out a little drawstring bag, something made from scrap quilting squares. She dumped the contents into my hand.

A bone-tooth key.

Magic from the key tickled with energy in my palm. Its chain a dingy brass. A crinkled ribbon of cloth secured it in place. Someone powerful created that key. I hurriedly handed it back to her.

"Bone Layer brought it over to my mother, for safekeeping."

I looked at her, surprised to hear this. "Bone? Why?" He had Grandmama to manage things.

She shrugged. "He told her 'the truth will set you free.'"

"Set her free?" I hand her the key back.

Adaire shook her head. "Not her. *You*." She glanced past my shoulder at the sound of voices moving closer.

"Free from what?"

We both looked over as a voice hit the door and heaved the couch back into place.

"Hell if I know—maybe he was talking about jail?" We stood. Aunt Violet tumbled into the house, drunk as a skunk, laughing as Joe Lucky Sr. pawed at her playfully. They both straightened and mocked sober at the sight of us.

Aunt Violet eyed the couch, then Adaire's hand as she tucked it behind her back, shoving the key in her shorts pocket.

"I was just leaving," I said, frazzled by what Adaire had told me.

"You ain't gotta leave, baby girl. Joe was just going home. Wasn't you, Joe?"

This was news to him. She shoved him out the door before he could protest.

Aunt Violet turned back around. Her short dark auburn hair flamed on top of her head, fierce as her brown eyes. Red and glassy from too much booze, but they were sharp enough to see something was awry.

"Don't forget this," Adaire called to me before I got out the door. She was bent over the table, scribbling something on a piece of paper real quick-like. "It's the list of herbs Mr. Webb needs to heal up the gout in his foot." She walked over and shoved the paper in my hand, then nodded once solemnly.

I gave her a look as I opened the paper. *Find the scales of justice. She holds the truth.*

Adaire died that Saturday. That was why the visions were no longer clear. And it had worried her what the fogginess meant. She'd never experienced that before; she said neither had Aunt Violet or Wyatt. She kept bringing it up, going over and over what she'd seen—or couldn't see. I blew off her concern, telling her to stop pouting because her gift delivered a dud. I should have listened. Paid more attention to her fear. Maybe if I had, I could have helped her figure it out. Maybe I could have saved her.

Of course, she wouldn't have been riding her bike if I hadn't borrowed her car.

I unfold the tiny piece of paper with my cousin's hurried handwriting on it. I didn't have a clue what she was telling me back then, but I think I do now.

Find the scales of justice. She holds the truth.

The truth about Adaire or me, I'm not sure.

The kitchen light pops on.

Oh, shit!

I drop to the ground and roll under the porch. A random tuft of weeds pokes me in the face. Something skitters across my thigh. I stifle a squeal.

Seconds later, there's a creak from the porch door as Grandmama opens it and calls out for Bone Layer. But it's late, and I know there's no task or chores that need to be done at this hour.

Through the wood slats of the porch, I watch Grandmama scan the yard suspiciously, scowling at the night. Not that her milky eyes can see, but she senses things. I hope not my breathing just below her feet.

There's a rustling noise from the one-room smokehouse as Bone Layer emerges. He comes out the door, and his eyes land straight on me. Panic forks my heart.

He stalks across the yard with purpose, lantern shining from his hand. I shrink deeper into the darkness, praying it will conceal me. His thunderous footsteps rattle the porch. Dust sprinkles down. I shield my eyes.

"God has given us a purpose, and a cleansing must be had," Grandmama says quietly to him. Bone Layer hums a deep noise that sounds like he understands what she's talking about and the gravity of what it means. "It's time. Fetch the bones."

ELEVEN

Sins of the Past

There's nothing like somebody suspecting you of murder to keep you up all night.

Oscar's got my nerves all frazzled with talk about me going to jail. And it's spooked Grandmama enough she sent Bone out in the middle of the night to gather bones kissed by moonlight for a protection spell. Probably to ward off Stone's ghost that might come for us.

I get out of bed like usual at the crack of dawn to help Grandmama prepare for our rounds. We sell tinctures for fresh eggs. Trade pies for fruits and vegetables. Rarely do we get actual cash from someone. Eventually, I'm sent on my way to run my errands, delivering herbs to our clients like usual, while Grandmama prepares more jams for the coming weekend's market.

That bone-tooth key itches in my pocket all day.

"Please explain to me again how going back to the scene of the crime will clear your name instead of getting you arrested?"

Raelean *snap-pop*s her bubble gum as she side-eyes me. Her brown hair flames around her head as wind rushes through the rolled down windows. Her blue Camaro purrs like a kitten, but the AC is for shit. Nice of her to drive me around, though.

She only questions this because she can't see the whole picture. I can't, either, to be fair. But it's there, I just need to collect all the pieces first.

"The sheriff thinks I might have murdered Stone—which… threatening to kill him publicly at the courthouse like I did, probably wasn't one of my better ideas."

Raelean hums an agreeing sound.

"And Stone didn't leave a suicide note," I go on, "which makes the whole thing extra suspect. Between that and Ellis dying, it looks like I'm picking off the Rutledges one at a time."

"And my question still hasn't been answered." Raelean frowns.

A deputy mans the main road to keep the media and any lookie-loos from corrupting an active crime scene. We can get there from the backside, though, if we sneak across the abandoned pecan orchard. Raelean's car squeaks and grumbles over potholes in the dirt road.

"Adaire said I had to find justice."

"She specifically told you to go to the scene of the crime?" She raises a skeptical brow.

"No." I roll my eyes at her. "But I have to start somewhere. She said I would need to be set free. And now they suspect me of murder."

"She could have been a little more specific," Raelean mumbles.

"I told you, it's not an exact science. There's not a map with a *go to X and find the treasure*. She's shown snippets of things. They're like puzzle pieces, and you have to interpret what they mean."

"Maybe justice is simply that the bastard is dead." Raelean shrugs like that's good enough for her.

"It doesn't feel like justice," I complain to the window.

Weeds and scrub have reclaimed the field's road. Sticks and branches from the narrowing path threaten to scratch up her paint job so she stops before we can get to the end. We'll have to walk the rest of the way.

"It isn't just about what Adaire saw," I say as we high-step it through the weeds. "It's also what Ellis said. *She's here.* It makes me wonder if he was talking about Adaire, her spirit. Then he called my name, desperate, like he wanted to give me a message from her?"

"Why, though? Ellis probably didn't know Adaire even existed." Raelean's logic stings. But still, something about it feels off and I want to find out what that is. "Look," Raelean starts in, "even if there's something to it, you can't arrest a dead man. Especially not based on the rambling words of a dying boy or some vague clues from some ominous vision—not that I question Adaire's abilities." She raises an innocent hand. "I'm just saying."

"It can't hurt to look, now can it?" I duck down low behind a tree as we get to the side road. Raelean crouches next to me.

"No, not at all," she whispers. "Why, what's the worst that could happen? Oh, wait, you could get arrested for trespassing on a crime scene!" She bolts her eyes wide with a wild expression to exaggerate her point.

"Well, then you better shush so we don't get caught!" I harshly whisper back.

From the scrub of weeds, we can see Deputy Billy Parnell blocking the end of the road with his vehicle. Billy totters around, attempting to juggle crab apples. He's a dipshit. How he made the force is beyond me. Slim pickings, I'd guess. Raelean and I dart across the road, unseen, into the woods where Mr. Rutledge's body was found.

"Don't you think the cops have collected all the evidence already?" Raelean shuffles double-step to catch up with me. "What exactly are you hoping to find?"

"Justice," I say dryly.

Raelean grumbles.

An octagon of yellow caution tape ropes off the main area, but nothing here looks any different than the rest of the forest.

"This must be where they found the burned crow." Raelean points to a pile of ash that sits off to the side. The bones gone now, taken into evidence, I assume.

"Don't you think it's odd a man like Stone Rutledge would burn a crow before he hung himself?" I ask.

"Maybe it wasn't him. Maybe it was those punk-ass kids who said they saw you tiptoeing around the forest that morning. Kids are always setting shit on fire," she says, shaking her head. It's possible, but I don't know how likely.

"What if something else was burned here?" Something about it don't sit right with me.

"Like what?

"Evidence, maybe? I don't know."

"Whatever it was, it don't look like much. What did Adaire tell you again? Specifically," Raelean asks.

"That Bone Layer gave Aunt Violet this key." I tug it out of my pocket to show her. I found it again in Adaire's nightstand after her funeral. It felt too important to just leave there. I hang it around my neck for safekeeping. "He told her the truth will set me free." I start from the center of the taped-off area and walk a spiral, searching for clues. Though Raelean is right; it's been picked clean already. "Adaire could barely see anything past that Saturday, the day she died. Then she wrote this." I pass to her the piece of paper.

"'Find the scales of justice. She holds the truth,'" she reads aloud, then hands it back. "So you'll go to jail and will need to be set free?"

"At the time, I thought Adaire might have been messing with me to teach me a lesson about the situation I'd gotten myself in and how I needed her help to get out of it. But then it consumed her, what the fogginess meant, and no matter how hard she tried, Adaire couldn't see hardly anything past Saturday."

For four days, she scried. At first, it was anything and everything surrounding Dickie and the race. When that came up dry, she started scrying with that bone-tooth key Bone Layer gave Aunt Violet for safekeeping. After that, she was on the trail of something. She refused to tell me what, though, until she knew more. Said I was *static interference*, whatever that meant. Now I think she only said that to spare me, because whatever she found out, I'm pretty sure it had something to do with her dying.

Raelean squints. "I still feel like she could have meant justice was had with Stone Rutledge dying."

I shake my head. "No, it's more than that. It was urgent for her to tell me this. Almost desperate. When I tried to get her to elaborate the next day, she just said she was looking into it."

"Looking into what?"

I shrug, then stop as a pair of lines outside of the perimeter catch my attention. Fresh tire marks cut a trail through the mud. I follow the path of the rutted ground through the trees to see where it leads.

After a good piece, Raelean asks, "Is that a farmhouse?"

She points a sparkly blue fingernail. A sliver of white siding peeks out past the edge of the woods off in the distance.

Fear spikes inside me. The memory of this house and what happened to the twin babies that night was something I tried to forget. Sharp and cutting, it digs its way back to the surface.

He stepped into a hole, a grave or something.

"This is where the Latham boys found Ellis," I say, a bit mystified, as we approach the farmhouse I thought I'd never see again.

I tried to find it once. But it had been too many years and too far away to relocate it. I'd just turned fourteen, and Grandmama had pissed me off about something. I had a good mind to find the babies' grave and call the police myself, tell them some kind of story that Grandmama was the one who killed them. But roads in the hills are windy and many, and finding that place was like looking for a black cat in a coal cellar. Besides, bike-riding around for hours worked some sense into me. And I realized they'd probably know I was lying.

Or worse, Grandmama would tell them it was me who murdered them, even though that was only half the truth.

In my memory, I can still see Stone Rutledge's low-to-the-ground Corvette bumbling its way over the driveway. The wailing of that woman whispers on the winds even now. From the looks of it, nobody has been here since.

There's something about returning to the scars of your past that reopens the wounds. Raw and festering, seeping with guilt. I can almost feel the hell fires burning my feet.

"Hold up." Raelean gently grabs my elbow and stops me from beelining for the house. She nods toward the north end of the property. Through a break in the trees, I can see the flashing blue lights of Deputy Parnell's car parked off in the distance on the main road.

Quietly, we slip around the edge of the woods until we are safely on the south side of the house, blocked from his view. It's not until we're walking in the thick of the overgrown weeds of the yard that the decrepit house comes into full view. Dingy white clapboard siding droops like aged skin. The rusty red metal roof peels back, exposing its ribs of dried-up wood bones. It's a rotting corpse, wasting away in a forest of summer green.

A shadowy presence inhabits the house and the land. Eyes from the woods watch us. Something darker knows we're here.

"I'm not sure about this," Raelean says, low and quiet.

"Stay here, then." I push aside the prickling of my sixth sense and walk to the spot where Bone Layer parked our truck once before.

Behind the house, deeper in the woods, I can just make out another area of yellow police tape. I assume it blocks off the section of trees around where Ellis was found; it's about where the grave of the babies would have been. Black ferns devour the small space, crawl up the pine trees like parasites. A stain, rotting the earth. I turn away, unable to shake the weight of my contribution all those years ago.

Raelean wiggles the doorknob, but it's locked. A laundry room window facing the carport has a cracked pane. I manage to slip my hand through, without cutting myself on the jagged glass, and unlock it. The window is just plain stubborn, but I work it high enough to shimmy in.

A frail wooden drying rack collapses under my weight. The crashing sticks sound thin, snapping in the emptiness of the room—my entry as graceful as sneaking into Adaire's room.

"You alright?" Raelean cups her eyes as she peers through the windowpane.

"Grown-ass woman floundering on the floor like a damn toddler," I mumble to myself. "Yep. All good." I thumbs-up and then crawl off the broken rack—leaving my dignity behind—and unlock the back door to let her in.

"Have you been here before?" Raelean's voice falls flat against the hollow of the room. Her eyes search mine, trying to read what I'm not saying.

"I came here once as a kid." I leave it at that.

The air is dry and stale like clothes stored in a musty wooden chest stuck up in the attic. There's a loneliness that accompanies a home that's been unlived in for years, a sadness for the life not being lived under its roof.

One step from the laundry room to the kitchen and every

detail comes rushing back. Even where Stone and the rich panicked lady stood on the linoleum checkerboard floor.

"What do you hope to find here?" Raelean pokes her head into one of the rooms down the hall.

Answers, I think to myself. To which questions, I'm not sure. All of them, really.

I find the only room that sticks heavy in my memory, where death took those babies.

The furniture no longer a burden to the room. It doesn't stop my mind from seeing it there, ghosting on the floor. The long gauzy curtains—tattered at the ends—barely sway in the breeze. I'm taken back in time to when that wooden potato box slid out into the hallway. Guilt seeps in. Sorrow lingers heavy in my chest for the wrong I wish I could undo.

Solemnly, I turn to Raelean. "I'm not sure what I hope to find. But you know how sometimes there are things that tumble into your life? Random coincidences you shrug off to just that?"

"Yeah?" She stretches the word, unsure where I'm going with this.

I quirk my head at the garish wallpaper covering the hall-way. Large roses on a dreadful dark—almost black—hunter green. I trail my hand along the thorny vines of rose stems, curling their way down the hall, until I end up in a living room at the front of the house.

"But then sometimes there's that niggling feeling in your gut that says maybe these aren't coincidences at all. Instead, they're just an intricate web of unknowns. Each thread you discover tells you a piece of the story. Until, eventually, it all makes sense."

"I guess." Raelean scrunches her nose at the horrid wallpa-per, same as in the photo the sheriff showed me of my mother. The regal chair she sat in is long gone, but this is where she reigned. Then it hits me.

"We're looking for a box," I say, suddenly realizing it was here on this floor where it sat. "My mother had this key. It goes to an old wooden box that's about yea big." I illustrate the size with my hands.

"So now we're looking for a box?" Raelean raises a questioning eyebrow, her face as flat as her voice. Those blue eyes of hers scan me pitifully. It makes me feel like a lost child who can't find her mommy in the grocery store. "Look, sweetie, I know you miss Adaire," she says softly. "But it's like we're on a wild-goose chase. Whatever this is—" she circles a finger in the air, referring to us in this house "—it isn't going to bring her back. Whatever you think you'll find, they will never implicate Stone Rutledge, not now that he's dead, anyway. And *none* of this helps clear *your* name."

Her words sour my mood. I hear what she's saying, I do. She thinks I'm desperately grasping at straws, searching for answers as to why Adaire is dead when I should be saving myself. But for some reason, I can't let it go.

"You're wrong," I say, rather sure of myself, despite having no evidence to back me up. "And yes, we're looking for a box. Adaire gave me this key." I tug at the brass chain hanging around my neck, then tuck it back into my shirt. "Sheriff Johns showed me a picture of my mom in this house with this box. I don't know what the hell any of it means, but if Adaire told it to me, then it means something. If you don't want to help me, fine. You can leave. But if you think there's even a tiny chance Adaire was trying to tell me something important before she died, then I'd appreciate it if you could help me search the house."

Raelean stares at me for a long scrutinizing moment without budging a lick. Her hot pink lips pucker tight as she tries to decide if she's going to ditch me or help. "Fine." She turns on her heels. "But hurry it up," she says over her shoulder, "because, if we get arrested, it'll be your ass I throw under the bus. I'll check the bedrooms, you check the kitchen." Raelean marches her short self down the hall into the first of the rooms.

I close my eyes and breathe a sigh of relief.

Then a solid *thunk* hits the kitchen window. A familiar sound. I bolt my eyes open and catch a glimpse of a dazed bird flying away. To the right, something flickers inside the dark recess of the kitchen pantry.

Curious, I step inside and close the door behind me. The darkness drinks me in, except for the thin line of light peeking between the knotty pine boards. A breeze drifts through the fine crack. I feel around for a handle or a knob, finding none, but the wall wobbles as I fondle it. With both hands pressed against the wall, I lean into it and push.

The wall depresses inward slightly. When I release the pressure, it pops open with a spring, revealing a now-present door. Its seams hidden between the tongue and groove of the wood. I stick my finger in a knot with a rotted center and pull open the door.

A hole opens into the ground. Three dirt steps disappear into a narrow cinderblock hallway. A hint of light promised at the end of the hall.

There's a crash from deeper in the house. "I'm alright!" Raelean hollers. Followed by a few choice words.

I shake my head, smiling, then descend into the root cellar.

The natural cold of the earth chills the air. Something grazes the top of my head—I duck. An errant cobweb from the ceiling clings to my hair.

The dank smell of earth brings forth a faint memory of déjà vu, my mama's promises of an ocean I've never seen. Down the hall, the light grows, seeping through the cracks of a slatted door. Hinges groan as I push in.

The skinny rectangular window along the ceiling streams sunlight through the broken filmy glass. It struggles to stretch across the room. A skeletal shelf cowers in a corner, tincture jars and wares stacked between its thin bones. No box. A braided rag rug covers the floor, it wobbles when I step on it. Pressed against the far wall, a homemade worktable. Papers scattered on top. Collections of old Appalachian folk magic and medical herbs, similar to the ones Grandmama and I use. Tucked like a bookmark inside a textbook, a pamphlet for pregnant teens. Scrawled in the corner, an appointment reminder for a free women's clinic. Whether it was for a health checkup or for alternate plans, I'm not sure.

I flip through a few spiral notebooks, one filled with math equations, the other chemistry notes. Aunt Violet told me my mama was smart but didn't go to college on account of getting pregnant. Maybe she would have done something with herself, if not for me.

Below hangs a ratty curtain, I pull it back—nothing but dust and rags and a milk crate full of old records.

I drag the crate out from underneath. Layers of dust cake the tops of the now-brittle albums. I thumb through and unearth greats like Jessie Mae Hemphill and Etta James. Bluesy, soulful tunes that push me back in time to those fuzzy childhood memories with Adaire. Incredible how a song can sink you into your past so vividly. I pick up a forty-five single by Patsy Cline. A smile spreads across my face as the memory bubbles to the surface. I press the small record to my chest, letting my mind drift.

The music taps like a heartbeat against my chest.

A slow, powerful *thu-thump*.

Thu-thump.

Thu-thump.

The sound pushes through an old Victrola as a warbly voice croons a lonely Mississippi song. The smell of rosewater perfume, old-fashioned yet timeless, tickles my nose—something Adaire stole from the old lady who babysat us. My skin grows sticky thinking about the sweltering summer heat when she and I listened to those stolen records in that cave. My mind wanders on as I breathe in the memories.

"I remember those," a heavy voice eases from the doorway. I smile at its familiarity, remembering all the nights he whispered to me in my dreams. Slowly, I open my eyes to find Rook leaning against the door frame. He saunters barefoot into the room. Shoes don't shift when he goes from man to crow. It was something he explained after I caught him barefoot at a carnival once, where I couldn't save a man who had choked on a chicken bone. The rooty smell of earth and pine trail in with him. His cool black eyes hold a steady gaze on me. I can't tell if he's deciding whether or not he should trust me, or if he's just taking me in now that he's a man again.

"How did you find me?" I pull at the bottom of my shirt, suddenly feeling exposed in my cropped gray T-shirt. Self-conscious, I run my fingers through my hair, knowing it's probably windblown from the ride here. I hope like hell Raelean didn't hear him come down here.

His face lights up. "I can always find you." He's right. Like somehow my mourning heart summons him. Maybe it does.

He flicks through the stack of 45 singles. A soft chuckle tumbles out of him. "You and your cousin." He shakes his head. "You two would belt out the lyrics from that cave. Loud enough to scare the trees."

I hide behind my palm, wrestling back a laugh.

"Do you remember that place? In the woods?" he asks, big grin on his face.

There's a small scuffing sound from the floor above us, Raelean rummaging around.

We both wait quietly, and after nothing further, I whisper, "Remember? Of course. That was our secret escape. And those trees, I'll have you know, they were our captivated audience." I pretend to be offended, knowing good and well we sounded like wild chickens.

I love the ease of my playfulness with him, like no time has passed since we were together last, despite the years.

"There wasn't a tree we didn't climb or a song we didn't sing. Summers were *our* time. We loved those woods."

Reality rolls back in like a bowling ball to pins, and it smacks me in the face.

"I'll never see her again." My words crack as my heart reminds me she's gone.

"Hey." Rook steps up, tilting his head so I will look up at him. "She's always with you." He holds out an open palm, offering it to me. It's a gesture that lingers a moment until I realize what he's doing.

This hand that's carried many souls over.

The gravity of what this might mean pushes deep into my chest. Did he walk Adaire over?

I lean forward, tempting a curious touch. Here's the boy I've loved since we were children, now a man, the flesh of him alone enlivening. And now he's offering me a chance to connect with her again.

Cautiously, I trace two fingers across his palm, longing to feel some tiny shimmer of her.

"Did she suffer?" I swirl the tips of my fingers in a circle, as if in doing so I could conjure a piece of Adaire and it keep it for myself.

"She was at peace," he says, not completely answering the question, but it's enough. "Go ahead." He nods at his outstretched hand.

Unsure and a little bit afraid, I slip my hand into his. The flesh of his against mine…something I've dreamed of, longed for. There's a tingle between them. My body tuning into the energy of those who crossed over with him. They flicker by, as if he's sorting through to find the one.

Then I feel her, or I think I do. Her presence lingers there between our touch. Not the whole of it, but a soft echo. Like the lingering scent of someone's perfume after they've already left the room. It makes me long for her even more. To bring my cousin back, even if it's only so I can say goodbye.

"Did she say anything? Before she…" I ask, yearning for a crumb.

"I wish I could give you more, but the dead usually don't talk to me. I only see brief glimpses of their joys. The kindness in their heart. The sadness for those they must say goodbye to." It's the depth with which he says this that surprises me, earnest in his attempt to convey the weight of what he is. He pulls us closer together, wrapping me into that soft scent of pine.

"It's a beautiful, emotion-filled light," he says. "Like a warm summer day that kisses your face." The backs of his knuckles grazes my cheek.

I close my eyes, vividly recalling one of the many times Adaire and I sunbathed on the rock by the quarry pond. It's as if Adaire is passing me one of her favorite memories.

How sad, or rather bittersweet, it must be for Rook, to feel love and sorrowed goodbyes. I am only experiencing this tiny moment, and it's almost too much. I cannot imagine how that must weigh on him. His gift a price he paid when I talked the death out of him and brought him back to life—if you call his split time as a crow a life. Both of us hold a shared burden for the miracles we can do.

"It's like an embodiment of their essence," he says. "You get a sense of who they truly were in life. Adaire was lovely."

I huff a small laugh. Lovely is not how I would expect Adaire to be described. Ornery. Grouchy. Surly. Not lovely. But I like the idea that all that gruffness she projected in life covered up her true self. The side of her Davis must have fallen in love with.

"Thank you for that." I pull my hand from his.

"Do you remember this place? When you first came here?" he says out of nowhere, his eyes leveling.

"Yeah…why are you asking me that?" From down the hallway, I hear the loud clomping of Raelean's heels on the stairs. An urgency kicks in my chest as our time together is slipping through my fingers like sand.

Rook turns and steps backward toward the sliver of broken window at the top of the root cellar. A panicked desperation floods me, causes me to step forward. I don't want him to go. His eyes clip to the door, then back to me. "Adaire wants you to remember," he says. Rook drops back into the dark as Raelean walks in.

"Girl, you've gotta see this." Raelean's voice injects itself into the room, just as Rook's form fades to black and feathers unfold. "Holy shit!" Raelean ducks as the crow flaps and flutters over our heads, then out the cracked window. She stumbles against the worktable, scattering its contents. The tin canister she's carrying gets knocked from her hands and rolls across the floor. "What the hell was that?" She eyes the window Rook just escaped through.

"I—I think it was a crow." Worried, I watch her face, trying to see if she saw more than a bird. "Its nest must have been in the window."

"That scared the bejesus out of me." She rights herself, a hand pressed against her bosom like she's recovering from a heart attack. "Good lord, girl, do you always chat it up with wildlife?"

"What? I wasn't…" I squat down to pick up the notebooks she knocked over, trying to avoid the curiosity in her eyes. A stingy, desperate need to keep him a secret—my secret—riles up inside me. It's one thing for people to believe you can talk the death out of the dying, but start telling them you know a man who is sometimes a crow…that's too big a leap. It was for Adaire.

"I heard you talking to someone—unless you were talking

to yourself?" She pops a questioning brow, like maybe she's misjudged my sanity.

"Don't be ridiculous. I was just reading aloud." I flap one of the notebooks I retrieve from the floor. Scraps of paper fall from between the pages and flutter to the ground. A photo lands face up. I tilt it toward the light. It's a picture of my mom. She's younger, maybe early teens. She stands next to a little girl, holding her hand. They wear shapeless shift dresses with a drop waist. My mother's is navy with a white collar and sleeve trim. Reminds me of the clothes they wore on old episodes of *Laugh-In*. But it's the protective way my mother clutches the Bible to her chest that feels so weird to see. My mother looks so...wholesome, compared to the woman I grew up knowing—the handful of times she bothered to be my mother. The little girl has an unsettling gaze, in contrast with the smile on her face. She's not someone I know.

I flip it over to the back. "'CFI Baptist Conference, me and Gabby Newsome,'" I read what my mother wrote on the back.

"Holy shit." Raelean snatches the picture from me. "Is that crazy Gabby?" She leans in to get a better look.

"You know her?" I stand and take the photo back.

"I've heard of her. How have you not? She's the sister that lives on the third floor of the Rutledge mansion. I've seen her up in the window before, standing there like a damn ghost. They say she's got more than a few screws loose."

"Stone Rutledge has a sister?" I ask, confused.

She waves a dismissive hand. "No, his wife's younger sister. You know Becky, out at the Watering Hole? Last year, she worked at the big house—and damn, if they don't get paid a fortune to keep quiet about what goes on there." Raelean picks up the tin that rolled across the floor. "They brought Gabby home after she'd been 'abroad' for a few years—I think she was locked up in a looney hospital. Becky says Gabby is always running away. A few months back she went streaking, buck naked down the hill into Clementine's."

"That was her? I heard about that, but someone said it was one of the bus tourists."

"A lie the family used to cover it up. It's impossible for the staff to keep tabs on her. They aren't even allowed in her private quarters. They don't want anyone to know anything about her. Rumor has it she offed her pet canary at Christmas dinner last winter. Fine china, big-ass candelabra kind of feast." Raelean fans her hands wide. "Ripped its head right off. The rest of the family politely smiled and continued to eat their Christmas ham, like decapitating pets was an ordinary thing."

"Jesus." I study the picture again. They look happy, standing formally next to each other in front of a group of kids. What made my mom go from a church mouse on the honor roll to an absentee parent with an insatiable wanderlust that I've always known? It's like I was born and a switch inside her flipped.

"Maybe. Look what I found upstairs." Raelean sets down a faded brown button tin with an Easter lily on the front. "It was hidden in the top of a closet. Don't ask me how I managed to get it down, almost broke my neck. Get a load of this…" She peels off the tin lid, and inside is a single piece of paper. I recognize Adaire's chicken-scrawled handwriting immediately.

If you find this, then I was right.
The riddled tongue will guide you to see.
Ask her about the droplet of rain.

"It's Adaire's handwriting," I say as I pick up the piece of paper.

"Oh, wow. Really?" Raelean leans on the workbench, getting a better look. "Why couldn't she just say 'here's everything you need to know, now go clear this whole mess up?'"

"Because there was nothing to see yet. Hell, she couldn't see clearly around her own death. I don't think she knew Stone would die, or Ellis for that matter, or if she did, she didn't tell me. She just said I'd need to be 'set free.' And it seems she learned something about why."

"Huh." Raelean works a piece of gum between her jaws, sifting through the items on the table like leftovers at a garage sale.

"I don't know. Maybe Adaire was scared to tell me what she found out," I say absentmindedly. *Remember this place. Remember when you first came here.* That's what Rook said. "But whatever she figured out has something to do with my mother, the first time I came here was with her. Something about this house—and this little girl—" I flap the picture "—led Adaire here. This Gabby knew my mother, maybe knows more."

"Hey, look at this," Raelean says. "It fits." She holds the faded button tin over a spot devoid of dust on the workbench. "It matches up exactly." She sets the tin down to show me, then picks it up. Down again, up again. "What do you think it means?"

"It was moved." I state the obvious. "Adaire moved it on purpose." A thought occurs to me. "Where did you say you found this tin again?"

"The bedroom with those paper-thin curtains. Freaking room has a creepy vibe if you ask me."

It's the room where the woman gave birth—misbirth—to those twin babies. Adaire is the only one I've ever told about that horrible night. What if those babies' deaths are what gets me in trouble?

"Why did she move it?" Raelean knocks the dust off her fingers.

"The better question… What was in it before? Whatever was here, Adaire thought it important for me to find."

Raelean studies the lone note in the empty tin. "You think whatever it was will clear your name?"

"Maybe. I hope so. What do you think she means by this—*the riddled tongue will guide you to see?*" I swirl the phrase around in my mind: riddled tongue, riddled, tongue. "What if she's talking about her?" I point to the picture.

Raelean quirks her head. "Gabby?"

"Yeah, I think maybe it could be." The idea of this feeling more right as I consider it. "She *has* to be the riddled tongue Adaire's referring to. Don't you think?" I look to Raelean for confirmation that I'm on the right track.

"Maybe." Raelean shrugs. "If she's as crazy as they say she is, I bet she's full of nonsense. My nana had dementia and she was always talking in circles. A riddled tongue, so to speak."

"Stop calling her crazy, we don't even know her."

Raelean sighs, nodding in agreement.

"What if Gabby Newsome knows something? But do we think Adaire even knew who Gabby Newsome was?" I ask. I'd never heard a peep about some unwell woman who lived at the old sugar plantation; just goes to show the family did a good job keeping a lid on that little secret. But still.

"Her mom worked at the Watering Hole, right? And well, Becky worked there, too. Hush money or not, a few rumors about the Rutledge mansion still got out."

It *did* make sense, sort of. Assuming Raelean was right and Gabby was a real person who lived in the mansion, all locked up and hidden away.

"Well then, what about the droplet of rain? She can't mean that literally."

"She said to ask her—you'll just have to go and see for yourself."

There's a sudden *pop-crackle* of tires rolling over gravel, and we both duck out of the window's view. A car door closes, and a static garbled voice mumbles over a walkie-talkie.

"Copy that." We hear Deputy Billy Parnell's voice from

the driveway. "Ma'am, if you could just wait a minute." I peer through the cracked window to see who he's talking to.

Someone steps across the lawn into view. And it's not Billy.

Lorelei Rutledge walks with purpose out toward the woods, telling the deputy she would appreciate him respecting her right to mourn in private. She slows about halfway, her eyes seemingly lost to the ground, searching. Like maybe she's mustering her feelings before approaching where the Latham boys found her brother? Of course, it's not but fifty yards out farther from where her father hung himself. This place's meaning forever changed to her now.

"I can't see," Raelean whispers, tipping high on her toes, trying to peer out the window with me. I press a finger to my mouth for her to hush.

Deputy Parnell speaks frantically over the radio, trying to get orders on what to do. "She's insistent," he says through gritted teeth to the person on the other end.

Lorelei turns around, as if maybe she's changed her mind— a batch of flowers fisted in her hand. With her back-and-forth struggle, she almost seems tortured by whether or not she wants to pay her respects. Lorelei's knees give way just as the deputy comes up behind her to inform her she's not allowed to be there.

"What is she doing?" Raelean asks once she finds a box to stand on. But the film and grime cloud her view. I'm wondering the same thing as Lorelei runs her hand over the dirt.

"Let me see." Raelean presses her cheek right next to mine as the deputy hefts Lorelei to her feet. She shoves a fistful of dirt in her pocket. Her memorial flowers scatter to the ground.

We drop below the window's view like skittish mice as the deputy escorts Lorelei by the elbow off the property.

"Did you see that?" I ask Raelean after we hear the deputy's car leave.

"No, because somebody's fat head was taking up all the viewing space." Raelean claps the cobwebs and dirt off her hands. "See what?"

"She took the dirt."

Raelean pauses in her grooming. "What?" She looks at me like I'm an idiot.

"She grabbed a handful of dirt and shoved it in her pocket." I gather up the tin with Adaire's note and the picture of my mother and Gabby.

"Is that, like, some hillbilly curse or something?" Raelean asks. At my eye roll she adds, "Jesus. Sorry. I don't know what you backwoods folks do around here," she adds playfully as she punches my arm.

"No, she must have picked something up with it."

"What?"

I shake my head. "I don't know, but I doubt she came all the way out here for just a handful of dirt."

We sneak out of the root cellar, once the coast is clear, and hightail it out of there like thieves, across the lawn and back through the woods to Raelean's car. The rumble of the Camaro's engine sounds extra loud, seeing how we almost got caught.

I drop my mother's picture inside the button tin with Adaire's note.

"Raelean," I say, "you think Becky still has connections at the Rutledge mansion?"

TWELVE

The Riddled Tongue

Ten dollars will buy you a one-hour tour of the Sugar Hill Plantation if you're dumb enough to fork over the cash. Which I was. It's the easiest way I could figure to sneak up to the mansion's elusive third floor and talk to Gabby Newsome, especially since I am enemy number one in this house now that two Rutledges are dead.

Luckily, none of the family's vehicles are in sight. Not Lorelei's gold Firebird Trans Am, Mrs. Rutledge's white convertible, or Stone's red Corvette. The murder weapon that killed Adaire. It seems horrifically unfair that they're still sporting around town in that thing, like a hunting trophy proudly on display.

I shake off my angry thoughts and focus on what I came here to do, though I might have sprinkled a handful of walnut dust and graveyard dirt along the front stoop as I entered, inviting whatever darkness wanted inside for a visit.

A young girl in cheap period-specific antebellum attire has started the last tour of the day.

"William Tobias Rutledge purchased the land that eventually became Sugar Hill Plantation after an inspired visit to the Caribbean." She details a general list of what we will see today.

I wrench the brochure in my hands—the only souvenir my ten dollars got me—and I keep an eye out for the second hallway on the left that Becky said would lead to the family's private stairs.

The tour guide drops her regal flair and opts for a more somber tone. Now she's telling of the sinful past that rots the South's history, and the whole room quiets. She's brutally honesty in her description of the horrible conditions here. The whole antebellum South sickens me and heavies my heart. She waits a poignant quiet moment, letting us digest that hideous truth before continuing on about what type of candies were created using the Sugar Hill crop.

She airs a hand toward the main hallway for the tourists to follow. I drop back until I'm at the tail end of the pack and jump the velvet rope at the second hallway. A long corridor leads me to a set of unmarked stairs I disappear up.

This mansion is regal as hell: detailed woodwork, refined antiques, ornate decor. Jesus, I'd be a spoiled brat if I grew up here.

Once I arrive at the top level, I use the master key Becky was able to get a copy of—took her more than a week to get it—and unlock the door to their private floor. Stepping through the entrance, my mind travels back to when Aunt Violet brought me out here to talk the death out of Mrs. Rutledge's father, Mr. Godfrey Newsome.

She should have never dragged me there to save that rotting man.

In elementary school, a lot of kids thought Lorelei and Ellis

Rutledge were ghosts. There were stories about two children who haunted the third floor of the Sugar Hill mansion.

I can still recall seeing them in the window as we pulled up. Side by side they stood, Ellis next to Lorelei, a dish next to a spoon. The boy was bloated like a balloon. Puffed so full he was ready to pop. The girl no less unforgettable. Gaunt eyes and skeletal thin, with a sour expression marring her face. Pitiful-looking kids who were unloved and uncared for despite their wealth.

When I was younger, I didn't know they still had all-boys and all-girls boarding schools that parents shipped off their children to. That was only something you read about in V. C. Andrews books. But the Rutledge twins come from old money. People like that can't be bothered with raising children.

Inside, the formal receiving room was a vast soulless space—even with its many antiques and oil paintings. There we sat at a play table, finer than any kitchen table I'd ever seen but small enough for children.

Not a word between us three kids as I waited to be called.

Red velvet plushed over the chairs. A miniature sterling silver tea set graced the table. Fifth grade felt a little too old for teatime, but they were a year or two younger than me, so I guess it was fine. Their manners were intact, but their personalities devoid of emotion. Aunt Violet gushed about how wonderful it was to have a tea party on real china.

"Isn't this a delight?" she asked.

Adults don't hide their nerves from children as well as they think. It was the way she glanced over at Stone Rutledge, still as a statue, waiting for her to finish placating me, that gave her away.

Aunt Violet had brought me there to do the death-talking—without grandmother's permission. But Aunt Violet's taste for whiskey outweighed her fear of her mother.

Then we were alone.

We three kids.

With our fine china, petite cakes, and sugary hot tea. Tiny sterling forks scraped quietly. Teacups clinked delicately.

The crinkle of Ellis's curls fought against the slick, glossy gel trying to tame them down. His plaid button-up shirt, freshly starched, made me a little embarrassed my cotton dress wasn't ironed. He inhaled the sweets and gulped the tea eagerly, shooting me smiles from that rounded face of his. He seemed nice. Friendly, even, like maybe we could play again sometime if they were allowed.

I don't think they would have been.

The girl's blue floral dress with puffy sleeves was made of a fine polished cotton. Something fancy enough to wear to church on Easter Sunday, but here she wore it in the middle of the week on summer break. She didn't offer any smiles. I would have thought her sad, had it not been for her grim stare. Maybe she didn't want to share her twin brother with me. Or maybe she didn't want someone of such a low caliber playing with her fancy tea set. I couldn't help but feel like Lorelei Rutledge hated me, even though we'd never formally met before that day.

She picked at her icy cubed cakes—petits fours, I believe they were—never eating them. Just decimating them into crumbs with the illusion of being consumed. I remember wanting her cakes if she wasn't going to finish them, my stomach rumbling all the while.

And death was there, too, slipping underneath the doorway from their grandfather's room. It clung to the air, thick as molasses. Smelled like a horse's stall that was sorely in need of a cleaning. The old man's soul-song a scattered sound of piano keys twinkling with no rhyme or reason; the disjointed tune set my teeth on edge.

Then Aunt Violet called, and I walked into the room past Stone. He was unable to look at me. Shame was there, tucked in the corner of his eyes. That and sorrow, like maybe he felt bad for me and what I was about to do. I wanted to touch his hand and tell him I'd be alright; it wasn't the first time I'd been called upon.

Velvet curtains stretched all the way to the ceiling, letting in a sliver of light. It was hard to make out the details in the dim, dusty room, but my eyes found Godfrey Newsome's as he struggled to cling to life.

The bed was a majestic beast, with its tall brooding wood balusters and bloodred bedding. Mrs. Rebecca Rutledge sat on the opposite of her father's bedside, eyes desperate and scared. It was a high bed, up to my chest. A stern, firm piece that looked uncomfortable to sleep on. I stood next to it, held out an open palm for old man Newsome to clasp. Cold and bony, his grasp was frail. He smelled of cigars and urine. I bent over to whisper the secret scriptures into his palm, and then I talked the death out of him.

Death curled itself in my belly like the gnarled roots of an old oak tree. It twisted inside me, a skeletal creature stretching to be born. It went on like that for more minutes than I wanted to endure. When it was done, a wad of death-ooze hung in my throat. With a garbled hawk, I spit it free in the fine teacup Aunt Violet held out for me. The black sludge slivered down and settled in the bottom.

Aunt Violet scuttled me out into the sitting room. My knees trembled like a fawn, weak and dizzy from the sickness that was coming. As I was ushered out, I saw a door on the other side of the room that was cracked open. It closed abruptly, the hem of a dress fluttering in its wake. We were sent on our way with a fistful of cash and not so much as a thank-you from the family.

Something made me turn around as we drove off. The tall dark figure of Stone Rutledge loomed in the upper window. It was impossible to know what he was thinking as he watched us go. Whatever it was made me feel sad and lonely. Forgotten.

Details of the sitting room haven't changed much all these years later. An oriental red carpet, just as fancy as I remember, covers the floor and matching velvet curtains hang alongside the windows. Stuck in the center, a round table with a large bouquet of fresh flowers just like before. Across the room, double doors lead to the tearoom, where I once sat with the Rutledge twins.

I smooth a nervous hand over my thin cotton dress, reciting in my head the script I plan to use. That I found this old picture of my mom and Gabby… How well did they know each other? I'd work my way into asking about the button tin, and if she knew it's importance for my mom. Doubtful, but Adaire didn't leave me with much else to go on.

Then, before my nerves give out, I'll ask her about the droplet of rain.

Not that great of a script.

Two light knocks on the door and a woman's voice on the other side gives me permission to enter.

Thirteen years it's been since I sat in this room that now houses an adult-sized table and tea set. Yellow balloons bunch around in various spots. Fresh flowers decorate a party table. A tiered cake, the center of attention, is beautiful enough for a wedding. A smattering of gifts are set in the corner. Fear hops in my chest. They're getting ready for a party—and parties typically mean people. Holy hell, if I get busted for being here, I'll be in a heap of trouble.

A woman samples one of the pastel mints from the silver candy dish and pops it into her mouth before she turns my way. I freeze for a half-second, not sure if this is Gabby.

"You're early for my party," the woman says, but then her brow dips in confusion as she realizes I'm not who she expected. It takes me a minute, but I slowly start to place her.

Her curly brown hair is riddled with wiry gray sprigs. The bags under her eyes too dark, like she's lived a heavy life. Her dress a cheery blue, with a refined lace looks like something straight out of *Southern Living* magazine.

"I..." I start, but all those practiced words just slip out of my head. "Happy Birthday, Gabby?" is what rolls out of my mouth. I hold my breath and hope I'm right. Then I waggle my plastic sack with the old tin as if I've brought a gift and that makes my presence here legitimate.

Her face lights up. "Don't you mean congratulations, silly?" She eagerly fans a hand for me to join her at the table already set for tea.

"Yes, sorry, I meant congratulations." I sigh with relief. Though I'm unsure what I'm congratulating her for.

"You must be one of Lorelei's friends from college." Gabby pours steaming hot tea into our cups, eyeing me with an eager curiosity. Across the table, slouching in his seat, a giant teddy bear with a gift bow tied around his head. A dainty teacup of his own sits in front of him.

"We know each other" is how I leave it.

"Sugar?" Pinched between a pair of dainty sterling silver tongs, she holds an anticipatory white cube, awaiting its fate.

They don't match her tea set. The tongs. They don't have the fine dotted trim of the silver creamer and sugar bowl. Of course, the tray doesn't belong to the set, either, as it is scalloped while none of the other pieces are. Like the antique dining table we're seated at, similar to the chairs, but not the same, though they try to be. A bunch of one-off pieces. It's like the family doesn't trust her with the good stuff, and she hasn't noticed they're knockoffs.

"Yes please." I hold out my cup for her to drop the cube into but she doesn't.

"Whores don't get sugar."

I fumble my teacup and saucer. *What did she say?*

She politely drops the cube into her own cup.

"I saw you through the window." She inclines her head toward the one she's referring to, then takes a delicate sip of her hot tea.

The window she's talking about looks down on the rear of Clementine's. I clear my throat. Heat flushes up my neck, warming the back of my ears. I might have fooled around with Ricky once or twice behind the restaurant. Had no clue we could be seen from up here.

I sip my sugarless tea.

There are a few quiet seconds of spoons stirring and cups clinking against saucers until I finally speak up.

"The truth is, Gabby," I start, "I didn't come here for the party. I came here to—"

"Apologize for the whoring?" she asks, her voice upturned again. My eyes bulge.

Now, if this would have been any other person, I might have chewed them an earful about being such an asshole, but with the shock of it all—and the fact I'm here to get information—I grit my teeth.

"Uh, no. I didn't realize… That was just… What I was trying to say—"

"Shh." Gabby gently presses a finger to her lips, then glances over to the corner.

I follow her gaze to the two brand-new cribs with giant gift bows attached to them. A chill slithers up my spine. My eyes jump around the room to the rattle on the cake, the stork on some of the balloons, and the ABC blocks that spell *Congrats*.

Is she pregnant? Becky said they kept Gabby under lock and key. Maybe that's why they sent her abroad, to hide a pregnancy the family would have a hard time explaining? So if this is a baby shower, the family must be throwing it.

Which means Lorelei and Mrs. Rutledge and whoever else will be joining us any minute. Wary, I look at the clock and

wonder how long I have before they arrive. It's hard to believe they'd still press on with a party after what happened to
Ellis—to Stone.

"You know," Gabby starts. She tilts her head, curious.
"What I don't understand is who gave you permission to
play with my dolls?" She genuinely looks perplexed. My eyes
dart to the teddy bear, frowning at us from across the table.

"I didn't. I don't think I understand—"

"Now, now, don't you tell a fib." She wags a finger at me.
"Of course you did. I saw you. It was very naughty of you to
make them go night-night. Naughty! Naughty!" Her voice
shrieks.

What is she going on about?

"It's interesting, if you think about it." She pours a bit of
cream in her tea, takes her time to stir it with her dainty
spoon. "You are a made thing, birthed and all, but you're
not..." Gabby pauses to find the word "...normal." Her voice
drops as she says it. Her head dips, and a wicked look blooms
in her eyes. "But that's why they say you're the Devil's kin,
isn't it? You're simply a tool, and he puppets your strings.
Dancey, dancey." She bounces her hands and wiggles her fingers as if she's operating a marionette. "Die, doll, die," she
sings. A wild expression cartoons her face. "Close your little
eyes. When you sleep, the death you keep. Die, doll, die."
Gabby claps her hands, thrilled by her little performance.

"Gabby, I'm not sure who you think I am—we've never
met before, I think you might be confused—"

"Confused?" She huffs a laugh. "Why, you're the baby
murderer, aren't you?"

Her words slip into my gut, flipping it upside down.

Slowly, the memory comes into focus. The old farmhouse
and its ugly floral wallpaper, and Gabby in the back bedroom,
screaming.

Her eyes gleam, as if this is the fun part of the game she's been playing in her head. She can see the realization spread across my face.

My teacup trembles against the saucer as I set it down. "Gabby, I was a child who didn't understand the power I had or how it could be used. I didn't know what it was being used for, who it was given to," I say with the utmost regret. My hands smooth out the wrinkles in my dress. "I should have apologized to you a long time ago. I just didn't know who you were. I am sorry, though, for what happened to you."

"It was your fault, you know. I knew it the second I saw what you did to Daddy." A memory flashes: the crack of the door and the swish of the skirt. It was her, watching from the other room. She saw me talk the death out of her father, saw the mucus that came up after.

"I was trying to save your father. Your sister, she called my aunt and asked for the Sin Eater Oil for you."

Suddenly, she straightens up. "You're not here for the party. So, what did you really come for?" she asks, folding her hands in her lap.

I swallow hard, not sure where to start.

From my purse, I pull out the photo of her and my mother. "You knew my mother once." I slide the picture across the table.

Gabby picks it up delicately. Fondness for the memory softens her features as she admires it. A light smile edges out, as if she's slipping back in time.

"Do you remember her? Darbee Wilder?" She's still studying the photo, lost in that day long ago. "She had this old button tin." I pull it out of the bag to show her. "Do you recognize it? Do you know what she kept in it?"

Gabby rears back as if I laid a snake in front of her. "Lies!" she hisses and pushes back from the table. "That's what was in it! Sin and lies," she says through snarled teeth. Abruptly, she stands and paces in tiny circles. Picking at her nails. Her eyes dart to the tin box and away.

"You should go," she whispers, as if she doesn't want anyone to hear. "Go, go, go." She quietly shoos me with her fingers.

"But Gabby—"

"No." She shakes her hands frantically in the air, batting away the memories I've unearthed. "Go." She points a rattled finger toward the door, wearing a hole in the floor with her back and forth.

The swing of her moods is jarring. It's obvious this woman isn't of sound mind and pushing her further probably won't get me very far. Reluctantly, I take the picture of my mother and the tin and shove it back into the plastic Walmart bag. I stand, about to leave, but the thought of walking out that door feels too final. And it will be. Once this household—or the sheriff—learns I snuck in here, I won't get back in. And I'll probably never see Gabby Newsome again.

This opportunity is now or never.

"Tell me about the droplet of rain."

Gabby's head jerks sharply my way; she freezes in her tizzy. Eyes dart to the door, to the balcony, to the windows, as though looking for someone secretly lingering.

"You know about the deer?" she whispers. There's a guarded, yet eager hesitation, but it's clear she's hoping for a yes.

I pretend to be concerned there are ears nearby as well. I give her a small nod. The tension in her body slackens as a huge grin grows on her face.

Gabby curls her hands to prance. "Bumpety, bumpety. Hop, hop." She jumps forward twice. "Out came the deer and nobody stopped." She shakes her head with an exaggerated no. "From its pocket, fell a blue drop of rain." Her hands cup together as if she's holding the droplet. "She whispered the recipe to see again." Gabby stood tall and proud as if she just recited the Pledge of Allegiance in front of the entire class.

She shushes me. "No one is supposed to know."

"Know what?"

"About the deer." Gabby fidgets with her fingers again, warily eyeing the door. "But I kept it." A childlike mischievous grin fans across her face.

"The deer?" Now I have images of a deer stowed away in the closet or locked out on that balcony.

"No, silly. The blue droplet of rain. But don't tell, or she'll get so mad. Lorelei's always mad." Gabby nervously straightens the napkins on the food table. Tweaks and turns the nuts bowl and the mints tray, eyes always flitting to the door.

A coil of unease settles itself in my belly. This is exactly what Adaire was telling me. *Her riddled tongue can guide you to see*, I remind myself.

"Can I see it?" I flash an eager grin and match Gabby's secretiveness as I slowly rise out of my chair. "Can I see the droplet of rain?"

Gabby steps back, guarded and unsure. She drums her fingers across her bottom lip, considering.

"I won't tell." I stand tall and hold high my three-finger Girl Scouts promise.

The edge of her mouth lightly curls upward. That's a promise she's willing to trust.

"Yes, yes, you can see." She bounces over to a desk in the corner and picks up a pink flowered box. When the lid opens, up pops a tiny plastic ballerina. I had a similar jewelry box when I was younger.

Her fingers scrounge around the trinkets and other treasures she keeps in there until… "Here!" She plucks a single item and holds it out for me. I open a palm to receive it. The tiny blue glass hits my hand like a weighted stone.

A cobalt blue bottle stopper.

The very one that matches the perfume bottle that holds my Sin Eater Oil, that sits next to Grandmama's recipe box.

The whooshing in my chest muffles my hearing. The earth waves under my feet. My thoughts trip over themselves, trying to calculate two and two and coming up with orange. A cold chill races up my spine. The mystery of this deer story feels imperative to unravel.

"Where did you say you met this deer?"

"Near the woods." She holds her hand out for me to return it to her. Instead, I pull back. This dwindles the joy lighting her face.

"This deer had a pocket?" My words a little firmer.

"Mmm, huh." She murmurs and nods eagerly, but she catches onto my wariness. "But don't worry about the deer." She misreads my concern "It's just sleeping."

"Sleeping?" I step closer. She steps back, bumping into her baby's crib.

"Yes." She turns nervously and fingers the white lace layered around the edge. Then she lovingly looks inside the small crib. "Sleeping like an angel," she whispers lightly and with a soft push, the cradle rocks. She hums a rhythmic cadence.

"Bumpety, bumpety. Hop, hop," she sings. "Out came the deer and nobody stopped." She shakes her head to the other crib. "From its pocket, fell a blue drop of rain." She playfully twinkles her fingers downward. "She whispered the recipe to see again. Sleeping!" Gabby twists around to me, eyes bright with joy. "A long forever nap. Like Stone. Like Ellis."

A wave of unease crashes over me.

"Like my babies!"

Slowly, I turn my attention to the two cradles. A faint dirty handprint stains the frilly lace on one. The realization of what she's saying dawns on me.

I peer over the edge, praying to sweet Jesus I'll see two beautiful baby dolls.

It's my fears that are answered and not my prayers.

Two dirty swaddles lie in each crib. The same meager blankets Grandmama wrapped those twins up in all those years ago. Threadbare and stained brown from rot. I stumble back, almost tumbling over the settee.

A haunting sneer spreads across that thin bony face of hers. Gabby tilts her head, almost gloating at the stark fear she senses in my reaction. She walks over and reaches into the crib, running a delicate touch over the foul empty blankets.

"Precious, aren't they?" She sighs a blissful motherly sigh. "My family gets mad when I sneak out, but you won't tell, will you? It'll be our little secret." Then she straightens and turns to me. "You didn't even ask me what the deer was going to cook." She seems affronted, and it takes my brain a chugging minute to catch up.

"A recipe to see?" I pluck the words from her little rhyme.

"Yes!" She rushes over to me before I can back away. "A recipe to see!" She thrusts herself right up in my face, then grabs my wrists, and we start to spin. "A recipe to see. A recipe to see!" she sings. "Devil's Seed Child. Devil's Seed Child, a recipe to see!"

We dance in a circle.

A wave of sickness flushes over me. My mind can't let go of this sleeping deer. This dead deer with a pocket. A pocket that carried the blue stopper that belongs to a perfume bottle that's been in my family for generations. No clue how long that stopper has been missing, I've only ever known the mismatched one that we have now. My gut knows what she's telling me, but my head doesn't want to think *who* this dead deer is.

What if Adaire found the stopper at the farmhouse, among my mother's things?

Gabby stops abruptly, her face realizing something. "You won't tell, will you?" And before I can promise my silence, a dark malevolence shadows her face. For a split second, her eyes eclipse to black orbs, then the orbs are gone in a blink. So fast, maybe I'm wrong.

Or worse, maybe Gabby Newsome isn't running herself anymore.

She grips my wrists tighter. "You better not tell!" she screams into my face. Specks of spit flying from her mouth.

"Let go!" I twist my wrists and wrench myself free, frantically distancing myself from her.

"You'll burn in hell if you tell!" She charges toward me, angry fists shaking above her head. I trip, knocking against the table of food. Mints scatter across the floor. Scrambling to get away, I twist and turn and race out the door. "Burn in hell!" These are the last words I hear screamed at my back as I fly down the family's private stairs.

I thrust through the kitchen, past the surprised staff, and rush out the back door. I'm not a half step outside when I'm tossed back by the sight of Stone Rutledge's pristine red Corvette parked right in front of me.

Lorelei casually pulls her shopping bags from the back seat of her father's car. "Oh, perfect, can you help us with these—" She freezes at the sight of me. Her face twists to rage.

It's not until I hear the bags hit the ground that I see her fist flying through the air. It cracks against my cheek with a wicked crunch.

Stars spark.

Darkness drops over my sight.

Gravel from the driveway digs into my elbows.

"Stay the hell away from our home, you freaking psycho!" Lorelei screams over me. I press my palm to my throbbing cheek. My head a clogged, dizzy mess. Rebecca Rutledge has stepped out of the car now and is just standing there, glaring down at me with a smug look. Perfectly happy to watch her daughter assault me.

The back door swings open, and Gabby flies out. "Devil's Seed Child!" she screams joyfully at the top of her lungs.

"My brother's dead because of you!" Lorelei kicks me in the shins, and I curl to block her. "And you show up at my house!" She kicks me again.

"You are a naughty, naughty girl!" Gabby stomps her foot on the stoop with every word.

My hands tremble from rattled nerves. The pristine front grill of Stone's car a menacing smile as they both scream at me.

Lorelei bends over, grabs me by the shirt, and pulls my face to hers. "You think you can come here and do what? Beg for forgiveness?" she asks, but I don't answer; I can't find any words. Her necklace swings violently at her throat. "You come around here again and I'll—"

My hand snakes out, and I capture the gold coin dangling from her ribbon necklace. "The scales of justice," I whisper as I see the image. A tiny constellation of stars diamond around the image of a woman holding the scales.

Lorelei steps back, confusion edging across her face. She tucks the ribbon inside her shirt protectively.

Find the scales of justice. She holds the truth. These were Adaire's words just days before she died. Lorelei shrinks back, fear spiking in her eyes. I push myself up to stand.

One of the cooking staff bursts through the kitchen door. "What's going on out here?" A few others bustle out the door behind him. He assesses the situation; his eyes jump with recognition when they land on me.

"Call the cops, you nitwits!" Rebecca barks at them.

But I've already turned to leave, headed down the hill toward Clementine's, where I parked Adaire's car.

THIRTEEN

Let Sleeping Dogs Lie

"What in the hell do these crazy riddles have to do with anything?" Davis shoves himself out from under Miss Belinda Jones's jacked-up bumper with a smooth roll on the mechanic dolly. Grease smears across his forehead. Black stains his rough-hewn fingers. He stretches open his palm toward the rubber mallet. I hand it to him.

"I don't exactly know yet. But they have to mean something."

"Why's that?"

"Well—"

"Oh, hey," he interrupts. "I almost forgot. Wyatt called here looking for you." His tone drops a bit. "He said Violet wants you to bring Adaire's car to the Watering Hole tonight. She's got a buyer."

"Awesome," I grumble, as I'll now be without a reliable set of wheels since I still don't have enough cash to fix my car. Davis slides himself back under.

Harvey's Metal Boneyard is a giant corrugated shed stuffed full of rusty parts, stacks of old tires, and a hoard of outdated equipment. The Yancey's junkyard garage used to be the main place you could get car parts before they opened the auto store over in Mercer. Pick what you needed from the lot, and Mr. Harvey would work his magic. After Davis's father passed, he resigned himself to the fact that as the third generation Yancey, he would have to take over the family business. But Adaire, to Mrs. Yancey's approval, convinced Davis he was too smart to spend his life as a grease monkey in a dying junkyard business, not with his love for science and medicine. Next to the greasy tools and soda cooler against the wall are Davis's EMT-training books. During the day, he works on cars and in night school, he learns how to work on bodies. I'm pretty sure his final exams are coming soon. Something I don't want to think about.

Hanging on the wall between the screwdrivers and wrenches is Blue's old collar. Adaire and I had no idea that the dog we saved that day would find a home for many years with her future sweetheart. That dog was a good boy, once he got used to you.

As my eyes scan the room, they settle on a package, unopened, beneath Davis's textbooks. I slide the books slightly to the side. The package doesn't say who it's from, but I don't need to know because I recognize Adaire's handwriting. A sweet pink ribbon ties the bundle up tight. Davis's greasy fingerprints patter all over the outside of it, probably from the many times he's picked it up, ready to open it, only to change his mind. Maybe he should save it for his birthday next year, a belated present.

The old diner bar stool creaks when I sit on it. I hold a cold Orange Crush bottle against my throbbing cheek and tell him the rest of my Gabby adventure.

Davis rolls out from underneath the car and pins me with a

scrutinizing look. "Gabby said she got the glass droplet from a dead deer. What's that got to do with Adaire?" His voice edges with anger. There's a thin line of patience he's holding on to. If I tug too hard, that line will snap.

"Well," I say, in a more tender tone, "it's been in our family for years. Where else would Gabby have got it from?" I hold up the blue stopper to the light. "Droplet of rain, Adaire called it in her note. Gabby called it that, too."

"You're not making any sense," he growls.

"*Gabby* wasn't making any sense," I say, more to myself, then I snap the lid off with the bottle opener and take a long, refreshing chug.

Out front, a crow lands on a rusty oil barrel and stares directly into the garage. I sit taller, unsure if it's Rook or just an ordinary crow. It pecks around on top of the barrel like it's trying to get at something.

Davis gives the bird an uninterested glance before he rolls back under the car. He bangs out a few muffled thuds with the rubber mallet.

"And I don't understand this 'recipe' she was talking about, either," I say when he stops pounding. "Maybe it just means to see something again. As in we've seen it before, now we get to see it again."

The crow stays put. Eyes locked on mine. Then it caws twice as if calling to me. I pop off my stool to see what it's getting at—

A loud clank drops from underneath the car, causing me to jump.

"Got it!" Davis rolls out, holding up the prized piece, a bar with red plastic fringe dangling on the end. He watches the startled crow fly off. His eyes pan back to me with heavy concern.

"What's that?" I pretend like I didn't even notice the crow and saunter back over to Davis.

"Handlebar to a pogo stick." He tosses it in the trash barrel with the remaining stick, now a red pretzel knot. "Miss Belinda ran over her granddaughter's toy."

"And it jacked up her car that bad?" The twisted bend of the front bumper a gnarled grin.

"Yep." Davis scrubs his hands with a bar of Lava soap. "She'll need a new one. Bent the tire rod, too. I'll have to order one of those as well." He leans back against the sink, drying his hands on a red rag that's nothing short of filthy.

"New bumper," I say more to myself as a thought occurs to me. Not an hour ago I lay on the Sugar Hill's driveway, face-to-face with Stone's car. Not a scratch anywhere on it. "Hey. If Stone's car hit a bicycle, wouldn't his bumper be jacked up? Like this?" I say to Davis. Before he can answer, I add, "Now that I come to think about it, I don't remember seeing any damage to his car when I put the witching jar behind his tire. A little strange, don't you think?"

"He probably had it repaired." Davis shrugs.

"And why has Lorelei been driving it around? Where's her car?"

Davis gives me a confused look. "Who knows. Maybe she sold it. And maybe you're misremembering about Stone's car; we had a lot on our minds that day at court. It's nothing. Just let it go."

Except I can't let it go.

"But that doesn't make sense—why would she sell a perfectly good car? Why would Stone's even be drivable after the accident? I didn't even get to the part about the necklace!" I'm about to tell him about the scales of justice and the ribbon necklace Lorelei had with that symbol—

"What are you doing?" Davis sharply cuts me off before I can finish my thought. "Why is any of this important?"

"It's important because... Well, I'm not sure, but I think

maybe—" Then I stop when I see the grimace on Davis's face. "What?"

He glances down and away, like it pains him to have this talk, but it's got to be done. I can feel the color wash from my face.

He glances back up with a seriousness that ages him. "I talked to Raelean," he says, as if this is supposed to mean something.

"And?" I smart my hand on my hip, not really in the mood to be lectured.

"She said at the farmhouse you were…you were talking to a crow." He picks up one of his tools and polishes it clean with the same red rag.

Oh, so this is where he's going. I clinch my jaw and hold back an annoyed swear. "I told her I was reading something out loud."

"That's what you told her." He spears me with a look, one that says he doubts my story.

"All little kids have imaginary friends." I wield a stern glare right back at him.

"At ten, maybe. At twenty-four?" He raises a brow.

Damn Adaire for telling Davis about Rook. I mean, I never said she couldn't, but it isn't anyone's business. I brought a dead boy back to some version of life, and it cursed him with the duty of a Soul Walker. I think it bothered Adaire he only returned when death visited me. Like my *relationship* with him was wrong somehow. That doesn't change the fact he and I are bound, symbiotic, my gift and his duty. As though either of us really had a choice in the matter.

"We both know what this is really about," Davis says. I don't like his condescending tone. "You gotta stop clinging to her. It's not a healthy way to grieve."

"Oh, so you're the expert on grieving now? Not all of us can continue on with life like nothing ever happened."

Davis points an angry finger at me. "That is *not* what I'm doing."

Crackled voices push through the ambulance authority's scanner, something Davis keeps in case extra hands are needed. He pauses long enough to hear it's not a medical emergency, then he turns back to me.

I pull my lighter and a small joint from my empty box of playing cards I keep them in. "What's your point?"

"My point is you're different. This…this…" He waves a hand up and down at my brown-and-orange-striped shirt. "You're wearing her clothes, for God's sake."

It's Adaire's shirt, one she made from a vintage serape tablecloth she found at a garage sale.

"You've picked up her bad habits, too." He raises a brow at the stubby joint I'm poised to light.

"She smoked when her visions came on too strong. It's helping me—" *to numb myself* is what I want to say "—to get over her."

"There's no getting over her. Don't you get that? We just have to make it through. And not like this."

"Like what? It's a little weed, no big deal."

"It's not just the weed. Jesus, Weatherly, you're going through men faster than Miss Belinda goes through new bumpers. Jimmy Smoot. Rodney Wheeler. Ricky Scarborough." He ticks them off on his fingers.

"Oh, so you're my daddy now?" I light the blunt.

"Never. I'm your friend. And I'm worried. In the last month and a half, you seem adrift." His words hammer out a chunk of that wall that's been holding me up. "You're not thinking clearly. Listen to what you're saying. You're over here talking about a mentally unstable woman and a dead deer and rain as if any of it matters."

"It does!"

"But it doesn't." Davis says this as if that's the final word.

"The court deemed it was an accident. Stone is dead. Why can't you let sleeping dogs lie? Leave that family alone before you stir up more trouble. They've suffered, too, you know."

I know he's right, but it doesn't stop the niggling feeling that there's something more. If this isn't about Adaire dying, what else was she trying to tell me?

"You're making this about something that isn't even in your control," he says.

"What do you mean?"

"Adaire's visions were vague, something she always had to interpret. But you want justice for her so bad you're reading into them, inventing some mystery that's taking you on a wild-goose chase, when maybe the truth is simply it was a horrible accident."

"It wasn't an accident!" I rupture. "It was *my* fault. Mine!" I jab a finger into my chest. "If I wouldn't have borrowed her car that day, she wouldn't have been riding that stupid yellow ten-speed." I stop abruptly as my voice catches in my throat. I haven't said it out loud yet, but as soon as the words left my mouth, it hit me—it was all my fault. She was on that bike because of me—and worse, I wasn't there to save her.

"Weatherly, it wasn't your fault. She let you borrow her car, and I know Adaire, she'd do it again no matter the reason. She'd have done anything for you." His voice is lower, softer now, as he tries to reassure me.

"Maybe. But I wasn't there to save her, either. Of all the times I would have been glad to have this god-awful gift. The one time I would have actually wanted to have that power, I wasn't even there."

"You can't save them all. Trust me, I know." He jerks his head in the direction of the ambulance scanner and I realize, at least logically, that he's right.

But I'm still sad and so, so angry. Why did she have to go off on her bike? That's when I'm struck with another thought.

"And what was she out doing, anyway? Did you ask yourself that? She didn't have to work at the diner until that night and Aunt V was going to drop her off. I was supposed to pick her up after her shift. There was no reason for her to be on that bike."

"This is exactly what I'm talking about," Davis says, flailing his hands. "Just because you don't know why she was out riding her bike, doesn't mean she was doing something mysterious. Maybe she went to get food. Maybe she needed cigarettes. Maybe she was just riding her bike! Sometimes, the most obvious answer is the right one."

"This isn't some bullshit in my mind." I whir a hand next to my head. "It can't be." I toss my soda bottle into the trash, and I snatch my keys off the desk. "And it's up to me to fix it," I say.

"Jesus, Weatherly, where the hell are you going now? What do you think you're going to do?" Davis asks as I spin on my heels and head to the car.

"First, I'm going to drop off Adaire's car to Aunt Violet." The car door yelps a wretched scream when I rip it open. As I turn the key, the engine sputters and guzzles from being startled awake.

With one hand on the wheel, I look Davis dead in the eye. "Then I'm going to find justice. She holds the truth." I hold up the bottle stopper, as if all the answers are in that tiny piece of glass.

His frown turns to pity as he steps away from the car.

"I'm not wrong," I say to him as he shakes his head and walks away. "I'm not wrong!" I yell at his back, but he doesn't want to hear it.

FOURTEEN

Devil's in the Details

You can always count on at least three barflies buzzing around the Watering Hole at any time of day. Friday at happy hour, the parking lot is jammed full. The bar used to be an old service station in the '50s, until they built the bypass on the other side of town. Then the long building sat abandoned for a good fifteen years. Until liquor licenses were allowed—for the county only. Within twenty-four hours, Gary Dunlap painted the windows black, built a square bar corral in the middle and slapped a hand-painted Watering Hole sign over the old service station's name. It's been packed ever since.

Quietly, I look over to the car's empty passenger seat, wish like heck Adaire and I could take one more trip down that old country road to our house. We were always laughing about something. She loved this car, the cracked vinyl her favorite shade of red. She always said it felt like sitting in the mouth of a beast. I pull the purple-and-white tassel from her graduation cap off the rearview mirror. The tiny brass '83 flickers in the sunlight. It's faded and ratty but holding it now, I think about that night after graduation where we stole beers from Wyatt's cooler. Man, he was pissed. We sat on the hood of this very car—a graduation gift to herself—and drank those beers, talking about a road trip to the beach someday.

A road trip we never got to in the last few years. Life just happens like that. You get caught up in doing everyday things; working, saving up money, figuring out the next steps. Next thing you know, time slips out from underneath you. Then life throws you a curveball and snatches away your best friend.

I take one last look around the car, try to soak up all those memories Adaire and I shared here. The door makes a frowning sound when I close it. I try not to think about a new owner sitting in the front seat soon.

A haze of cigarette smoke hovering in the top half of the bar greets me as I step inside. It does nothing to mask the strong odor of dirty bleach-water and fried food. Some new song by The Judds croons from the jukebox like an anthem. The so-called kitchen is a row of eight deep fryers that'll serve you one of four dishes: chicken nuggets, cheesy fries, mozzarella sticks, or mountain oysters.

I wave hello to Raelean, who's delivering an order to a table in the back. I'm hoping she can give me a ride home on her break because if Aunt Violet is more than an hour into a shift, you can count on her being too buzzed to drive.

I belly up to the bar and drop the keys on the counter. "Hey, Vic," I say to the bartender who's drying a beer stein. Vic's slippery grin reminds me of a cat before it pounces. It's as sleazy as his greasy black hair, reminds me of Danny Zuko. Searching the room for Aunt Violet but not finding her, I ask, "Aunt V here? I need to give her these keys."

He hangs the chunky beer glass on the hook. "Yep, she's in the manager's office, talking with someone."

"Tell her I've caught a ride home from Raelean." And I start to walk in Raelean's direction when he stops me.

"Nope. She specifically said she wanted to talk to you. That it was important. So you can wait your sweet little ass right here." He leans against the bar with both hands, lathering up that grin. "Now tell Vic what you want?" I ask for a glass of water. As I sit there drinking and avoiding any more eye contact than is necessary with Vic, I hear the door to the manager's office and voices as they exit.

"Oh, shit." I duck behind the register as Deputy Rankin strolls out. I don't recall seeing a deputy's car in the parking lot.

"Damn if it ain't a busy day for the law." Raelean lays her serving tray on the bar and gives Vic a table's drink order. "Heard they were out at the Rutledge place earlier today, too. You wouldn't know anything about that, would you?" Raelean side-eyes me. I lean farther out of Deputy Rankin's line of sight when he passes.

"Let's just say I won't be parading myself around town anytime soon." I sit upright once he's gone. I don't bother telling Raelean what Gabby said; she'd have the same reaction as Davis. "Hey, can you give me a ride home? Aunt Violet is probably already toasted."

"Sure." Raelean adds limes to the cocktails they ordered. "But she hasn't been drinking lately."

"Yeah, right." I huff a laugh.

"No, seriously, she's gone cold turkey." She stacks the last beer on her tray.

I think Raelean is so used to drunk Violet, she's recalibrated her barometer as sober Violet. Besides, I'd notice if Aunt V got sober. Wouldn't I?

"Becky just came in. She can cover for me, and I can drive you home—it's about time for my dinner break." Raelean spins on her wedge heels, tray full of food perfectly balanced on her small hand. I walk over to the manager's office.

Behind the desk, Aunt Violet is sorting through a stack of bar tickets. Her black hair—box-dyed and short—flames into this swooping wave on top of her head, the tips frosted. Her eyes, a crimson brown, flit up to me as I tap out a knock on the door frame. My hand a little shaky, I can't help but wonder if Rankin was asking about me.

"You're not bartending tonight?" I ask, stepping into the cramped space. Alcohol signage and paraphernalia litter the faux-wood panel walls. Two filing cabinets shoulder up a tottering overstuffed bookcase on either side that could come crashing down with a good sneeze.

"Lord, no." She swipes a dismissing hand through the air as she stands. "Gary has me doing the books now. Don't look at me like that. Your Aunt V has a brain, you know." She leans in to hug me, but stops short and snags my chin. "What in the hell happened here?" she gasps, examining the bruise purpling up my cheek.

There is no part of what happened today that I care to share. Instead, I tell her I had a run-in with a glass door.

"Mmm, huh," she says rather dryly, side-eyeing me, knowing it's a lie but she doesn't press further. It's a small town, the truth will eventually make its way to her. I'll deal with it then. "Let's get this fixed up." She frowns at the bruise, then scrounges in her overstuffed purse until she finds her makeup bag. Aunt Violet wears enough foundation and makeup for the both of us, but I don't mind her fussing—might spare me a few questions later on. "Look, sugar…" She dots out some concealer before blending it with her thumb. "Have the cops come to talk to you again about Stone?"

I feel my stomach tighten instantly at the mention of Stone's name. "Not since they first brought me in for questioning. Why? That why Rankin was here?"

"Yeah, he wanted to know if you stayed the night at the house the night before he died." She glances out in the hallway to make sure no one can hear and then closes us in her office. "But don't worry none, I covered for you. If they ask, you tell them we had leftover spaghetti for dinner. Maybe drank a few beers. And went to bed around one a.m. And you didn't leave until the next morning, say like, before nine." She dusts on a little bit of powder, then leans back to observe her work.

"But I did stay the night with you that night." Though I snuck in through Adaire's bedroom window, and I tell her that.

Aunt Violet pauses in dusting my cheek. Her brow crinkles up in confusion. She stares at me, unsure how to process this information. "Wait, you're saying you stayed at the house the night Stone was murdered?" The way she asks, it's like she's going to need a little proof to verify my story. "When did you get there?" Her voice shakes a little.

"I… I'm not sure, probably two thirty, three a.m. I was pretty drunk."

She chews on this a bit. "Okay then, if they ask, it was between one and two. Then we have similar stories." She nods, satisfied, as if this tiny change will matter somehow.

"Oh-kay. But you believe me, Aunt V, don't you?" Aunt Violet, with her nervous hand, closes her powder compact, unable to look at me. The color drains from her face.

Suddenly, this tiny office feels smaller and stuffy with the door closed. "You believe me, don't you?" I ask again.

She swallows hard, nodding. "Yeah," she says slowly, as if lost in thought. That nod of hers picking up pace as though she has to assure herself this new information is okay. "Yeah. Don't tell the cops you snuck in the window, okay? Stick with what I said: we ate spaghetti, had a few beers, and went to bed between one or two in the morning. Left before nine the next day. Okay?"

I watch her warily. She truly believes she's covering for me. My own family thinking I'm capable of something so brutal as murder. "You know I didn't kill Stone, right?" I ask, but honestly I'm not certain she does.

Her head jerks up, and then looks me straight in the eye. "That man deserved to die, you hear me? No one needs to feel guilty for avenging their family. But if you say you didn't do it, then you didn't do it." Aunt Violet smarts a nod. I release a sigh.

The office door swings open, causing us both to jump. Raelean shoves her head in and pauses, picking up the intensity in the air. Then she pops off. "Hate to interrupt your little family meeting, but if you want a ride, it's now or never."

"Coming." I move to follow her out, and then I pause. "Hey, Aunt V, is it true what Raelean said, you're sober now?"

A soft smile tugs at the corners of her mouth. "Yeah, doll, nineteen days and counting. I started thinking about my baby girl. And if her dying isn't a reason to get my act straight, then I don't know what is. Now, you get on out of here and keep your ass out of trouble. And the next time someone clocks you in the face, I better hear you gave it back to them twice as good." She chucks me on the chin. "Glass door, my ass. Get out of here."

She smacks me on the butt to get going.

Some rowdy Hank Williams Jr. song tune blasts from the jukebox. There's a boisterous conversation going on between a group of guys hanging around the pool table.

"Now maybe we won't have to hear you bellyaching about not getting first kill of the season," an old guy says to Jimmy Daughtry, and the crowd erupts in laughter.

Raelean catches Jimmy's eye as we pass. "Hey, sugar, why don't you come over and sit in Jimmy's lap and celebrate with me?" He gives his legs a hearty pat.

"Sure thing, Jimmy," she says, giving him a half second of hope. "Right after I'm done dropping off baby formula for the newborn your wife is home taking care of—bastard." The last part she huffs under her breath.

"You're no fun!" he hollers as we step out of the cigarette haze and into fresh early evening air.

"What's he celebrating? Wasn't his baby born, like, a month ago?" I ask as we walk over to Raelean's blue Camaro.

"Yeah." Raelean totters over the gravel in her heels. "He's celebrating the fact he doesn't have to buy any meat for the next month. But his truck fender paid the price for it."

I eye the damaged truck as we pass it and freeze as I catch sight of an antler sticking up out of the truck bed.

"A dead deer," I whisper to myself.

"That's right." Raelean tugs open her car door but pauses to watch me a second.

"A dead deer caused that kind of damage to his truck." A rhetorical question.

"Yeah. Why? What's turning over in your head there, Weatherly?"

Davis is wrong. Stone's pristine bumper is not nothing. Lorelei driving her father's car is not nothing. Gabby talking about hitting a dead deer is not nothing.

"You know what? On second thought, don't drive me home. Drive me to the police station."

FIFTEEN

Dumber Than Dirt

The shadow of a bird sails along the highway, following slightly ahead of Raelean's car. She's rambling on about how lousy the Watering Hole tips are and how maybe she should make her way over to Nashville and find an up-and-coming music star at a honky-tonk to hang around with.

The crow shadow splits and divides, from one to many, and I smile.

They speckle the sky, a soft black veil. Their ebb and flow like ripples in a river against the orange and purples of the eventide.

"Whoa." Raelean leans forward over her steering wheel to get a better look. "You seeing this? There's so many." Her voice a marvel.

And yet it's only the one, Rook just divided. "We're in the hour of crows," I tell her. "It's when the day is no longer but the night is not yet."

Raelean eases back, watching me. "That sounds really beautiful and creepy as shit. Jesus, Weatherly." She shakes her head. "Are they gonna, like, swoop down and peck our eyes out or what?"

I huff a small laugh. "No. It means the crows are gathering at the end of the day for a night's rest."

As we come upon the cluster of buildings ahead, the crows veer off route into the canopy of the trees. The smell of a far-off summer rain fills the car.

"You've got to be dumber than dirt to be going in there after what you've already pulled at the Rutledge mansion."

I glower at Raelean. "Some friend you are. Oh, wait, don't pull into the sheriff's lot," I say as we approach the building. "Do a drive-by first and let me see who's there."

Law Road, named after Jessup Law and not the sheriff station, always has a steady flow of passersby. The garbled rumble of her Camaro chugs as we slow down so I can make sure Oscar's deputy Bronco is there—he's my only chance at not getting arrested immediately.

"Shit," I say when I don't see it. "He's not here."

It's only Callie, who mans the dispatch desk. Everyone else must be on call. I have Raelean park the car over at Quickies, probably the last place for miles that still has Classic Coca-Cola.

"There's always a dominos crowd that gathers on Friday nights," I say to Raelean. "I'll wait there until Oscar gets back."

"I'd wait with you," Raelean hurriedly says as I get out, "if I didn't have to get back to work."

I lean into her open window. "That's fine. I'll figure it out." Off in the distance, a dark figure steps within the cover of the trees, disappearing behind the deli.

"But if you're still here later," Raelean says as she starts to drive off, "or need bailing out of jail…"

"Yeah, yeah." I clip a wave, hoping that won't be the case.

I wait for her to ease down the road, out of sight, before slipping behind the deli myself.

Just like at the mansion, as soon as I'm behind the building and catch sight of the picnic table, I'm transported back. Two summers after Papaw passed, I walked down here by myself once. I asked Bubba Dunn, the owner, how much bologna and crackers I could get for a dollar. I think he must have felt sorry for me because he gave me the bottled Coke, the bologna and crackers, *and* a few five-cent bubblegums. I thought I'd hit the jackpot. I skipped outside with my loot to the picnic tables by the pond out back.

It was the clattering of the trash can lid that scared the devil out of me. I about dropped all my goods. Then I saw him, young Rook cowering behind the trash bin he had just been pilfering through. He was longer than his clothes with how much he'd grown since the summer before. Rough for the wear as well. It hurt my heart something bad, knowing he had to scavenge food from the trash. Shame kept him from looking me in the eye, but it was me who deserved the shame. Never occurred to me he didn't have a home—or a dollar— to get himself something to eat.

We shared that bologna and Coca-Cola while we counted turtles sunning on a log. We bragged about how many tadpoles we could catch in a single scoop. And discussed how a dragonfly got its name because it didn't look anything like a dragon or a fly really.

When I finally asked him where he'd been the past year, Rook couldn't remember. Time had a way of disappearing for him. Long gaps between being a boy and a crow.

"Why are you back?" eleven-year-old me had asked him. Not intending to sound rude or ungrateful; I just didn't understand.

"The deaths. The souls. They always bring me back to

you." He said this in a way that stole my heart. He's held it ever since.

That week, Mr. Allen Roberts had died—that's why Rook had returned. I tried to save the old man after he fell off a ladder, trying to pick peaches from his tree. But it seemed the good Lord wanted him home, and there was nothing I could do. Or so Grandmama had said.

Waiting for me now, Rook sits on the top of that same picnic table, bare feet on the bench seat. Handsome as the devil now, too.

"You following me?" I say, smirking. I take a seat next to him. The road and the sheriff station's parking lot are both in view from back here.

"Should I be?" He thumbs my chin to the side, getting a good look at my cheek. Heat flushes my face; I wonder if he saw Lorelei clock me.

We sit there a few quiet beats. Suddenly, I feel thirteen again, about to have my first kiss.

A car comes down the road and I perk up, but it's not Oscar.

"Are you waiting for him?" Rook's soured gaze focuses across the road at the sheriff's station. It's the way he clamps down his words that makes me realize he's aware Oscar and I were together once. Guilt sends my eyes to the ground. I had wondered if that's why he's stayed away these past few years. I've also wondered if there were women he was with in those lost gaps of time. But I don't have the nerve to ask or desire to know.

"It's not like that between Oscar and me. Not anymore." I look up at Rook. "It hasn't been for a long time."

The tension in his shoulders loosens; the softness in his eyes returns.

"I need to talk to him, about the case. I have a theory," I start. "About how Adaire died." I tell him about Adaire's visions, my time with Gabby Newsome, Lorelei's necklace—

that got me a busted-up cheek—the damaged car bumper and supposed dead deer, and well, everything.

Rook doesn't doubt me like Raelean. Or think I'm off my rocker like Davis. In fact, he listens intently to everything I have to tell him as if it's gospel.

He nods, understanding. "Then I hope Oscar will help you." I hope he will, too.

The back door to Bobby's deli kicks open, startling us both. But it's only the butcher taking out the trash. He eyes us briefly, then goes back to dumping the bag when we prove to be nothing of interest.

A random crow lands on the power line near the road and caws out once. "A friend of yours?" I say, not holding back a laugh.

He laughs. "We really need to do something about that smart-mouth of yours." His eyes dip to those very lips. My thoughts tip sideways.

The crow squawks again, annoyingly loud. Then it dashes off into the trees. Another car comes down the road, still not Oscar.

A thought occurs to me. I quirk my head at Rook. "Do you know who I am when you're in that form?" I ask, genuinely curious.

He bobs his head. "Kind of. When I'm here—" he fans a hand in the air, referring to Black Fern "—when I'm near you, the crow lets me have control." It's odd to hear him refer to the crow as a separate being. But I guess he must be. "Through his eyes, I see souls. I can find you that way."

I love the idea of this. "And when you're not here?"

His brow scrunches up. "It's like a smoky dream. Everything is dim. There are flashes of sights and sounds but a dark filter covers my memories. And I feel far away. I'm not Rook or the crow but something else. Something lost."

"So you're not free." It isn't a question. It's a realization that he's bound to me, my gift, and the mercy of the crow.

"Time passes in odd gaps for me, and the crow does most of the living," he admits.

But that's not living at all.

"Hey." He ducks into my line of sight. "I'm here because of you."

He is. But Davis's words keep shoving themselves around in my head. *You gotta stop clinging to her. It's not a healthy way to grieve.* What if Rook is something inside my head that I created to cope? I touch his hand to anchor myself.

He feels real.

Across the street at the sheriff's station, I notice Oscar's Bronco has returned. Must have missed it while we were talking.

"Don't go anywhere." I stand. Rook does, too. "I might need a rescue."

"Let's hope so." He falls backward and scatters into the crow before his body even hits the ground.

Drops of rain begin to dot the thirsty pavement as I cross the street and head toward the station. The front doorbell announces my arrival with an electric *biz-bong*, a frazzled sound that's crankier than my alarm.

Callie Wilson—a woman who's birthed four kids and looks like she's going to pop with number five—does a double take as she sees me. Thankfully, she's tied up on the phone with another call ringing its next place in line. I pan a small wave hello.

Oscar, standing in the office hallway, looks up from the paperwork he's flipping through. "Well, you're making my job pretty easy today. Come to turn yourself in?" His disapproving stare tells me everything I need to know. Then he straightens a little taller when he spies the shiner bruising over on my left cheek, despite Aunt Violet's attempt to cover it up. "What the hell?" He tilts my chin to the side to get a better look.

"Assault and battery?" I try.

Oscar frowns. "Is this before or after you illegally entered the Rutledge's private quarters?"

"Does it help if I tell you I had a ticket for the tour?" I wince, wishing I still had that crumpled brochure.

"What would help is if you would stay away from that family and let me do my job, Weatherly. You stirred up a hornet's nest out there today. They called in the sheriff personally. Apparently, you upset Mrs. Rutledge's sister something terrible. Do I even want to know what that's about?" Before I can answer, Oscar's attention slides over to the glass door as headlights pan across the building. He lets loose a long sigh and a soft swear. The Rutledge's shiny red Corvette parks out front.

"Rebecca and Lorelei are coming in to file a restraining order," he mumbles. Something the court usually deals with, but I'm sure the judge can't be bothered while he's out fishing. "You better pray they don't press charges, too."

"Please, hear me out first." I glance urgently over at the door; if they see me here, it'll be all over with. "I swear it's important. I found evidence today, evidence to help the case." The urgency in my voice is enough to give him pause. He notices the plastic Walmart bag I'm holding. "Please." I lay my hand lightly on his arm. Oscar's posture softens at my touch. It feels wrong to use our past to implore him, but I'm desperate.

"Go wait for me in there." He points a finger in the office he just walked out of. "And for God's sake, keep out of sight and your mouth shut. Got it?"

I zipper my lips shut and slip into the office just as the door chime buzzes another staticky *biz-bong*.

"Hello, Mrs. Rutledge. Lorelei. I'm Deputy Torres." There's a quiet pause where I can barely hear that it's Rebecca talking. "I've got a small matter to deal with first, but Callie here will help you get started on the paperwork. I'll be right along shortly. Callie, can you show them to the break room, maybe get them a cup of coffee? Thank you." Then Oscar's silhouette shadows over the frosted glass door and he enters.

"This better be good." He points to the chair where he wants me to sit, while he perches on the edge of his desk. His folded arms a stern warning.

"I think Lorelei Rutledge killed Adaire." I vomit the words. That handsome face of his slips to annoyance. "You said you have evidence for *your* case. Adaire's case is closed."

"What if I find something that opens it back up?" I tug that Walmart sack up in my lap protectively. The drizzle of rain outside picks up pace, tapping louder on the building's tin roof.

He exhales heavily. There's only a hairbreadth of his patience left. "I'm listening."

"Adaire knew she was going to die. She saw it coming." That's how I start. This, Oscar does not question. He already knows what I can do, and I'm sure he's heard whispers of the other peculiarities that run in our family.

"Three days before she died, she had a vision. She knew I was going to be in trouble. She told me Gabby had the answers, and she gave me a key." I debate if I should tell him that I think it belongs to that box that's in the picture they have of my mom. "She said 'find the scales of justice, she holds the truth.' Then today, after Lorelei assaulted me, she had on a necklace, the scales of justice—which is the astrological sign for Libra in case you didn't know." He stares at me flatly. "Now I thought it would be justice for me, but now I'm thinking she meant justice for herself. We found this tin box."

"We who?"

"I," I swiftly correct.

He lifts a questioning brow.

"*I* found this tin box *with* Adaire's instructions, so kind of like we did it together." Jesus Christ, Raelean would murder me herself if I got her into trouble.

"Found where?" He growls his words.

"Out at this farmhouse—"

"You were at the crime scene?" He snatches up the box, his anger coming at me like a dagger.

"Not technically. Well, maybe…but that box was inside the farmhouse, which was not part of the crime scene. *Technically*," I reiterate.

He reads Adaire's note. "She was right about what? What's this droplet of rain? Riddled tongue? Where are you going with this story? This is all just random blather. Where's the evidence?"

"I'm getting there! Jeez, Louise." Out front, the door chime announces another person's arrival, shrinking my borrowed time. "Gabby is the riddled tongue, she talks in circles. She gave me a blue glass droplet. It's a family heirloom, my family's." I show him the bottle stopper. "When I asked her where she got it, she said she got it from the pocket of a dead deer. She was there when they hit a deer; she said so herself. Except I don't think it was a deer at all but Adaire. And I don't think it was Stone Rutledge or his car that hit her."

Oscar's incredulous flat stare says the last of his patience just evaporated. He stands, throwing up his hands. "I cannot believe you wasted my time with this tall tale. Rain droplets and a deer with pockets and riddles hidden in empty tin boxes." He tosses the button tin on his desk. "Seriously, Weatherly?"

The door rattles with an urgent knock, Callie peeps her head inside. "Sheriff called, um…" She slips a look to me, then back to Oscar. "It's pretty serious. He needs you out at the Rutledge place, ASAP."

Oscar turns his scowl on me.

"What?" I hold my hands up in innocence. "I told you everything. I swear!"

"I'll be there in a sec," he tells Callie, and she smartly ducks out. "I'm not finished with you." He grabs his deputy hat and Bronco keys.

"Hey, what about what I just told you?"

"It ain't evidence." He snugs that Stetson hat onto his head and goes to leave.

"Stone's car doesn't have a scratch on it," I blurt. It's enough to keep him from leaving. "That red Corvette doesn't have a mark on it. Go look for yourself." I fan a hand toward the front door.

"It's called a repair shop, Weatherly." He shakes his head and grabs the doorknob.

"Not repaired in a week, though," I pop again. He pauses. "The court hearing was a week and a half after Adaire's death. Stone's Corvette sat on Main Street that same day. Shouldn't it still have been in the shop? Talk to Jimmy Smoot. He towed Stone's car *after* that day in court because of a flat tire. He would have seen if there was some damage, right? If he hadn't had it repaired yet? If Stone's car hit—" The words catch in my throat. "If he ran over something," I say through gritted teeth, "deer or otherwise, where's the damage? No car gets repaired that fast. Not around here. Especially not an expensive sports car like that." There's a nugget of question in his eyes now.

"It's still not evidence," he says as he turns.

"Lorelei's driving her father's car," I try to get out before he closes the door in my face, but I'm too late.

"Where's *her* car? Huh?" I say to the empty office and drop into his desk chair. "Ask rich girl about that, will ya?" I give his Rolodex a spin with my finger.

I don't get more than two swivels back and forth in his desk chair when I notice the tab on the folder Oscar was perusing through when I arrived. *WEATHERLY WILDER*, reads his scratchy writing. An icy fear creeps up my neck and flushes my skin.

A ding at the front door. I glance up a half second. When nothing comes of it, I spin the folder around and open the manila flap.

On top is the medical examiner's report for Papaw. A diagram of his body and notes scribbled in the margin, a document that's painful to read. Underneath it, a complaint filed from Mrs. Phillips about the time I "healed" her husband. I remember how ungrateful she was that I talked the death out of him; she gave me an earful about it, too. Then a Xerox copy of Dr. York's notes from the day I tried to talk the death out of Ellis Rutledge. The next page is from a yellow notepad where Oscar has written down a few names and dates, people I've used my gift on. There are several more Oscar doesn't even know about.

But it's the words scribbled in the margins that catches my attention.

Unknown drowning victim???

My soul drops to the floor like a sheet.

Hand quivering, I slide the next page out. It's only a few sentences. Three, actually. An intake call to dispatch from fifteen years ago.

Augustus Wilder called in to report a drowned child he and Jonsey Hayworth found by the river. But when the deputy arrived to collect the body, Augustus informed him they were mistaken. It was only a patch of waterlogged dark carpet hung around a downed branch.

Somehow, I feel naked. Exposed. My secret lying here for all the world to read. If only they knew what they were reading. But clearly Oscar suspects something.

One small note turns over in my head. A patch of carpet? Adaire saw a vision of a boy by the river. I could have sworn Papaw and Bone Layer found that boy. I kissed him. Made a wish on a crow feather and brought him back to life. Didn't I?

Yet, the police report is telling a different story.

Two more doorbells ring out front. Urgent voices jostle

around on the other side of the office door. From the silhouettes of Stetson hats, I can tell it's a room full of law enforcement. I slam the folder shut. A rumble of thunder stampedes above. Two counts later, a crack of lightning zips across the sky. It lights up the sliver of window above the file console behind Oscar's desk. And it's clear that's my best way out now.

Feetfirst and belly-side down, I wiggle my way out and hope like hell someone out front doesn't notice two flailing legs kicking out the side of the building.

The four-foot drop is enough to give my heart a good scare. The button tin and all its contents dump on the ground. Hurriedly, I pick up Adaire's note from a tiny puddle and dry it on my shorts. Once I'm sure I've got everything back in my little collection plate of evidence, I spin on my heels and run smack-dab into Rook's chest. A liquid purr pours down my body at the sight of him. Rain soaking his black hair and spiking his lashes. His firm body pressed up against my palm.

"It's you." Surprise lifts my voice.

"Were you expecting someone else to rescue you?" Rook raises a scornful brow. The parking lot lights barely reach this far back, but there's a wolfish glint in his eyes.

"I was just…" I thumb over my shoulder to the window I just crawled out. "There was no other way I could… I didn't actually expect you to—" Nerves tangle up my tongue.

A sly smile slides across his wet lips.

"You." I sour my expression to one that I hope appears unimpressed. "If you consider this a rescue, then you're sorely mistaken. I was escaping just fine on my own." I swipe the pounding rain from my face, looking more like a drowned cat by the minute.

Voices of others out front push their way toward us. Rook slides an arm around my waist and spins us into the dark shadow of the building.

The rich smell of pine and earth shove itself in my face. I become acutely aware how smooshed up I am against him with a fistful of his drenched shirt clenched in my hand. My heart thunders inside my chest.

A commotion has us both looking toward the rising chaos. Light flickers from inside Oscar's office.

"We should go." Rook's words whisper against my ear. Before I can agree, he grabs my hand, and we disappear into the woods under the cover of the rain.

SIXTEEN

A Conjuring from My Dreams

Woods—especially at night during a storm—have a way of making you feel like someone's watching you. We run a little faster to the only place I know no one will come looking for me.

Breathless, I stop and peer up at the old cave Adaire and I used to explore. Exposed tree roots finger like a thick brow over the cave's opening, a dark eye. Kudzu vines string down the hillside, an endless flow of green tears. Rain runs down the mountain, creating a thin veil over the opening.

My hand grips the top rung of the chain camping ladder Adaire and I left hanging here years ago. I look down behind me. Before I can ask Rook if he's coming, he leans forward, his body shrinking into a dark blur, then shifting into the feathered form of the crow. One becoming the other before he can even come close to touching the ground.

Incredible.

A wisp of wind and a flutter of wings swoop past me.

There's a dark gap as he shifts back. Rook stretches out his hand for me.

"Show-off," I mumble and take ahold. His grip firms as he hefts me up with one swift pull.

Face-to-face, we stand there. Only the drizzling rain and our ragged breaths keep us company. Years of scattered moments is all we've ever had. We stare at each other, getting a good look to hold us through the next lapse of time.

I marvel at the man standing before me now, towering. Moonlight shines on his pale skin, a fine marble. His jawline smooth yet angular. Strong. There's a depth in his eyes, like he's lived centuries from the few souls he's carried over.

He's a conjuring from a dream. Desire fully imagined and alive.

The drum of my heartbeat jumps as he reaches up and pushes the wet strands of my hair out of the way. My breath hitches at the slight touch. That Mona Lisa smile of his twinges at the corner of his mouth.

A clash of thunder punches the night, splitting the sky. It sets off a cascade of loud squeaks and shrills above our heads.

"Shit!"

We duck as a colony of bats flap and flutter erratically around us. Rook bows himself around me, protectively. One by one, they dart for the cave's opening, shrieking out into the night.

Once the chaos quiets, still cowering as I search the ceiling, I ask, "Are there any more?" Barely any light filters in the cave. The dark a fathomless hole to nowhere.

Rook tugs from his pocket a glimmer of silver and flicks it to life. The flame, a dancing wick, instantly shrinks the cave's illusion of depth. He scans the lighter near the ceiling, and two more stragglers take off.

"I think we're good now," he says after finding no more. Feeling confident enough, he straightens to his full height.

"Shoes don't shift but a Zippo does?" I nod to his bare feet.

He shrugs. "I think the crow just hates shoes." He pans the light around.

The shallow space of the cave is not more than twenty feet and a hell of a lot smaller than my ten-year-old memory recalls. The rock ceiling slants so you have to duck lower on one side. The scent of moss so heavy it tastes like earth when you breathe in. The stone floor only allows the vines to grow in between the cracks. Leaf litter claims everything else.

An old puppy and kitten poster curls on the stone floor, long faded. A cracked vanity mirror we used to play dress-up in front of leans against the back wall. The purple velvet of an old Wicked Witch costume crumbles between my fingers.

"This place is… Wow," Rook stresses, really taking in the space for what it was.

"Yeah," I say, just as breathless.

From under a clump of weeds, a rusted candelabra pokes out. Rook pulls it free. Dried wax bleeds down the ornate arm. He squats in front of the raised slate of stone, setting the candelabra upright. He heats the wax in one of the sconces until it's soft enough to hold the stub of a crumbling candle.

The flame flickers a jagged dance across his face and the room comes alive. All of mine and Adaire's childhood litter is strewn about the space. A flood of memories comes blazing back to life.

Rook inspects a rusted *Welcome Back, Kotter* lunch box where we kept the arrowheads and Indian beads we found in the creek bed.

"We used to come here after school and on Saturday mornings," I say, then rummage through a milk crate with old toys, moldy magazines, and a Polaroid camera crammed in the bottom. I click the button a few times and nothing. Corrosion crusts over the batteries. I use a plastic pick-up stick to chip the white flakes away, then reinsert the batteries and flip it over—

A spider skitters over the camera lens, and I squeal, dropping it. The camera cracks against the stone floor, and a bright flash ignites inside the cave. Rook shields his face, blinded.

"Shit. Sorry." I pick the camera up as it grumbles a motorized complaint and spits out a photo. Stuck partway in the shoot, I rip it the rest of the way out. Only half an image forms as I fan it to life. Mostly of my shoulder.

I pick up a plastic pencil box filled with worthless treasures: stretchy colorful bands of nylon to make pot holders, a few Barbie shoes, a fluffy ball key chain with googly eyes. I shake it and watch them dance, then settle at the bottom.

Another Polaroid, which I forgot existed, hides at the bottom of the box. Taken from down below, it's Adaire and me, sitting at the cave's opening, feet dangling, our arms draped over each other's shoulders. We're grinning ear to ear, like the world was ours for the taking. I can't recall who took the picture, but I remember it was the first day of summer after third grade. We were both sporting fresh Dorothy Hamill haircuts.

"We loved this place." My voice a whisper. Here, we were queens of our own world. No adults to tell us what to do. Just living in our imagination and having a blast doing it.

"I miss her," I say, not particularly to him, but it fills the silence. I close my eyes. I can almost feel Adaire here. Smell that cheap Brut cologne she stole from Papaw to spritz up the cave so it didn't smell so musty. Never was she conventional.

I catch Rook quietly watching me. Self-conscious, I tuck the photo in my jean shorts back pocket and turn my attention to a stack of magazines.

"I want to show you something," he says, and I turn to him as he blows out the candle. He gently grabs my hand, and we stand. "They never completely leave me. All the souls, I mean. I want you to see it."

The whites of his eyes turn black. An energy builds in his palm and pushes into mine. A soft glittery blue light swims its way up my arm into my chest. My vision tunnels to black until it *pops!* Illuminating light crackles in the air surrounding him. Floating iridescent dust particles. I reach out to touch one. It tingles the tip of my fingers with a soft electrical buzz.

"It tickles," I say, giggling.

Rook's body is alive with these glimmering fragments.

"Soul remnants." He waves his arm back and forth in the air. They seem to cling to him like staticky bits. He releases me, and the illumination douses.

I blink in the darkness until my sight adjusts.

"That's incredible. How are you even…you?" I ask.

A light smile plays on his lips, and he shrugs. "You should know, you're the one who made me."

I huff a laugh. "True." But I don't know how I did it. Well, I know how—I whispered the secret scriptures of a Death Talker to a dead boy. What I don't understand is how that extra part of me brought him back to life.

"Do you remember the day we met?" I ask. The silence of the night gobbles up my words.

"I remember you said you kissed me." I hear the smirk in his words.

I chuckle. "Of course you do." Silly how I'm blushing over something that innocent. "For the record, it was more like a life wish or a prayer for life or—"

"Mouth-to-mouth?" he says, and I want to sock him.

I do my best to tuck in the grin wanting to slip out. "I believe what you mean to say is thank you. So…*you're welcome.*" He laughs at that.

"I remember the beginning, though," he says. There's a pensiveness to his voice that gives me pause and I look at him. Really look at him. He relights the lone candle in our crooked candelabra. He seems to sink into his memories as shadows play on his face. "I remember being hungry. So hungry." His hand absently moves to his stomach as the ghost of the feeling sneaks over him. "I didn't know my name or where I was from, but I was alive. It didn't make sense to me how knowing that mattered, because I couldn't remember dying. Just knew that I was alive. Again." He lifts his head. "Because of you."

His words strike me, in a good way. The gratitude in his voice thick. It makes me see how much more important my gift could be in the right hands.

He empties out the milk crate and flips it over, setting the candelabra on top.

"Was the crow always with you?" I ask.

He scrapes the leaves off the stone ledge, making a place for us both to sit. I bunch up the pile of old costumes and a dingy quilt for our backs.

"I think so. I didn't quite feel whole to this world, if that makes sense?" He scoots back, stretching out, ankles hanging off the edge. I sit beside him, cross-legged. My bare knee presses into his thigh. There's something about our touch that feels deeper than anything I've felt before. It's like we're part of each other. That day forever bonding us. A Death Talker and a Soul Walker.

"Where did you go?" I ask him. I don't remember what happened afterward. I woke up a few days later, after the death flu had run through me. I tried to ask Papaw about it, about what had happened to the boy, but he wouldn't say. Only that I should never try to talk the death out of the dead again, and I haven't since.

Rook pulls at a dry leaf that's tangled in the fringe of my cutoffs. He twiddles it between his fingers. "I found myself wandering along a highway. Lost. The sun disappearing behind a truck stop. I felt no sense of direction toward home or if I had one. But hunger pushed my young feet forward."

I swallow hard. In all these years, I never heard his half of the story. I soak his every word into my bones.

"This woman—Alma I think her name was—found me. A scrawny child hidden away in a dingy truck-stop bathroom in the middle of the night."

The thought of it breaks my heart. I squeeze his hand, a silent sorry.

"She eyed the empty lunch box I'd stolen from the mechanic's garage. It only had a crust of a sandwich and a capful of cold thermos coffee. It barely dented the ache of my hunger. I'm sure it alarmed her, but she acted like happening upon me was all in a day's work."

His amused smile eases my guilt a bit.

"Half hour later, with a clean state of Georgia souvenir T-shirt and belly fully of pancakes, I was snoozing away on the red bench of a booth. Until the voices of law enforcement came to collect the 'runaway.' That's what I heard them call me. I couldn't say I was a runaway, but I also knew I no longer had a home.

"Then came this nudging. It was urgent and pressing. Something from inside myself told me to get up. To go outside. It wasn't my own voice, but it came from within. So strong, I couldn't deny it. The lawmen chased after me, out the diner's door. They tried to stop me. Acted like I was a wild animal about to bolt.

"The pavement was freezing underneath my bare feet. My breath puffed white from the cold. Stars littered the sky, and I yearned to go there." Rook pats his chest where the desire lay.

"The officer told me not to be scared, that I was safe now. I opened my mouth to tell him I wasn't scared, but instead a *caw* came. A cry so loud it felt unearthly. And in a wink, my vision tunneled until the lawmen disappeared, and my mind slipped into black."

"The crow." My words a whisper in the small space.

He nodded thoughtfully. "That's how it is every time, just before I disappear from here. I'm grateful for him, though. The crow. He got me through that first winter."

An errant firefly wanders into the cave, like the pulsing light of a stray soul.

Rook's story weighs heavy on my heart. His, too, it seems, as he sits there, letting his thoughts swirl a bit longer. I think he had to get his story out of him, as much as I needed to hear it. It reshapes everything I thought about him, how I brought him back, what it meant afterward.

And what it means for the way forward.

What if he's trapped in this life because he is this half version of himself? A slave to the souls he carries. Do they keep him alive, those souls? But if he's not a Soul Walker, he wouldn't exist at all.

But what if there was a way to set him free? To release him of this duty? I made him, when I talked the death out of his dead body. Maybe I could set him free. But would he return as the boy I'd saved or as the crow? Or neither.

"Don't do that," Rook says. His hand comforting mine. "Don't let your mind wonder if you could have done this or should have done that. This is where we are now. Live in the now. It's all we can do. Okay?" He tips my chin up when I don't look at him.

"Okay," I say back to him, trying to push away the guilt that lingers.

"Besides…" He scoots forward, sits up taller. "Look at this incredible paradise you have here." He fans his arms wide as if marveling over this gift he's been given.

"Ack. Don't call it *that*. It's just a—"

"Treasure trove, a time capsule to your childhood. What's this?" Rook mocks an overexaggerated surprised face. From the corner, he pushes aside a pile of leaves and unearths the old crank-style record player Adaire and I played with. The cracked wood lid lies helplessly on its side. The nest from some animal clogs the front where the speaker doors open. He pulls the debris out.

"Oh, wow, it's still here!" I hop up and help him move it. "I think I can get it to work." We set in on the stone ledge. I fiddle around with it a minute until sure enough, I get the old Victrola's handle to crank. Some record, the label worn away by the elements, sits on the center stem.

Warbly muffled music pushes through the front. The sound a scratchy static until it hiccups as the needle hits a melted bump in the vinyl and skips to another part of the song. It hits the dip on the other side, starting itself over.

"I think that's Dolly Parton," I say, and I strain an ear, trying to focus on the woman's voice before the loop jumps and repeats again.

"Go ahead," Rook urges me. "Sing me something terrible. You know you want to."

"You are an asshole, you know that." The album finally gets past the warped spots, and I let loose. Crooning to "Jolene," begging her not to take my man, even though she can. I'm pretty sure Rook's sides are about to split from laughter.

"What are these awful lyrics?"

"They're about a floosy of a woman trying to steal Dolly's man." I try to sound indignant on her behalf. I flip the forty-five over to play the B-side.

Rook gently grabs my hand after I drop the needle. His thumb and forefinger fiddle with the gold initial *R* ring on my pinky. I know what he's thinking without saying it. I feel it, too. How much time do we have left before the crow makes him leave? Maybe he's only here long enough to help me with Adaire's death—a restless soul with unfinished business. Eventually he'll be gone again. Something I'm not ready to think about.

★ ★ ★

I don't remember when we finally fell asleep, but it's the chattering of birds that wakes me. Not a soft musical twittering, but a loud squawking at odd intervals.

It takes my brain a stretched second to register where I am. The early-morning sun streams through the tree canopy. A filtered light plays along the cave's stone wall. The night's rain layered on top of the earthy smell.

The rattle of the chain ladder shuffles back and forth against the kudzu vines. Quickly, I turn on my side and find Rook is not there. I prop myself up on my elbows, about to ask him why he's climbing up instead of flying, when Davis's head pops up.

"I've been looking for you everywhere." He sounds like an indignant father, and I feel like a teenager who got caught sneaking out to see her boyfriend again.

I sit up, rubbing the sleep from my face. "Yeah? You going to turn me in for some kind of reward?" I pull out a twig tangled in the ends of my hair.

He rolls his eyes unnecessarily.

"Yeah." He sets a to-go carrier of coffee from Clementine's at the top. "Because I buy coffee for all the people I send off to jail." He pushes himself over the edge into the cave. A spider's web catches on his head. He swats at it, almost spilling his cup.

"Okay. You wouldn't be that kind of an asshole." I stand, grateful for the coffee even if he forgot to bring sugar.

Davis pops the top of his Styrofoam cup and blows over the top to cool it. His eyes scan the scattered objects around the cave. He softens at the sight of it all. It's only mine and Adaire's old playthings. But from his point of view, it's a welcome reminder of the woman he still loves.

"So then why are you here?" I ask, trying to loosen my words so they don't sound so snippy.

"Well," he says in a thoughtful way, "because Raelean told me you were an idiot and went to the cops." He lets that sit in the air. I grit my teeth. "So I decided that, one—" he ticks of a finger "—I should check to see if you needed me to bail you out. And, two—" he ticks off another finger "—I figured if you were stupid enough to go to jail over this, then maybe you were right."

I raise a questioning brow.

"Maybe Adaire was trying to tell you something."

I hold back my victory, *Yes!* and settle for, "Okay. So now what?"

"I've been thinking about what you said."

"I've said a lot of things. I'm curious which one stuck."

He scowls at me a half second. "There's only so many repair shops in a fifty-mile radius that work on Firebirds," he says, snagging my full attention. "So I made a few calls."

"And?" I say, when he doesn't elaborate.

His eyes dip down to my bare feet. "Get your shoes on, I'll tell you in the truck."

SEVENTEEN

Dead Man's Curve

The inside of Davis's truck smells like an oil pan mixed with vanilla air freshener. The ashtray is overflowing with orange soda bottle caps. The floorboard is cluttered with changes of clothes for one job or the other. It's a vintage 1954 Ford truck, something he and his father rescued from the Dillards' old barn and rebuilt.

"So you found Lorelei's car?" I ask, after he tells me he called around to every tow truck company in the neighboring counties.

"Nope." He cracks his window to spit out the gum he'd been chewing. "No one had a record of picking up a gold Firebird on or around the day Adaire died. So then I got to thinking...that shit is traceable. If I was covering up a hit-and-run, I'd pay them to not make note of the car's make and model. So I called back around, asked if they picked up any cars off Highway 19 around those dates."

"And then you found her car?" I'm needing him to get to the point.

"No. But I find it awfully curious that Gunther's American Motorsports got pissed I called back a second time. Before the man slammed down the phone and hung up on me, he told me not to worry about cars he may or may not have towed from an accident. Thing is, I never told him the car had been in an accident."

"Oh, damn," I say, and I lean back against the seat. Cars get towed for all kinds of reasons, so if he said accident... "He knows something, doesn't he?"

Davis slowly nods.

It takes us about an hour to get over to Mercer to Gunther's American Motorsports. During our ride, Davis informs me that, once he passes his final EMT exams, he's going to start looking for jobs down in Galveston where his grandmother lives.

"Big Mama isn't getting any younger and Mom wants to sell the junkyard and move down there to take care of her. Makes sense to sell. I'll be too busy working at the ambulance authority to run it. She never liked the business, anyway, just held on to it after Daddy died." He says all this, talking to the road ahead of him and as if none of it's any big deal. Like stepping out of my life is an easy thing to do and several hundred miles between us doesn't matter to him. "I figured, since most of Mom's family is down there, I should set up roots there myself."

I want to ask him, *What about Charleston?* Adaire and him had had plans to move there so she could attend that fancy design institute while he worked as an EMT for a big hospital. I guess their dreams were only her dreams.

Of course, I feel shameful the second I think it. Davis loved Adaire. *Still* loves her. I'm happy for him, I really am. He's following his dreams in the medical field. And Galveston has a big hospital he can work for. I imagine it would be too painful for him to live their dream without her. But the idea of leaving her behind is even worse.

"Mom got a really good offer from a junkyard company over in Alabama." Davis's voice brings me back to the truck cab with him. "I think she'll make enough to retire. But you know Mom." He turns to me, flashing a big smile. I try my best to mimic it. "She doesn't know how to sit still for five minutes. She'll have a part-time job somewhere, I'm sure."

I nod, happily agreeing, doing a good enough job faking my enthusiasm because Davis doesn't give me one of his pitying looks. Instead, he veers off the highway into Mercer and through the city streets until we finally find Gunther's.

The paint on the building looks faded, now more a muted mauve, probably from years spent in the overbearing sun. Seems fitting that a giant cartoon rat with a long beard and sunglasses drives a souped-up hot rod across the building— we ask the first employee we see, who points out the owner, Billy Gunther, who bears the same rodent-like front teeth and red scraggly beard. Except he looks like he's on the south end of retirement, hunched over and hobbling around.

"That's not who I talked to," Davis says. "The guy I spoke with had a young voice."

We decide to go inside and talk to the woman at the front desk, with spiky long nails, teased high hairdo, and skintight T-shirt, boobs spilling out of the V-neck.

Candy, or rather Candy Kane, as her name badge reads— damn, if her parents didn't do her wrong—manages the phones, cash register, and impatiently waits on customers all by her lonesome.

"What can I do for you, sugar?" She eyes up Davis like he's her next dessert. He does look handsome, even if it's just his Harvey's Boneyard mechanic uniform—the tough growling bulldog logo oversells it, though.

Davis leans heavily on the high counter, melting her with his gorgeous brown eyes. I bite my lips to keep from laughing.

"My boss called yesterday afternoon. He's looking for..." Davis fishes a scrap of paper from his pocket and squints to read it. "A 595-A front clamp, full wrap manufacture color code 194/200." He politely stuffs the paper back in his pocket and throws her a smoldering look.

Well, that gets her purring. It's Greek to me what he said, but apparently she speaks mechanic.

"That's pretty darn specific, but I'll see if we can order you one." She bobs a seductive eyebrow, then pecks away on a computer a few seconds. "Turbo? Or a sedan?"

"Turbo."

"Diamond black bezel or halogen headlight?"

"Diamond."

Peckety-peck a bit more.

Davis lets loose a long whistle when she quotes him a price. "That is *way* out of my client's budget." Davis stretches his neck as if he's trying to get a look-see at the parts cars parked out back. He leans in closer to her. "Come on, you don't have a little something in the back I can get for cheaper?"

She bites her lip and dashes a look over to the garage, then leans in conspiratorially.

"You didn't hear this from me..."

Hope flares inside me.

Davis zippers his lips dramatically.

"But Billy Jr. got called to pick up a brand-new Pontiac Firebird some spoiled silver spoon wrecked, hit a deer last month. Busted fender, heavy damage to the undercarriage."

I lightly gasp. Davis gives my hand a squeeze below the counter. His eyes stay focused on Candy. Intently listening. Holding on to that charming smile like he didn't miss a beat.

"We wasn't supposed to say nothing because she paid us to keep quiet so her daddy didn't find out." Candy exaggerates her eye roll. "But everything gets hauled to DeRoy's place," she whispers, then scribbles an address and a phone number down on the back of their business card. "Go see DeRoy, he'll take care of you."

"You're a lifesaver." Davis grips the top of her hand in thanks, and I'm sure she's about to pop.

My knee joints feel like Jell-O as we walk away.

"Well," Davis says from the side of his mouth, as we walk out and a younger rat version of Billy Gunther Sr. walks in. "Guess we're going to DeRoy's place."

"Shit, man." DeRoy's teeth are a brilliant white. Charm and swagger ooze off his handsome face. "We've got junkers that pick up and drop off cars anywhere from Ohio down to Gulf Shores." He rolls a lone truck tire over to an existing pile of equally exhausted tires. "Everybody wants this part or the other. But if we're talking about a vehicle as new as you're saying…" He picks up a fresh tire to haul back over. "Then some individual might have bought it. Owners sign the titles over, not us. Find the title to that car, you'll have the VIN number. Then you might be able to track it down."

I brandish a big grin over to Davis with this bit of great news.

"That is, if it was done all legal-like," DeRoy adds, deflating our hope. Chances of that are definitely slim.

It's a quiet ride back, as neither of us want to talk about hunting down the car that killed something so precious.

We're almost home when Davis speaks up. "We're gonna get that VIN number," he says like a promise.

I tilt my palm back and forth in the sunlight and watch as the rays play on the blue glass.

"Wanda up at the courthouse owes me a favor for changing her car battery. I'll see if she knows anyone over at the motor vehicles office."

I simply nod.

"Hey." There's something about the gravity in his tone that implores me to look at him. "I want to show you something before I take you home."

"Yeah?" I say to him, pulling down the car's visor as the late-day sun tries to blind me. "Show me what?"

"Something that's been bugging me." He flicks on his blinker to turn left at the end of the road, and I tense up.

I've done pretty good these last few weeks avoiding Highway 19. Hell, I take the two-mile loop on Shaw's Chapel Road just to avoid it. I haven't driven on it since Wyatt and Aunt Violet dragged me out there to stick one of those white memorial crosses on the side of the road where Adaire died. Raelean said it's really pretty, like Easter in the middle of summer, with all those fake spring flowers you can buy from Walmart.

For me, it feels like they decorated a crime scene. I've got plenty of ways to honor Adaire, and I sure as hell don't want to memorialize where she was slain.

Aunt Violet also said it's a place she can go to feel close to Adaire. Like her ghost is stuck out there on the side of the road, cars whizzing by, all alone, just waiting for someone to remember she once existed. I want to tell Aunt Violet that Adaire is right here next to me, next to her, next to all of us. But that doesn't make her feel as good as a cemetery of plastic bouquets.

My body clenches up as we get closer. It's a quiet stretch of highway through the back woods of a small town, but this road is so much more. Dead Man's Curve it was named back in the '50s, when a teenager took the tight turn too fast and flipped his car and killed himself. Since then, lots of young kids over the decades have dared each other to drive fast around the curve for kicks. Sure, there have been a few car accidents here and there, but only two deaths. First that teenager and now Adaire.

"Why you doing this?" There's no hiding the tension in my voice.

"'Cause I need you to see something?"

"I don't need to see anything out here." My foot presses the imaginary brake on my side of the floorboard.

"It's fine, Weatherly. Trust me."

"Davis," I say, my tone tight as the straight part of the highway disappears into a sharp right farther ahead.

"Davis," I say a little more urgent as the front of his truck gobbles up the highway.

"We don't have to stay long, I swear. I just want you to see—"

"Davis! Stop!" The terror in my voice has him slamming on the brakes. We fishtail lightly as the road peeks around the corner. That artificial patch of vibrant color that marks her death sticks out like a sore thumb stuck in the middle of nature.

Crawling from the ditches and up the embankment are tufts and tufts of black ferns. A cancer suffocating the landscape. Their thick presence here only adds to the fear this stretch of road holds.

Davis eases the truck over to the side of the road in case someone comes along. He waits for me to calm myself; I didn't realize how heavy I was breathing until the silence of the truck highlighted it.

"I need you to come with me," he says, regarding me like a newborn fawn. "It's important," he adds when I hesitate to follow.

The black ferns, despite their ominous color and spiky fronds, are soft as the brush against my ankles. A thick carpet beneath my feet as we work our way closer to the memorial.

Davis squats down low to the ground and points to the road ahead, just before the plastic garden. "What do you see?"

It almost feels like a trick question. I shrug. "Fake flowers. The road."

He nods. "Okay. What do you *not* see?"

I regard the pavement again, still not getting his meaning. "I don't know."

"This is the scene of a car accident, what do you not see?"

I remember the time Papaw and I were in a car accident, sort of. He had to slam on the brakes to keep from running over Mrs. Cole's young cocker spaniel, who had streaked across the road right in front of us. The sound of the squealing tires against the pavement were as loud as the dog's frightened yelp.

"Skid marks." I realize. Suddenly interested, I slowly move forward; all that anxiety about being here tries to rise up, but I push it down, as far as it will let me, because I need to understand what Davis is talking about.

He stands. "I know the ambulance picked her up here. But where are the skid marks?"

As I walk, I swing my foot back and forth, gazing over the weeds and ferns for glimpses of the ground underneath.

"You know what else I don't see?" I say, after making a few laps over the area. "I don't see pieces of her bicycle. Not a wheel spoke. Or a chip of a broken reflector." We spend a little time combing over the area, picking through the grass, looking for any evidence. We don't find anything more than broken beer bottles and fast-food trash.

Davis slowly nods, seeing the new conclusions I'm drawing. Things he hadn't considered.

"She wasn't hit here," I say. The realization sinking in. I walk farther down the road to where there aren't any trees and the landscape opens up to cotton fields. I stand in the center of the road and turn in a circle.

"We're at Three Way," I say, even though Davis already knows this section of the road leads three different directions. "Town of Black Fern is that way." I point down the curved road toward home. "Gas station where it forks toward Mercer City that way." I cast my arm a third of the way between north and south. "And what's that way?" I point toward the center of east and west, at the white peak of a home's roof hidden within the oak trees.

Davis speaks a whispered "Oh."

Sugar Hill Plantation. It hits me like a ton of bricks.

"But now the question is," Davis asks, "where does that side road lead?" He points to the field road the farmers use to maneuver their combines so they don't drive over the cotton. A smile slides on Davis's face. "Let's go see."

His truck bounces and shakes as he attempts to avoid the shallow mudholes and dodge the downed branches.

He and I are both surprised when, after not too long, the weedy dirt road turns into gravel, which soon after becomes pavement. The roof and shoulders of Sugar Hill Plantation are slowly revealed as we get closer.

Over the horizon, the tall pickets of a rusted green iron gate rise with a massive capital *R* in its center, lording over the dead. The historical Rutledge family cemetery. Gravestones here date back to the early 1800s. The land is filled with decaying jagged teeth in a carpet of green grass.

From the dilapidated condition of the fence, this entrance isn't maintained anymore, probably from lack of use. It opens with a gritted hiss and a howling yawn. I swipe the crumbly green flakes of paint off my hands.

I take off suddenly, needing to find something—anything—that will confirm the picture that's now forming in my mind.

Davis hurriedly tries to catch up as I rush down the road, looking for skid marks.

"Why was Adaire riding her bike that day? What was so important she couldn't wait until I returned her car?" I ask Davis, who's scanning the side of the road for any signs of evidence.

"Because she couldn't see Saturday clearly, it was too foggy," he says.

"Bingo." Now Davis is finally starting to see meaning in everything I've been telling him. "She discovered something. Something important. Something so urgent she had to address it right then and there. Enough to ride her bike for miles to get to it. Whatever it was, I think it was here." I halt so quickly Davis slams into me. Then he sees it, too.

Parallel lines of slanted *S* tire marks. Scattered within the dried crabgrass, chips of broken bike reflector. I hold up an orange piece to show Davis.

"Damn, Weatherly." That's all he can manage under the weight of what we've just discovered.

"Yeah," I say. This is big, and we both know it. But I still don't understand.

What where you doing out here? I silently ask Adaire, scanning the cemetery as if a giant lighted arrow will appear and point the way.

"We better go," Davis says quietly and tips his head toward the gardener pruning the roses out back.

We're a good piece down the road when Davis says he will try to talk to Wanda up at the courthouse and see if she can't find a car title or a vehicle registration for Lorelei and get a VIN number to track her car and find out where it ended up.

I pull the blue bottle stopper out of my pocket and turn it over in my palm a few times. A glimmer of light from the fading sunlight flickers through it.

A recipe to see.

For the life of me, I can't figure out what Gabby was referring to that could help me see what Adaire saw.

"Ha!" I say, realizing the recipe, or many recipes, are right in front of my face every day when I do the dishes at our kitchen sink. Right there in that narrow window is our family's magical recipe box.

"Drop me off at Raelean's instead."

"Are you sure? Because mom wouldn't mind you staying with us a few days until things cool off."

"Tell your mama I appreciate her. But I need to see about something first."

EIGHTEEN

Sins of the Father

Grandmama's recipe box has eyes.

No matter where you are in the room, it always seems to be watching you. Or maybe it was because no matter where I was in the room, I was always watching it. It's sat in that tiny window in our kitchen for as long as I've lived.

I've only ever seen Grandmama's family recipes in brief glimpses. Something I snooped over her shoulder when she didn't realize I was near. A few words here. Drawn sketches or instructions there. Never a fully detailed "how to" list of what to do. They are ways for her to fix things that medicine or practical means can't. Things that require unnatural remedies. Like how she knows just the right measurement of Sin Eater Oil to bake in a pie that would make you sicker than a dog or one that would kill you from a single bite.

Or a recipe to help an old blind woman to see the sins people try to hide.

And whatever is in there can help me see what Adaire's trying to tell me. I'm sure of it.

As far as magic keys go, they aren't universal. When I tried the bone-tooth key Adaire found under the floorboard in her house, all I got was a zap of energy telling me *Wrong lock*. If I'm going to break into Grandmama's recipe box, I'm going to need *her* bone-tooth key.

"Why do I have to do this?" Raelean scowls from the other side of my bedroom window. Her voice whisper-quiet so she doesn't wake Grandmama.

The night air is musty from the day's rain. The crickets and the bullfrogs celebrate with chattering conversations.

"Because you love me." I blaze my biggest smile. She harrumphs, neither agreeing nor disagreeing.

"Do you even know what you're looking for?"

See now, this is the sticky part. I don't have a clue what I'm after, just *a recipe to see*, whatever the hell that means.

"I'll know it when I see it." Or…I hope I will. She stands there, not budging. "Are you going to help me or what?"

She stares at me for another long cockeyed moment. "You do realize this is a me-always-helping-you, one-sided kind of friendship, right?"

Raelean's not wrong, but I'm not going to concede to it now.

"Okay, fine. If you want me to go to jail, then go on home." I make like I'm closing the window, sealing my fate.

She grumbles a few swear words and something about murdering me if she winds up in jail. "You owe me." She points a finger at my chest. "Twice now," she adds.

"You're the best." I blow her kisses, which she swats away like pesky flies. "Don't forget to be overly loud." I close my window and sneak over to my bedroom door and wait.

Anticipation revs up my blood. I wait a few seconds. Then a few seconds more. After a short piece longer, I strain my ears, wondering if maybe she's being *too* quiet. I'm about to go over to the window to ask her what's taking so long. Then I hear the *bang-bang-bang* clobbering of her fist on Bone Layer's smokehouse door.

Perfect.

I take a deep breath and ready myself.

I can't make out Raelean's exact words, but they're exasperated and panicky, enough that it will get Grandmama's attention. Seconds later, I hear the creaking squeak from the unoiled hinges of her bedroom door as she wanders out to investigate.

I'm relying on the fact that she has to know everything that happens around here.

"What's going on out there?" her scratchy voice demands from the porch as she makes her way to the smokehouse to see what all the thunder is about. That's when I make my move.

Quickly, I slip out of my bedroom and dash into hers. Leaving the lights off so I don't attract any unwanted attention, I blindly feel around in the dark on her nightstand for the bone-tooth key.

The magic from the key warms as my hand crosses over it. I snatch it up, fear and excitement fueling my blood. I skitter out of her room and into the kitchen.

In the backyard, Raelean apologizes for waking them up and gives the fake story that Violet is drunk and drove her car into a ditch again—which used to happen more often than not. She needs Bone Layer to pull her car out. I "borrowed" Aunt Violet's car, and Raelean helped me stage it in a shallow ditch to bring the lie home.

The recipe box growls at me from the window, reminding me I'm not allowed to touch it. I swallow back my hesitation and pull it down.

To my surprise, it doesn't bite.

One might expect a click or a snick as with a turn of a key

in a locked box. But no such sound comes. The lid simply pops open and the world inside is mine for the taking.

I pause, reveling in the power at my fingertips.

"Please don't be angry, Mrs. Wilder," Raelean says rather loudly, stopping Grandmama from returning inside.

Shit. Hurriedly, I thumb through the recipes, no idea which one I need. There's promised warts to plague a straying lover. One about talking fire out of burns and blood-stopping with Bible verses. Remedies for a broken heart. Rashes for your enemy. Some cards have a classic title, then list out the ingredients and their proper proportions—tongue of a cat listed specifically for stopping gossip. Other cards have sketched images of rare medicinal herbs or diagrams of body parts and what you can inflict on them. Just when I'm about to give it up, I find a card with a perfectly sketched image of our perfume bottle with a stopper that matches.

A Way to See, the scrawled handwriting reads. Hope thrums in my chest. I pluck the card from the cache.

"You know Violet," Raelean says, extra loud. "She's always getting herself in a pickle."

The porch creaks.

I shove the card down my tank top and snap the lid shut and return the recipe box back to the windowsill where it lives. Before I duck underneath the dining room table, I grab the bottle with my Sin Eater Oil in it.

The recipe card burns with awareness. The bottle stopper rattles lightly in my pocket, and I clamp a hand around it, trying to calm my nerves. Outside, there's the rev of Bone Layer's engine as he wakes the truck to fetch the wrecked car out of the ditch. Grandmama shuffles back inside the house.

Then I feel a soft buzz in my hand, and I open my palm.

The magic of the bone-tooth key thrums. Waiting for me to return it back to where it sleeps, next to Grandmama's bed.

Shit. Shit. Shit.

Grandmama stops mid-shuffle as if she's heard my thoughts. Her gauzy white gown sways slightly around her thin shriveled-up legs. My chest burns for taking such shallow breaths.

Please, God, I beg. *Push her to go.*

God doesn't give in to my pleas often, but tonight He's feeling generous. She moves on, *shuffle-step, shuffle-step*, back to her room.

The second her door closes, I make my escape. The bone-tooth key a damning piece of evidence in my possession. On the wall, Grandmama's baking apron hangs. I stow it in the pocket, hoping like hell she assumes she forgot where she left it.

I flee out my bedroom window.

Drink with the spirits.
Taste the death.
Walk the veil.

"That has to be the vaguest recipe of all time," I say to Raelean from her bathroom, putting on a fresh set of clothes she let me borrow after my shower: a WKRP radio T-shirt and red shorts. "I have no clue how I'm supposed to 'see' anything with these instructions." I towel dry the ends of my hair and run a brush through it.

Raelean's trailer is a tiny place with a bedroom at each end and a kitchen and living room in the middle. Her vintage melamine table, aqua-blue-rimmed in chrome, something that stepped right out of the '60s. We sit at it, she's across from me, the amber glass shade of the hanging light casting a yellow light on us.

The lined card stock, once white, has aged to a dingy beige. In the top left corner, a printed rooster sits, similar to the one on the outside of the recipe box, a set that dates back to the '40s I'd guess.

Notes scrawled at the bottom, probably in my great-grandmother's hand, talk about seeing the *sins of others, you'll need markers to reach them.* Markers can be objects from the dead or something associated with them.

"What in the hell are you making there?" Raelean tips a chin toward the jar I'm filling.

"A witching jar."

"I don't like the sound of that."

"It's nothing too bad. It's just graveyard dirt and objects from the dead."

A piece of orange reflector from Adaire's bike I took from the cemetery. The blue bottle stopper. Adaire's last note. The picture of my mom and Gabby. Stone Rutledge's cuff link—something I should have gotten rid of already. Random pieces I've collected that might help me.

I'm about to screw the lid back on, but I stop. I tug the initial *R* pinky ring off my finger and drop it in there, too. I don't know why I do it, but something about it feels right. That's how witching works sometimes, fueled by thoughts that pop in your head out of nowhere. But I've learned over time that ignoring those little hints typically means things don't turn out very well.

I poise the lid over the jar, leaving a small gap where I can whisper the secret words that bind these objects together and ask them to help me discover what it is I need to know. Quickly, I screw the lid on tight.

"And what do you need that for?" Raelean points at the perfume bottle sitting in the middle of her kitchen table. The yellow light above shines through the blue glass and casts a small green halo onto the table.

I flip the card around so she can see it has the same bottle drawn on it, a watercolor image—except this shows the bottle full of the black ooze of death, where the one here barely has a half inch in the bottom. A black smear was wiped off the corner of the card at some point; in the light I see a faint iridescent oily shine of Sin Eater Oil. From my Papaw's mama, since she's the one who passed her gift on to him.

"I don't have a good feeling about this." Raelean crosses her arms over her chest and gives a sour disapproving expression. One that says she isn't the authority on stupid, but she recognizes it when she sees it.

"Well, I need your help figuring out what this recipe means." It isn't so much a recipe as vague instructions. "'Drink with the spirits.' You think that means I need to have a beer in a graveyard or with a ghost?"

Raelean snorts at my suggestion.

I kick her under the table. "Okay, Miss Know-It-All. What do you think it means?"

She straightens up tall and takes the card out of my hand and stares at it. Thinking.

"'Walk the veil.' That sounds like a place that's neither here nor there, right?" I nod. "So maybe that's where you'll 'see' what you're trying to find? Like if you do these first two things, this will be the result."

Sounds solid enough to me.

"'Taste the death.'" She looks up at me. "When you talk the death out of someone, does it have a taste?"

"No. Not a taste, but it has a sound." Which I know doesn't make sense to her and probably isn't helpful. "And it has a smell." I suddenly remember. "That's similar to taste."

She shakes her head, mouth pursed. "Not the same thing, though." She studies it a bit longer. "That stuff right there... what did you call it—Sin Eater Oil? That's what you cough up after you talk the death out of someone, right? So it's kind of like death in a liquid version, wouldn't you say? I feel like this card is telling you to taste it."

"Drink my own Sin Eater Oil? I'd rather not die, thank you very much." I snatch the card back. The idea of putting death back into my body is enough to make my skin crawl.

"But wait," she says. "What if this recipe is telling you how to do it without dying? Maybe you're right. You need to do shots with a ghost."

"Now you're just making fun of me." It was a dumb idea in the first place, and I don't need her bringing it up a second time to rub it in.

But something about what she said stops me.

"Oh!" I stand, excited, realizing what it's telling me. "Sin Eater Oil can never be in a cup that's had whiskey in it." I fan my arms open wide with a voilà motion.

Raelean isn't impressed with my revelation. "Oh-kay?" She waits for me to elaborate.

"So. No whiskey or vodka or any alcohol for that matter can ever have been in a cup where you're going to put Sin Eater Oil. Now why is that?" Raelean holds strong to her unimpressed look. "Because I bet you something happens when Sin Eater Oil and alcohol are mixed. Maybe that's what gives the oil it's 'seeing' properties? 'Drink with the spirits.' Not with a ghost. *Spirits*. As in alcohol. I have to drink my Sin Eater Oil with some kind of liquor." I'm sure Raelean must have something around here. I check her pantry.

Raelean nods, catching on to what I'm telling her. "And if you do, then you can 'walk the veil.'" She air-quotes the last words.

"If this works, that pretty much makes me a genius." I waggle a bottle of Goldschläger I find. The gold flakes swirl in the bottom. Thankfully, there's a little more than a swig left.

"I'm fairly certain that's not how genius works." Raelean grabs a shot glass—which she has plenty of, too. She snatches the bottle from my hand and fills it up.

We both look at the perfume bottle of Sin Eater Oil.

"I ain't touching that," she says, eyeing it skeptically.

I pause. A knot twists in my gut. We could be mistaken.

Am I really sure this is what the recipe is calling for? I mean, if I do this and I'm wrong, then it could kill me, right?

And if I don't, I might not learn what Adaire wants me to know.

"Okay. Let's do this." I pluck the mismatched stopper from the top and carefully tilt the bottle over the shallow glass of Goldschläger. A slow drop of ooze slips toward the lip of the spout—I half expect a puff of smoke when the two liquids converge. The dollop of oil drops into the alcohol with a *plop*.

Instead, something much more enchanting happens.

Crackling veins of iridescent blue light fracture the thick black drop, setting the shot glass aglow. The alcohol seeps into the cracks, causing the oil to roil and writhe as if it's a living thing, born into something new. The oil gives in to the alcohol and melts into a thinner substance, diluting the liquid to an inky blue.

Tiny crackling embers pop, the last remnants absorbed. A faint blue glow haunts the glass.

"It's cold," I say, surprised when I pick it up. My fingers frosty numb as if holding a chilled can of soda. I give it a smell. The glowing liquid ripples from the closeness of my touch, alive and thriving...waiting for a kiss.

"Are you going to drink it all?" Raelean stops me short of taking a sip.

"Should I?" I look at the liquid, wondering if a sip is enough.

"What if you die?" Raelean scrunches up her nose.

I was ready to dismiss that thought until she said it aloud. I set the glass down and sit back. Dying isn't on my agenda today.

I stare at the inky blue liquid as it begins to fade. A realization slipping into my thoughts.

"Fuck it." I snatch it up—

"Damn it, Weatherly." Raelean jumps out of her chair with

a halting hand. Her urgency stops me cold. "If I have to call your grandmother and tell her you're dead, so help me God, I'll bring you back and kill you myself."

Something in my gut nudges, and a thought comes to me. "If I die, call Bone Layer."

"Are you freaking cracked?" Raelean huffs a laugh.

"You heard me." I look at her, stern. Not in a mean kind of way but with an unspoken understanding that says, *Follow my wishes, even if they don't make sense.*

The gravity of what we're doing forces Raelean to sit back down as she resigns herself to what's about to happen.

She nods. Once. Ever so slightly.

Here goes. I slug the foul-smelling liquid down. Frosty cold, it ices my throat, leaving an aftertaste of rotted fish and cinnamon. I cough and press a fist to my mouth, trying to hold it down.

I wait, not sure if I'm going to suddenly get slurring drunk or if visions will just reveal themselves in front of me. Or if I'll die.

Except nothing happens.

"I don't feel a thing," I say to Raelean, and set the glass on the table. When I do, my hand leaves behind a blurry trail, as though I'm moving in slow motion. "Whoa." I look around the kitchen expecting the whole room to melt into a dizzy haze. But it's the same sad kitchen as always.

"Are you seeing this?" I wave my hand back and forth to show Raelean. "It's kind of like a ghosting delay. Oh, wait, can you see—" I pause.

Raelean is sitting there, frozen-faced, her eyes affixed to the chair I'm in.

"Hey," I say a bit firmer and snap my fingers in her face. My hand an echo of itself. She doesn't even flinch. Then I notice the dust particles in the shallow kitchen light, how they no longer float, but are perfectly still. The second hand on the clock has stopped circling. And a drip from the faucet dangles in the air.

Everything in the room is frozen in time.

A melodic hum snakes into the silence, the sweet warm sound of a soul-song. Not inside my head, though. Nor my chest, like it does when another soul is preparing to leave this world. That beautiful hum, plucked from my childhood, is coming from outside. *Adaire.*

It snakes into the trailer through the cracks around the door.

The pull so alluring, I'm helpless to its call. I walk to the door and briefly pause, turning back to see the slow dragging of my body as it catches up with me. Raelean still sits at the table, staring at the spot where I just was.

I step out onto the porch—

The sight of Adaire standing there catches me off guard. Her back is turned to me, but I'd know that scratchy short hair anywhere. Her clothes the same we buried her in: black-plaid pants with her favorite red Journey T-shirt. The colors are muted, like the tones of a faded photograph.

When I call to her, no sound comes. Only a flatness of nothing refracts back to me. Black smudges the edges of my vision. A hazy frame around this in-between place I've stepped into.

Coolly, Adaire turns her head to look at me over her shoulder. I smile. Even though she sees me, her expression is emotionless. Then she turns around and walks off the porch.

I throw out a hand to catch her; my foot missteps off the porch—

And lands inside a house. Except there's daylight now, and instead of Raelean sitting at the kitchen table, it's Adaire. She hovers over a scrying skillet. Her thumb mindlessly rubs that bone-tooth key; her eyes lost to a vision. When I look into the black glassy surface of the water, I watch my mother cry as she reads a letter. I lean closer to see what the letter says, and tumble forward into the skillet—

Splash, through a ceiling, I land with a thud on the floor of an empty room. Not any room, a bedroom at the farmhouse. Adaire scoots a wobbly chair into the closet and disappears. When she steps out, the brown button tin of my mother's is in her hands. Eager to see what's inside, I cross the room toward her. A thickness in the air slows me. I strain to push through—

The tension releases and I flounder into a grand office. I flail my arms to balance myself. A gorgeous oriental rug lies under my feet. A stern bookshelf stacked with law books. Adaire sits in front of a massive mahogany desk. The tension in her nerves so visceral I can feel it, like static electricity in my mouth.

From over her shoulder, I see her gripping a handwritten letter. It's loopy swirls from the hand of a woman. Stone Rutledge, with his knitted brows and talking hands, attempts to reason with her. Her anger spikes a bitter metallic on my tongue, and she abruptly stands. The mixture of her and I in the same space, dizzying. I gasp as our souls collide. Determination pushes her out of the mansion. She turns back at the harsh call of her name—

My knees give way into a run. A spinning, churning motion that speeds the grass beneath my peddling feet—not my feet, but Adaire's. Decaying granite juts from the ground like rotted black teeth. Tombstones. Adaire's ramped heart, like the racked wings of a thousand humming birds caged in her chest. Her terror spikes as the metallic gold beast chasing her gains ground. She peddles faster. A deft nudge from behind sends her flying, head over feet into the ground. A crashing, crunching disjointed impact that blackens the world around us.

The smell of grass heavy in my nose as we lie broken on

the ground, staring at the sky. The copper of a thousand pennies fills my mouth and dribbles red down my chin as we gasp in wet breaths. A greedy tugging at my waist causes me to look down. Gabby Newsome pillages our pocket—plucking free a blue droplet of rain. *A recipe to see.* Her grin an excited dance upon her face. The letter in our hand flutters away in the wind.

The pain.

Dear God, the pain. A blinding white-hot throughout my body. The blackness drinks me in. My eyes flutter in slow blinks. I give in to death as the sinking ground swallows me whole—

Wide-awake, I stand—or rather fall in reverse until I'm upright again. An endless field of grass surrounds me in all directions. I spin in a dizzy circle until a jarring stop lands me directly in front of Stone Rutledge. His gaze blank. His coloring a thinned version of what it should be. Flint eyes tip up to meet mine, and then he turns and walks away.

Just as with Adaire, I follow the dead—

Into a dim, smoky room. Red wool rug back underneath my feet. Fresh vanilla smoke and leather clouds around me as Stone Rutledge steps through me with an icy chill and into an office. Vibrant and alive and much younger than the man I ever met. A broken man. The heaviness of his sorrow like an anchor dragging at the bottom of an ocean.

At the head of the desk, the family lawyer, the same one that helped Stone get the charges in Adaire's case dismissed. Stone scribbles a signature on the documents pushed at him, then leaves. His bitterness the taste of an acrid pecan shell. I follow as he storms out and past Grandmama, waiting by the office door. My heart stops at the sight of her, causing me to trip backward—

Into a grand bedroom. Stone Rutledge stalks over to the window, intently watching down below. I look past his shoulder to catch a glimpse of Aunt Violet's rickety green Ford Pinto as it eases down Sugar Hill's driveway. The sweet face of eleven-year-old me in the rear window, peering back up at Stone. An ache—like none I've ever felt—stabs my heart. I clamp my hand over my chest at the longing—

In my hand is a glass of whiskey. Not my hand but a man's. Stone's. Looming over the mahogany desk before me, a raging Lorelei. Her anger a scorching bonfire against my face. Exhaustion. To my very bones, I am exhausted. The disappointment I feel for her tastes like soured milk. Abruptly, Stone stands and hurls the whiskey glass against the wall, yelling—

A panicked sound lures me down a darkened hallway until I face Ellis. Soft and muted, the eyes from which he gazes upon me are vacant. A gray version of the boy he was in life.

Just as the two before him, Ellis turns and I follow the dead—

Behind a dark doorway, we peer through a crack and watch Lorelei and their father argue. Whatever they are saying ignites my fear. Ellis leans too far into the door and falls—

My feet gain footing and I duck under a tree branch as he runs through the woods. I chase him—or whoever's body this is that I've fallen into does. Anger sets in my blood, threatening to rage. I can't let him get away. I can't let him tell. I clamp a desperate hand upon Ellis's arm. Disgusted by my touch, he wrenches free and swings around to face me. I see an opportunity to stop him, and I can't control myself. I shove him, angry and hard. He trips, a flailing, twisting motion. Horror slashes across his face as he grasps at the air. His hand catches at my neck—then *snap!* He falls backward and impales himself on the stick jutting from the ground. He lets out a scream that could wake the dead and I—

I wake up.

Me.

Wholly me.

What the hell——?

The real world a throbbing echo around me. Those blurred black edges of the Sin Eater Oil haze fade. The hushed sound of rain tamps around me. The tree canopy above an umbrella.

I lie there a minute. Those foggy moments in time that the dead showed me swim around in my head, bobbing up and down, telling me a story. Telling me the sins of others.

It was Lorelei. She chased Adaire down, ran her over with her car. She chased Ellis, after he found out. Pushed him right onto the branch that pierced his neck and killed him. It was all Lorelei. Because Adaire found out something that was worth killing for.

I sit up, trying to get my bearings. These woods look about the same as any other woods around here. It's morning now, the sun rising over the east——at least my sense of direction is still intact.

When I stand, a bitch of a headache pierces behind my eyes, about as bad as when I've had too much to drink. I hold still until the pounding subsides.

It doesn't take me more than a second or two glancing around to realize I'm where death and Ellis met. The sharp branch he pierced himself upon only a few feet in front of me.

Scattered on the rain-mucked ground lies Lorelei's bouquet of flowers, now rotting. A small glint of gold catches my eye. I bend down, riffling through the leafy debris to retrieve it. A dainty gold chain, something snapped in half. Instinctively I reach up to my neck, that yanking snap from the hazy dream still lingering. *Lorelei's necklace.*

The scales of Libra hung around her neck from a flimsy ribbon. That was why she came back out here. Not to leave memorial flowers at her brother's death site. But to find her necklace that Ellis snapped off her neck the day he died. She didn't shove dirt in her pocket; it was the gold pendant. The scales of justice.

It had to have been Lorelei who chased her brother in the woods that day. That urgent need to not let him get away still heavy in my chest.

She doesn't want me to tell.

Ellis knew. He knew Lorelei killed Adaire. He knew his father covered for her. A sin Ellis wasn't willing to keep quiet about, so Lorelei killed again. I think Stone must have figured it out. You could see it in his face that day at the Lathams'. A lost and broken man who realized he had raised a monster. A Bad Seed. Stone couldn't live with himself over it and the part he played.

The sky starts wringing out the clouds like a wet rag, so I get the hell out of there.

It takes me a solid hour of walking before I find a passing farmer to drive me back to Raelean's trailer. The cold rain—rude and relentless—spills from the sky as I step onto her front porch. My urgent fist pounds on her door.

It rips open. "Where in the hell did you go?" Raelean's face is pained, her hair a sloppy bun on top of her head, smudges of yesterday's mascara and eyeliner darken her eyes. Even early in the morning she's pretty. "You vanished—actually vanished—into thin air. One minute you're sitting across from me at the table, about to drink that awful liquid, and then next you're gone. Like I blinked and made you disappear." She snaps her fingers as she says this last bit, emphasizing the quickness of my exit.

"I'm sorry," I urge, but she knows it isn't my fault. I hope. The tension in her shoulders relaxes a little. Her tiny front porch doesn't have a roof, and I'm getting soaked. As soon as she realizes this, she steps aside, tugging her robe up around her neck.

"I need you to drive me home."

I take the towel she hands me and dry off as best I can. Then I tell her what I saw in the hazy Sin Eater Oil dream, where it took me—though I have no idea how—what I think it means, and why I need to go home.

Her face fills with dread, but she exhales a resigned sigh. "Let me get dressed." I'm grateful she doesn't feel the need to question me any further for now.

From my little witching jar, I fish out my ring and bone-tooth key necklace and put them on. The other stuff I return to the button tin for safekeeping.

I take a deep breath. Readying myself to face whatever is waiting for me at home.

Because I'd like to know exactly what business Grandmama had with Stone Rutledge.

NINETEEN

Fetch the Bones

Raelean's windshield wipers work overtime the entire drive home. Once we round the bend to my house, she lets up off the gas as multiple sheriff cars clog our driveway.

"Are you absolutely certain you want to do this…?" Her voice is extra twangy. That cocked eyebrow of hers lecturing me.

There's a half second where I want to tell her to floor it and get us the hell out of there. But parked alongside the sheriff's car is a coroner's van. Raelean eases forward, seeing it, too.

"I'm not so sure this is about you," she says, stretching her neck to see what the fuss is all about. The backyard comes into view and she stops.

A small backhoe slams its massive digging bucket into the rain-soaked ground behind our house.

"What the hell?" I hop out of her car, apprehension ticking in my chest as I walk up the driveway.

The backhoe's hydraulic arm swings to the side and dumps

the dirt out of the bucket. Then back to the hole for another scoop.

The wrongness of it loosens my knees. The rain, the trees—the world is closing in around me; the air is suffocatingly tight.

Sheets of rain pour off our tin roof as I slip onto the porch. A deathly stillness lies there as the mechanical monster claws at the yard.

I stand silently next to Grandmama and watch the unimaginable—they're digging up Papaw.

Sheriff Johns hands me some folded papers. I take the official-looking documents and scan the pages.

"Search warrant from the judge," he says as I read just that. "Read it in its entirety to your grandmother. Let me know if you have any questions." He crosses his beefy arms, and we keep watching. I pass the papers for Raelean to see.

Digging up the dead feels wrong, unholy even. Especially on a Sunday morning. You lay someone in the ground, you expect them to stay there. But with Papaw, it downright pisses me off. I can feel my jaw locking up as the tension spreads through my body.

I want it to stop.

My feet are swifter than my judgment, and I march right past the sheriff to the porch steps and— Raelean catches ahold of my arm.

"It's gonna happen," she says. A lump gets hung in my throat. "Nothing any of us can do now." I want to tell her she's wrong, that I can stop all this, right here and now.

But somewhere inside me, I know she's right. It's enough that I step back.

I scowl over at my grandmother. As powerful as she claims to be, she can't stop them, either. Maybe she was never powerful to begin with. Maybe it was just my inflated fear as a child that she warped and manipulated for years. It makes me hate her all the more.

Whatever killed Stone Rutledge, they think Sin Eater Oil played a part. Doesn't matter to the sheriff that Papaw went septic from the way it built up in his body from years of the death-talking. To them, it looks the same. Two men from very different socioeconomic worlds. The most obvious link…me.

We huddle together in the shelter of the porch as the sky weeps. I'd do anything to go back to that cave with Rook. Crawl up in his arms and pretend this world doesn't exist. Just him and me, and that tiny piece of happiness we carved out for ourselves.

That backhoe keeps hollowing out my soul—dig, dump.

Dig.

Dump.

Dig—the man operating the backhoe stops mid-scoop and waves an arm at the sheriff.

They've hit the pine box. The blood drains from my face in a cold flush.

With the flick of his fingers, Sheriff Johns directs two men already out in the yard with rain slickers and shovels, ready to finish the job.

Seems like, if anyone should be doing the digging, it should be Bone Layer. He put Papaw in the ground, he ought to take him out. I look around, realizing neither he nor the truck are here.

It takes time, but eventually they uncover the pine box, wrap straps around it, and haul it from the earth. The thick pine, coated in a heavy protective layer of shellac and oil, hasn't degraded too much—Bone knows how to make a proper death box.

An angry burst of thunder cracks, followed by a zipper of lightning across the sky.

Papaw's not happy about this.

A man jabs a crowbar at the edge of the lid—I gasp and turn my back to it. Like a tree in the storm, my roots are being ripped out from underneath me. Raelean wraps a comforting arm around my shoulders.

My heart is a heavy lump in my chest, dreading the tiniest bit of evidence they might find. That they could use my gift against me. Might now have a reason to send me away for good.

Because I am the Devil's Seed Child. This town damned me and my soul a long time ago.

Grandmama just stands there in her oversized white dress shirt, dingy from age and farm work since it was once Papaw's. Her brown skirt a sack with an elastic waistband. An emotionless bag of bones bundled in fabric, that's what she is. Her heart a cold lifeless rock, unfazed by the depravity of what's happening here. I turn to face her.

"Do something," my voice pleads. "Don't let them take him."

"Quiet!" she snaps back. "Won't no good come of it. You've done quite enough already." And as she inclines her head my direction, I notice the brass chain to the bone-tooth key back around her neck. Probably knows what I've been up to if she realizes which recipe I stole. What do I care? Not like she'd go out of her way to help with the sheriff, anyway.

Anger penetrates my chest. Stuffs itself under my bones. Pries beneath the very core of me. I push past Grandmama and the other deputies on the porch and escape inside the house.

Raelean rushes behind to follow me inside. "Sweetie, maybe you should just—"

"Go home." I swivel around, hard and fast. Shock widens her eyes until they frown with hurt. I clamp down on the rage that's bubbling inside me, realizing I shouldn't have swung it at her. But right now I can barely breathe, much less carry on a conversation. I gather the last bit of kindness left in me. "I appreciate you, I truly do. I just need a little...a little bit of breathing room."

God love her, her eyes soften with that unspoken under-standing. She reaches out and gently squeezes my hand. "You call me later."

I nod. The screen door quietly claps shut behind her.

Water trickles from the kitchen faucet as I fill a glass. I down it, then another. Neither extinguishes the anger, the frustra-tion, the sadness, the *everything* that's eating me up right now.

I take a little bit of comfort in knowing the most damning evidence is back at Raelean's—the perfume bottle.

I reach for the faucet to fill a third glass when I notice what's missing from the kitchen windowsill. There's a spot now, void of dust where the familiar recipe box usually sits. There are plenty of recipes in there that can incriminate both of us, and for more than just Stone Rutledge's death.

Frantic, I scan the counter. Comb the kitchen shelves. Ran-sack the cabinets. Everywhere I search, I come up with noth-ing.

It's gone.

A half second of confusion muddles my thoughts. Why on earth would Grandmama hide the recipe box—to protect me?

I huff a laugh to myself. She wouldn't. She's protecting herself.

A squeak from the unoiled screen door turns me around. Grandmama shuffles inside the house. Her age and stature makes her seem frail and innocent, you wouldn't suspect she could even kill a fly.

"Are you going to tell me what you've been up to?" Her voice a heavy ragged thing that scrapes the earth. That de-finitive note of blame always lingers in her tone. It points its ugly dog finger at me, as if everything is my fault. "Or do I have to ask you twice?"

Her scornful blind eyes stare right at me. That hardened heart of hers is always looking for a reason to cut me down. I want to drill her with all the questions I have, but now ain't the time; not with the law as thick as they are out front. There is no doubt in my mind that if they pressure her in any way, she would turn me over, if it meant saving her own ass. That recipe box she would swear on the Bible was mine.

"I don't know where you've hidden the recipe box—" I drop my voice threateningly low "—but if you think for one second I won't tell the sheriff how you've used my Sin Eater Oil, you're sadly mistaken."

Grandmama's face slips smooth, almost ashen, as her mind registers what I'm saying. Her cloudy eyes dart straight to the windowsill, where the box should be sitting. For her ailing eyes, it's a rectangle of light. The black square that usually sits there is gone.

Her gnarled arthritic knuckles clutch the brass chain of her bone-tooth key like a fretting priest holding his rosary. She's scared. Holy shit, she's scared.

I ease back against the kitchen sink, realizing it's not Grandmama who's hidden the recipes. The only other person who's ever in this house is—

Out front, I see Bone Layer has returned and more deputies have arrived as well. That asshole has gone and hidden it to protect her.

I storm out into the backyard to confront Bone. The rain less angry than it was a bit ago, but still stubborn about sticking around.

"Excuse me, Deputy," I say to the officer who waits on the tiny porch of the smokehouse with Bone's shotgun in hand. The officer doesn't stop me as I burst into Bone Layer's sleeping quarters.

He looks up from putting on his church coat.

I don't remember the last time I came into Bone Layer's room—years, maybe. Only six shirts hang in a single rusty red armoire, a piece of furniture that's older than him and me. Made from Appalachian pine and painted with homemade milk paint tinted with red clay. Folded on a shelf are four pairs of work pants and a couple of undershirts. A single oil lamp rests next to his bed, along with his Bible. A pitcher and water basin for washing up nestle on a table next to the small wood-burning stove. Just the bare minimum of life's necessities. No modern amenities. Doesn't have to be that way. He chooses this life. This is Bone's own personal atonement, but for what, I don't know.

"Nice of you to join us," I smart off. Then, remembering my purpose, I add, "Where have you hidden it?" through gritted teeth. He knows what I'm talking about, too. I can see it in his eyes.

Usual Bone Layer–style, he doesn't say a word. He just sits down on his tiny bed, the covers stripped from the thin mattress and folded up as if they won't be used for a while. He swaps out his work boots for his church boots. The difference: scuffed versus not.

Bone Layer seems ageless at times, but now that I'm getting a good look at him, crow's-feet are scratched around his eyes. Gray peppers the fluffy tufts of his sideburns. Even his leathery hands are hardened and wrinkled from years of manual labor.

"Where are you going?" I ask at the sight of a small duffel bag sitting on the floor.

"Bone, you ready?" the deputy waiting outside the door asks.

Bone Layer nods, then his dark eyes turn to me. "I promised your mother I'd do anything to protect you" is all he says. These simple words knock me back a step. He walks out onto the porch of his one-room smokehouse and places his hands behind his back.

"Jonesy Elijah Hayworth," the deputy says, calling out Bone Layer's full name. "You have the right to remain si-

lent. Anything you say can and will be used against you in a
court of law…"

"Wait? What's happening?" I ask Oscar, though I'm not
sure when he arrived.

Another deputy interrupts us. "Coroner thinks it could be
the same poison. Take the pine box, too? It's not rotted," he
says to Oscar, who nods yes.

"And have the boys search the premises and collect anything that could be considered poisonous. Bag and tag everything."

The sheriff instructs them to load the coffin into the coroner's van. They haul Bone to the deputy's car, where he's placed
in the back. People are searching through things and taking
stuff—our things.

Oscar rests a hand on my arm to refocus my attention on
him. "Bone came into the station after they arrived to dig up
your grandfather," Oscar says, then pauses to make sure I'm
listening. "We have two bodies…infants." So they did find
them—and that's how Gabby got the blankets, they must have
been left behind. "They have the same marks from the black
poison that killed Stone Rutledge. Same as your grandfather.
Bone Layer claims he buried those infants. We suspect these
aren't the only victims he's poisoned."

"He didn't kill them!" I blurt, even though the truth
wouldn't be any easier to explain.

"He hasn't denied it, either, Weatherly."

"What's Papaw got to do with any of this? You trying to
pin his death on Bone Layer, too? Bone Layer loved my Papaw
more than anyone. You know that. He would never have poisoned him. Besides, the coroner already determined sepsis
killed Papaw. Are we just inventing crimes now?" Desperation and guilt thin my voice. *Tell him, tell him the truth about
the babies!* Fear locks my mouth shut.

"In light of the new evidence, the medical examiner is reconsidering your grandfather's initial cause of death."

"I killed them," I blurt it out, ready to take whatever is coming to me. Oscar flinches back at my abrupt confession. I shove my wrists at him so he can lock me up instead.

He rolls this over in his head. Then his scrunched brow softens. Those tender eyes of his brush over me as if he's regarding a child.

"Look, I know Bone feels like family to you. This isn't going to be easy on y'all, but I promise you... I'll make sure he's well taken care of as we sort this all out—"

"You're not hearing what I'm telling you. It wasn't Bone Layer. I'm the reason they're dead," I say, loud enough one of the deputies looks our way.

Oscar pushes me back into the smokehouse a little farther. "Enough." I've never heard him speak so harshly. "It's not possible. It happened a long time ago, you would have been a child yourself. Don't go stepping your way in front of this to protect Bone Layer. I said we'll sort it out. Trust me to do my job. Jesus, how many times do I have to ask you this?"

I promised your mother I'd do anything to protect you. It's hard enough for me to fathom Bone Layer was close enough with my mother to make such a promise, much less follow through with the vow. But that's exactly what he's doing right now.

"It wasn't Bone." My words so quiet, I'm not sure Oscar hears me. Or maybe I didn't even speak them out loud. My head is circling, and I feel like I'm going to drop from the dizzy spin of my thoughts.

"Now listen, we'll need your grandmother to come down to fill out some paperwork," Oscar continues. "We have a warrant to search the entire property, so if you know where there's poison—any type of poison at all..." Oscar pauses and raises a knowing brow. "You should tell us now."

"Um," I say distractedly. "There's rat poison in the barn I think. But no, nothing else I can recall."

More deputies flood the property, pulling barrels and boxes out of the barn. Someone squeezes past us into the one-room smokehouse, and I step out of the way. He starts to tear apart Bone Layer's room.

"No, you can't take that." I grab Bone Layer's cigar box of miniature taxidermy birds he hasn't finished yet. It's bad enough they have him; they can't have his stuff, too.

Oscar nods to the deputy to let me have the box. He instructs him to give me a minute and search elsewhere.

"This is a lot to take in." Oscar sits me down on Bone's bed as he kneels in front of me. "Just let us do our job. When you feel more on your feet, you'll need to drive your grandmother down to the station."

He tells me to pack some clothes for a night or two, as we're not allowed to stay here while they complete their search. I don't know where we can go, since Grandmama hates Aunt Violet.

Oscar leaves me there.

Sitting on Bone Layer's bed.

Swimming in my thoughts.

Along the inside of the rusty red armoire's door, a full-length mirror. Gray lines from its age wrinkle over the face. Sometimes if you stare at yourself long enough, you don't recognize the person staring back anymore.

I grab the armoire's thin door to close it and pause. A dark shadow of a box hides under Bone's bed. Squared edges, quietly tucked away in the recess of the corner. Nothing special about it, but a sweet hum warms my chest. It nudges me off the bed, onto my knees. I reach back until my fingers catch the corner of the box and slide it on out.

An old wooden chest. Hand-forged metal straps wrapped around it, with an unusual keyhole on the front.

For a bone-tooth key.

"Holy shit." I run a knowing hand over it. This is the box my mother propped her foot on in that photo the sheriff showed me.

I pat where the necklace lays under my shirt and pull it out. My hand shakes as I slide the toothy bits perfectly into the hole. Energy from the magic thrums through my body as I flip my wrist with a turn, and the lid pops as it releases.

The hinges creak in protest as I tilt the lid open, and I peer down inside and find one lone item.

A tiny red suitcase.

My heart skips. I can hear my mama whispering, a twangy, insecure sound, promising to take me to see that ocean. The tiny seashell she gave me sealing that promise. Why give the suitcase to Bone Layer?

Careful to keep an eye toward the door for deputies, I reach inside and pull it out.

On the front, a cartoon image of a little blond girl in a hooded yellow cape, carrying a basket of goodies. The metal locks spring open under the pressure of my thumbs. I begin to crack open the suitcase—

The sound of footsteps growing closer to the smokehouse stops me. Quickly, I slap the metal latches shut and stand. I dart past him out the door and head straight for the pickup truck.

"Ma'am, that's evidence," the deputy calls to me as I'm about to slip the suitcase inside Bone Layer's truck.

Quickly, I glance to Oscar, who's instructing another man to search under the house.

"You said we can't stay here tonight. Since when are my panties evidence?" I show Oscar the suitcase that isn't much bigger than two shoeboxes. I hope like hell he was too busy to notice I didn't get this from my room.

There's a slight hesitation, where he might ask me to show

him the contents. Fear ices over me. I glare at the deputy who's edging up in my space a bit too close.

"Rodney, go search the smokehouse." Oscar points where the deputy needs to get going.

I drop the suitcase into the truck bed with a defiant thud.

TWENTY

Somethin' Terrible

Getting arrested takes a heck of a lot longer than what the movies make you believe—Hollywood can't get nothing right.

It's a lot of waiting around for the law to do their job. Sign this. Authorize that. Make calls to a judge who is *not* happy about his Sunday afternoon golf game being interrupted. Most of the day we were waiting for Bone's arraignment and a bail to be set. Now it's starting to get dark. If another deputy tells me, "We're almost done," one more time, I think I'll crack.

At least we get to go home. They rushed the search of our house on account of the big storm rolling in. Didn't take them long to search everything. When you're as poor as we are, you don't own much.

All we are waiting for now is for Aunt Violet to show up with the ten percent of the assigned bail, and we can take Bone Layer home.

At the corner desk, Deputy Rankin hen-pecks on a typewriter as Grandmama stiffly waits there for him to finish. We didn't speak the whole car ride over. She knows something, but now so do I. And it'll take more than wanting to please her to part with my new knowledge.

Across the room, Bone Layer sits with his church coat folded nicely over his lap, his left arm cuffed to a metal pipe. A pipe he could rip straight off that wall if he wanted to. His eyes lost in a gaze to the nothing on the floor.

There's a lot of secrets locked up in that man. I really need him to part with one or two.

The torrential downpour outside has me worried as hell. Where's Rook right now? Does he have somewhere safe to go? All the years and all the storms, he's managed okay. It's flimsy reassurance, but I'll take what I can get.

My attention, on the other hand, is constantly being pulled back to the rain-drizzled glass door up front. Not at the door, but at what I can see just beyond, Bone Layer's truck and that small red suitcase that's waiting for me.

My fingers are itching to get at what's inside, but I can't chance opening it here, can't risk it getting confiscated by the sheriff.

I promised your mother I'd do anything to protect you. I keep replaying Bone's last words in my head. He wouldn't tell me that if he planned on turning me in, though, right? The practical side of my brain thinks maybe it's just the recipe box; he hid it inside there for safekeeping.

"It's a pitiful shame, if you want to know the truth about it," the heavy, burly drawl of Deputy Rankin says as he pours himself a cup of coffee and grabs a slice of Callie's marbled Bundt cake. My stomach growls at the sight of it; I haven't eaten all day.

He's not talking to me but to Billy Parnell. I must be invisible because neither one of them seem to notice I'm sitting just two chairs down.

"Somethin' terrible if you ask me." Billy's accent has that exaggerated Southern drawl that feels like he's talking in check marks, every syllable starts low and ends up high. "Sad how that pretty girl lost a brother and her daddy in a matter of days. Then all that crazy business with her aunt, too." He shakes his head with a frightful shiver. "They hauled her off real quick-like. A rag doll the way they tossed her in that hospital van." He takes a large bite. "Though maybe she's better off some-where else," he says with a mouthful of cake.

I can't say I don't disagree with him. Gabby definitely needs professional help. Poor woman, her family locked her away like a shameful secret. That's no way to live.

Billy leans into Deputy Rankin, dropping his voice. "You think he killed them all?" He pans his eyes over to Bone Layer as if there's some other person in the room arrested for murder.

The scowl I send Billy's way is lethal. He catches it from his periphery, realizing I'm watching *and* listening. He decides to shove another bite of cake into his mouth, then he makes himself busy pestering Callie at the intake desk.

Rankin bears down on me with one of those looks that says he thinks he's better than me because he has a badge. I bran-dish my fakest smile and hope it reads like a middle finger.

Deputy Rankin isn't wrong about Lorelei, though. Losing two loved ones like that...unimaginable. If she wasn't an evil bitch for murdering my cousin, I might have felt sorry for her.

Her and Ellis may have been twins, but it's clear they were nothing alike. Ellis didn't seem like he had a bad bone in his body. I'm basing that off the handful of times I ran into him in town, during those brief summers and on holidays when they were home from boarding school. But that stark fear on his face as he ran from me—well, not me, Lorelei.

Biz-bong!

The station's doorbell startles me back to the present. Oscar rushes into the building, shaking off the rain. He hands Callie a plastic bag protecting some evidence he found at the house. After he knocks clear the droplets clinging to his Stetson hat, his eyes land on me. He nods for me to join him in his office.

"It's been a crazy few weeks around here." Oscar's bronze hand glides over his wet hair. He fans an open palm for me to sit across from him. Same seat I took two nights ago.

"It's getting dark soon, and this storm isn't getting any younger," he says, grabbing up some paperwork and a pen. "We've got calls coming in that Davenport Road has waters rising. And we've already closed off the levee because of flooding. You should probably get Agnes on home before it gets too bad to drive."

"Well, I wanted to wait on Bone," I say, thumbing over my shoulder.

"Look." Oscar stops signing his paperwork. "I can't have you getting stuck on a flooded road and putting my boys in danger trying to fish you out of a ditch. They already had a tornado touch down up in Tennessee." He takes one stack of paperwork and files them on top of another equally tall stack. "Don't worry about Bone. Once his bail is paid and the paperwork is processed, I'll bring him home myself. Of course, he'll have to show up for court on Monday, but I'll get him home tonight."

Court on Monday. To press official charges for murdering those babies. And Papaw. And maybe even Stone. I'm wondering how, between now and then, I can make things right. "You don't have to do that. I can take Grandmama home and come back for Bone."

Oscar gives me an exhausted look; he's tired of arguing. "Have you eaten today?" He raises a brow, knowing the answer. It's the soft way he regards me that reminds me why I dated him in the first place. "Go home. Get something to eat. You could use the rest, Weatherly. I'll bring Bone home shortly."

I nod, standing. Food and sleep do sound good. "Hey." I stop, realizing something. With Bone Layer getting arrested, and that Sin Eater Oil dreamy haze last night, I had forgotten about what Davis and I discovered with Lorelei's car. It's too exhausting to explain everything, so I just tell him the basics. "I know now is not the time, but Davis and I found a place that towed a gold brand-new Firebird Trans Am to their shop."

Oscar's shoulders drop.

I throw up my hands in surrender. "I'm just relaying the information. The receptionist said a girl brought her car in after hitting a deer—"

"It's not illegal to kill a deer."

I grit my teeth. I'm about to pull all my hair out if I have to keep convincing people Adaire's death wasn't an accident. I let out an exhausted sigh.

"The sheriff's office has connections with the motor vehicles department, right?"

"Are you asking me to illegally get you information?"

"No," I say. "I'm asking you to do your job and investigate. All it takes is *one* phone call." I hold up a single finger. "Get the VIN number for Lorelei's car and find out where it is."

"I'll have one of my boys look into it." The dryness in his tone tells me he's not jumping on it anytime soon.

"Thanks," I say back to him, just as dryly. "I'll tell Bone you're taking him home. See you out at the house in a bit." I turn my back on him before he can say anything more.

Out in the main room, it feels a lot colder than sitting here a minute ago. I walk over to Bone Layer. He scoots his knees out of the way, allowing me to sit in the folding chair next to him.

The sleeve on his church coat has a button loose. I make a note to mend it. His dark eyes search my face. The complexity of who he is kept at bay by his stoic silence. Like all his knowledge is stitched up tight, filling him to bursting. If he doesn't let it out soon, I imagine his seams will split wide-open.

I don't even know where Bone Layer is from besides Appalachia somewhere. Or if he has kinfolk he still speaks to. And yet here he is, knowing my entire world.

"Why?" A loaded question that's asking him ten things at once, but mostly why he's letting them arrest him for something he didn't do.

Bone observes me for a time. I sit up taller in my seat. I want to tell him I'm grown enough to hear it all. Let it free. When he doesn't say anything, I think about cracking his head open just to get a look at his thoughts.

A small smile tugs at the corners of his mouth, so soft I almost miss it. "I remember when you were born." His words a warm vibration, tucking itself around my heart. "So tiny I could hold you in one hand." Bone splays his palm open—the size of a dinner plate. I don't speak, for fear this rare moment might evaporate.

The sparkle from Bone's eyes dwindles, his brow dips. "Your mother wasn't always who she is now." Bone Layer says this so earnestly I believe him. I think about the picture of my mother and Gabby at the big Baptist convention. My mama looked wholesome back then. Pure, even. "She was very different before…"

Before she got pregnant with me, and I ruined her life, I finish in my head.

"You were her greatest joy." Bone says this as if he heard my thoughts. "She wanted to do right by you. Sometimes that means making sacrifices. Someday you'll understand."

"Well," I say, "I won't hold my breath waiting for someday." Then I inform him about the worsening storm and how the roads are flooding and how Oscar will bring him home after they process everything.

The rain washes down on me in buckets as I dash out to the

truck. The windshield wipers swat the rain, pathetic-like. I pull around to the side entrance underneath the flimsy metal carport and wait for them to bring Grandmama out.

Rain wraps the awning in sheets, trapping me in its watery curtain veil.

I glance into the darkness of the truck's floorboard. I can't see my little red suitcase, but I can feel it. Calling for me to open it up already. I slip another glance at the door. My hand reaches down into the dark at the same time Callie rounds the corner to the short hallway with Grandmama on her elbow.

The suitcase is going to have to wait a little bit longer.

I stretch across the bench seat to open the passenger door.

"Drive safe now," Callie says, after she helps Grandmama into the truck.

Grandmama pats Callie's hand softly with a polite expression on her face as she tells her thank-you. Not two seconds after Callie shuts the door, she grimaces in disgust.

"Her belly smells of rot." Grandmama's cragged voice cuts through the silence. She only says things like that when she thinks someone has been an adulterer. I've seen Callie and her husband uptown with their family occasionally. They seem as normal as any other couple raising four kids. But they haven't gone to church in some time, and that's sin enough for Grandmama.

"Only thing rotten around here is you," I say, and I throw the truck into Drive.

"Don't you go smarting off at me, just because you've been lying and stealing and hiding secrets away."

The cab of the truck is icy cold despite the heat of the summer. Grandmama has a way of sucking the warmth out of everything. I kick up the wipers as fast as they will go, and it's still a sloppy blur on the windshield.

"What did you tell them about those babies?"

"Nothing they didn't already know." Her calm is infuriating.

"What's that supposed to mean? You and I both know Bone didn't kill them."

"No, he certainly didn't. Neither did I," she says with a poignant look in my direction. "Maybe I should have shared more with them?" The threat clear in her narrowed stare.

"Well," I say, shoring up my confidence, "maybe you should have. I guess you better get busy praying Bone doesn't decide to tell them how you ordered him to bury me alive with those dead babies. Wouldn't that be a hard pickle for you to explain your way out of?" I get the satisfaction of seeing her stiffen a touch.

A flash of lightning races across the sky and lights up the watery road ahead. I grip the steering wheel with two hands and slow down. A spray of water fans out from the tires, and we drive through it.

It doesn't matter what Grandmama told the sheriff. I've already made up my mind that come Monday morning I'm going to tell Oscar everything that happened the night Gabby Newsome's babies died, despite how crazy it's going to sound.

I've also decided I'm never going to give Grandmama another drop of my Sin Eater Oil.

If I think about it, Sin Eater Oil isn't the reason we are all in this situation right now. It's not why Bone Layer was arrested. Sure, Sin Eater Oil killed those Newsome babies. And it will keep killing folks or making them sick. But it's the death-talking that's the real problem. You can't have one without the other. That's when it hits me.

"You don't want me locked up, do you?"

"Am I supposed to want my only granddaughter to be hauled off to prison? Is that what you'd prefer?"

"No, that's not it, you need me—you need my Sin Eater Oil. Else you can't go on fixing up potions and shit, poisoning people around town, inflicting your own version of justice on everyone else."

"Shut your mouth. Don't you dare sass me. After all I've done for you, you ungrateful little beggar. Took you in after your mama left you, didn't I? Wouldn't have had a roof over your head nor food in your belly if it wasn't for me. Taught you how to use your gift, how to do something worthwhile in this godforsaken world."

Gift? It ought to be called a curse.

No, death-talking is not a gift once you take in the sum of it all. It's a burden. One I'm exhausted from carrying. It anchors me here to this small town. To this life. To her.

"You've barely taught me anything, none of the real magic, anyway. All those recipes you keep locked up for yourself, hoarding that so-called power. You try to control everyone and everything around you. Manipulating us all to do your bidding, acting like you're some holy saint sent here by God himself. Look at Papaw, you used him for years, and where did it get him? Six feet in the ground. Dead! From all the death-talking you made him do."

"How dare you—"

Something smashes against the windshield of the truck. I swerve in response. A smear of blood covers the fractured glass. Darkness eats up the road ahead where the truck's headlights shine until a flock of crows flies straight at us.

Bodies pound against the windshield. Caws of pain echo all around as bone crushes against steel. Until… BOOM! A single solid body punches the roof of the truck. Something large flies over the top, rolling as it hits the ground and flops to a halt.

A visceral image of Adaire being run over shoves itself into my brain. The agonizing, white-hot pain she felt. The iron taste that pooled in her mouth and choked out her last breath.

I stomp on the brake as we slide toward the ditch. The rain-slicked tires fishtail left, then right until the back of the truck whacks a tree.

My head strikes the door window.

Stars spark my vision.

The truck tilts to one side with a sloshing *thump*.

A long dark pause fogs my thoughts as my head struggles to comprehend what's happening. Ears ring. Only the dull short huffs of my breath anchor me to the present.

The headlights now shine in the direction we came from. Relentless rain punishes the pavement. A dark object lies in the road just out of the light's reach.

Not a single dead bird anywhere in sight.

Then I switch the truck beams on high. Rook's body lies lifeless on the ground.

"Oh, God, no." I shoulder open my door and out into the pouring rain. It bounces off the inky surface of the road. Scattered taps against the ground as the night sky weeps. Rook's black jeans are suctioned to his soaked legs. Long black eyelashes thick from the wet. His moonlit skin flawless as always.

"Wake up." I shake him, but he doesn't move. "Wake up!" I try again, but he only flops limp.

I lean in closer to him, trying to hear that soft whisper of his soul-song. The song I've tasted on my lips, drank into my body, and the life I've breathed back into him once before.

Once is all you get.

A little voice inside my head reminds me.

"No! No! No!" I try to make Rook sit up, but his arms are like slippery noodles in my grasp. "Wake up!" I scream. That's when I notice.

There's no blood.

No bruising.

There's not so much as a scratch upon Rook. He's perfect and beautiful and everything my heart desires.

And he's not real.

Everything I held to be true floats away. Rain drizzles down my face. I close my eyes, and I'm back in the comfort of

Adaire's room, nose to nose with her. Her ghostly words whisper in my head. *You have to let me go.*

From my pocket, I pull out a raggedy feather, one I keep for just such occasions. I make a wish to set Rook free.

And I let it go.

"Wake up! Ma'am, wake up!"

My eyes flutter open to find a strange man hovering over me. Confused, how is it I'm lying on the side of the road in the mud? Driver's-side door wide-open. A single foot still lodged in the doorway.

"Ma'am, are you alright?" the man asks again.

From my right, I hear a murmuring. Or, more precisely, it's the slow disjointed musical sound of a soul-song, calling to me. Through the truck cab, I see Grandmama slumped against her door. A silty mud from the embankment oozes through the cracks in her window. A trickling of blood dribbles down her face.

A blinding bright light pierces the night from the middle of the road, causing even the man who woke me to turn toward it.

We both watch as the glowing blue light glimmers, remnants of Rook's soul letting go of this world. Freeing him.

A figure steps through the brightness and calls my name.

Crackling, garbled voices swallow me into the dark.

TWENTY-ONE

Do Right by the Miracle

I can smell the death rolling off Grandmama, even through the hospital's wired glass. Doctors say if she makes it through the night, she'll have a good chance of living.

I don't bother correcting them.

It's a slow trickling of death that lasts the night and most of the next day. Inch by inch, it claims another piece of her. I can hear her soul-song fading, a feeble, pathetic sound. I'd always imagined it to be a loud pounding of a church piano or a fierce rumbling like thunder. Instead, it's the wheezy, raspy tune of a struggling accordion.

I could have talked the death out of her pretty easily when we arrived at the hospital.

But I'm waiting.

I'm not sure for what. Maybe I want her to suffer in this state of limbo between living and dying for as long as possible. Or maybe I haven't decided if I'm going to save her at all.

Down the ICU hallway, Bone Layer snores away in one of

the stiff waiting room chairs. I have no idea how he can sleep upright like that. It was a trucker who found our wrecked vehicle wedged between the ditch and the embankment. Not five minutes behind him was Oscar, bringing Bone Layer home.

I knocked my head when we hit the tree; mild concussion, the doctor said. They gave me some pills to nip the headache. If it wasn't for Grandmama being at the edge like she is, they would have kept me overnight as well.

"How much longer?" Aunt Violet says quietly beside me as we watch the machines monitoring her mother's fading life.

"It's probably about that time," I say.

I make my decision right then and there.

"Don't do it." Aunt Violet grabs my elbow as I move to go into the room with Grandmama. "She doesn't deserve your kindness."

"No." I nod, fully agreeing with my aunt. "She does not deserve my kindness, you're right. But it's not about what she deserves. It's about who I am as a person. And I'm better than her." Without any more delay, I step into my grandmother's room to save her.

We are alone.

Her and I.

And death.

Only the occasional beep of her heart barely holding on and the *shushing* push-pull of the oxygen machine to keep us company. I close off the thin curtains to the tiny room and make my way to Grandmama's bedside.

The stench of death is different for everyone. Grandmama's has the pungent odor of vomit. Reflexively, I cover my nose and push away the nausea.

I grab her bony hand. It's cold and frail, something easily crushed. The veins running over them bulge like blue worms living underneath her crepe-thin skin.

Leaning in closer, I hear her soul-song. It's a ragged, wonky sound. I move right next to her wrinkled ear and whisper, "This will be the last time I ever use my gift. You will never have power over me again." Maybe it's my imagination, but I could swear Grandmama winced at my words.

Then it's time.

I press my forehead to hers, grazing my hand lightly over her head and down her shoulders. Then over myself in the same way. Back and forth I continue from her to me, readying her soul to connect with mine so I might lure death out of her. Then I begin to whisper the secret scriptures my papaw taught me. The Bible verses that call death forward and allow me to talk it out. Verses I'm sure Grandmama has read herself many times before, unaware of their particular power.

The room grows cold, and death rises out of Grandmama's body.

Our soul-songs—mine an unnamed hymnal, hers a pathetic accordion—wait, poised between my two open palms, ready to clamp down on death and join into one.

Then they clap together—

An electric charge sends a shock through my teeth.

A squelch louder than any microphone distortion rips through my ears, numbing my body. It knocks me back at least three feet.

Our soul-songs clash, a violent scratching that rips and claws the wheezing accordion to shreds. I press my palms against my ears, hoping the pressure will make them stop ringing.

"What the hell?" My heart in an erratic panic behind my ribs. I work my jaw a few times to get the feeling back into it and the numbness out. The buzz in my ears simmers to a low dull hum.

For some reason, my soul and Grandmama's cannot seem to find the same frequency. Some kind of adverse reaction, an interference that won't allow them to work together. It's almost like nature is telling me water and electricity don't mix. Same thing that happened with Ellis. Except I haven't been drinking today. Maybe it means I'm losing my gift? Papaw carried the gift most of his life. I've only had mine fifteen years. Seems too soon to be fizzling out.

"Gifts from God are not self-serving." Bone Layer's deep voice reverberates in the small space.

"What did you say?"

His huge frame eats up the entire space of the doorway. Politely, quietly, he steps into the room and closes the door behind himself.

"God expects us to do right by the miracle. We cannot use our spiritual powers for personal gain. Something your grand-father learned when Agnes lost her first child at birth."

I glance to Grandmama as if I expect her to confirm this. She never told me about losing a child. Not that it's some-thing people freely share.

That chirping beep marking Grandmama as still alive steadily slows. The putrid stench of death thickens in the air.

"It's in the blood," Bone Layer says, stepping closer. He presses a hand to my elbow, and I pause. "The rules that bind you to your gift are sealed within your blood. Her blood and yours, they're the same. There's no stepping around it." His words seem to tilt the world underneath my feet.

A small kick of panic spikes in my chest, the idea that I can't save Grandmama. It's silly. Grandmama has done wrong by me most of my life. But the idea that she's dying and I can't stop it...

Desperately, I turn to Bone. "But I should try again, right?"

"There's no point, child. You can't save her any more than you could save yourself." Bone Layer drapes that large arm around my shoulders. We both stand there, watching over the old woman. Frail and shriveled. Helpless. The idea that

I've feared her most of my life seems impossible, laughable, looking at her like this.

I barely hear Aunt Violet come in and join us. We three stand there, shoulder to shoulder. Watching Grandmama fade.

It doesn't take long before the beeping stops and the alarms go off, alerting the staff to the emergency. We step back, let them attempt to revive her. But her soul-song has already slipped away.

There's no bringing Agnes Wilder back.

There's an emptiness that fills the waiting room. When family dies, you should feel sad; you might even grieve. But there's not a tear among us, just this empty space in the world. I'm not sad she's dead. Nor am I happy. It's simply a thing that has happened, and the *what to do next* hasn't come to me yet.

Life in the hospital dwindles down as visitors and patients come and go at the end of the day. Only the wearied-worn few of us who've dealt with the worst of it remain. There are hospital procedures for when someone dies. Which consists mostly of waiting around for someone else to do their job and then inform you they did it.

Bone Layer sits with a wastebasket between his feet to catch the shavings of wood from whatever he's whittling. Aunt Violet flips through some housekeeping magazine I'm sure she's read at least three times now.

"I couldn't save Grandmama," I say to the floor, unable to look Aunt Violet in the eyes when I tell her. I don't know why I feel ashamed. It's not like Aunt Violet had any particular love for her mother, either. I guess I just want her to know I tried. "Bone says there's this thing about my gift," I say, pulling at a thread on my jean shorts. "It's something to do with *blood of my blood* rules of God…" Which seems unfair the more I think about it. "You can't talk the death out of kin."

Another thought skips out of me. I couldn't talk the death

out of Ellis, either. Surely, that doesn't mean…? Of course not. It had to have been the beer I drank that day.

Bone Layer blows off the excess shavings clinging to the small wood piece, drawing our attention to him. He turns the chunk of wood back and forth, examining exactly how he needs to shape it.

Sitting there, staring at him, however strange our relationship may be, I realize he's one of the few people I've got left now. And there's a good chance he'll be taken away from me, too.

"You had a hand in this," I say to Aunt Violet. She cuts me a quick look, unsure what I'm talking about. "Rutledges wouldn't have known about my Sin Eater Oil or what it could do if you hadn't helped them out. Twice." I hold up two fingers so the weight of her actions hits home a little harder.

She begins to pick at her fingernails as if they're the most interesting thing in the world right now.

"You used me as a kid." I keep going. I don't know why I'm suddenly sour about it. Had my whole life to think on it, and yet right now all that bitterness is rearing its ugly head. Grandmama's gone. Adaire, too. Bone might go to jail. And it feels like people are dying left and right around here. The whole world seems to be sliding off a cliff. The weight of this is crowding on my chest, suffocating me.

"Bone might go to jail for something that had nothing to do with him," I tell her. "Hell, they still might come after me. Did you know what Rebecca Rutledge was going to do with my Sin Eater Oil? How she planned to use it?"

Aunt Violet's crossed legs start to jog. What I'm dumping on her shoulders and forcing her to deal with—to face—sets her on edge. She fumbles in her purse for her pack of smokes, pulling them out like she's about to light up. Then she remembers where she's at—hospital waiting room—and stuffs them back in her purse.

She sighs.

Something long and deep, like the last fight in her is gone, and she's decided to lay it all out there for the good Lord to sort through.

"I didn't know for sure," Aunt Violet mumbles, still not quite ready to look at me. "But I knew she intended to do something bad with it. I wish I could say that if I knew *how* she was gonna use it, I wouldn't have given it to her. But I'd be lying to ya.

"I was bad off back then. Worse on the bottle than I ever got to be. Your uncle Doug had died, and I was stuck raising two kids on pennies with a shit job. I ain't saying that's an excuse." She gives me a clipped look. "I'm just saying my head was too clogged full of bullshit, and I wasn't thinking about how it would hurt you or him—" She thumbs over to Bone Layer. "Or nobody."

She pauses and steals a look at me, making sure I am hearing her. I am trying to, at least.

"I just needed to get through the hard part life had given me back then. Seems like the hard parts are always coming at you, though. You know? You just about get one thing dealt with, then you're thrown another. I wish I had a clean slate to work with. A clear head so I can right all my wrongs. Get my life straight for once." Aunt Violet looks at me again, really looks at me. Like she sees me and all the hurt I've been run through.

And I see her, too. She has a good heart with all the love to give, despite all the shit she's pulled. She sits up taller, a small moment of clarity washes the shame off her face, like she's suddenly remembering that life ain't over for her yet. It's not too late to fix things.

Aunt Violet's chin gets to quivering. Her eyes glass over. She cups her hands around mine. "I'm going to do right by you from now on. You hear me?" Tears slip down her cheeks.

Mine, too. "I already lost one baby girl. I don't want to lose you, too. Okay? I'm sorry. I'm so, so sorry." She pulls me in for a tight hug. I bury my face into her shoulder and let the sobs come.

The front doors to the hospital split open and Oscar steps through. I pull away from Aunt Violet, wiping my face clear.

"I came as soon as I heard," he says. The way he crosses the room so intently toward me, it almost feels like we're still dating. It's odd now to see him out of his uniform and in regular clothes. The green T-shirt looks good against his tan skin. And those broken-in pair of Levi's jeans are my favorite on him.

Aunt Violet and I stand as he approaches.

"So sorry about your mother, Violet." He brushes an empathetic hand over her arm. "You two doing alright?" Oscar asks both of us, but he's studying my eyes to get the true answer.

"It feels a bit different, now that she's gone." *Lighter,* my mind decides. It does feel lighter the more reality sets in. Hopeful, even.

"You know if there's anything y'all need, I'm just a phone call away," Oscar says. We both nod. "And, hey," he says to me, "if you feel uncomfortable staying at the house alone…" It's almost like he's about to offer me his place. "Um—" he glances at Aunt Violet "—you can probably stay with Violet. Or Raelean. Just know you have options."

I consider reminding Oscar that Bone Layer will be just out back in the smokehouse, but maybe not after the court makes their decision.

"Yeah. I'll be alright."

One of the doctors interrupts us, and Oscar gives us our space. As the doc starts talking, Davis arrives, still in his ambulance uniform from the night shift. He frantically looks around until he sees me. He gives a quick wave, letting us speak privately with the doctor.

The doctor wants to know which funeral home we'd like to send the body to. An odd horrified look moves across his face as we inform him we take care of our dead ourselves. It's a rare practice, but it's still legal in Georgia. I probably won't do it ever again, but it's our way of things, and I know it's what she would want. Besides, I have a few particulars I want to send Grandmama off into the afterlife with.

It'll take a few days with the paperwork that must be filled out before he can release her body to us. Aunt Violet follows the doctor to make everything official.

As soon as they step away, Davis swoops in with a big hug.

"Girl, you have been through way too much," he says into my hair. I appreciate the fact he holds on a little longer.

"I got your message. I was on call over in Camden. I had no idea the wreck was you. I came as soon as my shift ended," he says as he releases me. "Don't worry about the truck. I used the wrecker and hauled it back to the junkyard. Looks like a busted axle, but we can get that fixed. How's your grandmother?"

There's a blank look on my face, and I don't know how to say the words. So instead I answer, "I couldn't save her."

Davis gives me another long hug, telling me he's sorry. I've never understood why people apologized when someone dies. Sorry only goes so far with grief, and it's never far enough.

"Today was a rough day for you. When you're feeling a little better, let's talk some more." Davis's words are a bit ominous.

"Talk more about what?"

He hems and haws, uncomfortable.

"Spit it out already," I burst at him.

"Okay." He holds his hands up in innocence. "I found something out that helps us. Helps with Adaire's case. Wanda, my friend at the courthouse, called me back."

I straighten at this bit of news.

"She got me the VIN number to Lorelei's car."

As a man wheels his elderly mother through the hospital lobby, Davis tips his head for us to head out front away from prying ears.

It's muggy outside with the heat of the evening mixing with last night's rain.

Davis waits until the hospital's sliding doors close before he continues. "I was able to track the car to a salvage lot in Ohio. I called the owner of the lot, and he confirmed he had it."

"What kind of damage?" My pulse jackhammers inside my ears.

"He found no visible signs of blood or hair from 'hitting a deer.'" He air-quotes his words.

"Okay. Lorelei probably cleaned off any visible evidence on the grill. Maybe there's something on the underside?"

Davis nods. "That's what I was thinking, too. Then I realized, even if they do find something, it could very well be from an animal."

I uh-hmm in agreement, but my gut is telling me otherwise.

"But then he told me something I didn't expect," Davis says. I freeze. "He said whatever the car hit, it rubbed yellow paint on the bumper."

The realization hits me. "Adaire's banana bike."

Blood or hair evidence would be nice, but they could match the yellow paint to the bike. Which I'm pretty sure Wyatt put in their tool shed out back.

This piece of news lights a hot flame in me. "I knew it," I say through gritted teeth. "I knew that bitch killed her."

"It's enough to reopen Adaire's case and interrogate Lorelei," Davis points out. That and the fact he and I discovered Adaire wasn't even hit in the location where the accident happened. Not to mention Stone's car doesn't have a scratch on it.

Davis and I quiet up when Deputy Rankin strolls past us

into the hospital. *What is that asshole doing here?* I think to myself.

"There's more," I say after the deputy is inside. I tell Davis about walking the veil and witnessing the sins of the dead. Sure, it's not evidence for a court, but it definitely confirms that what I saw in that Sin Eater Oil haze was true. Lorelei mowing Adaire down with her car like she did.

"Why?" Davis shrugs. "Why would she have it out for Adaire? What'd Adaire ever do to her?"

That's a great question. And, before today—with my grandmother dying—I probably couldn't have answered that.

"I can't talk the death out of kin," I say to Davis. "That's why I couldn't save my grandmother." At Davis's scrunched brow, I add, "What if it's why I couldn't save Ellis Rutledge? It's never not worked before, and Bone told me about the rules with kin."

Davis sways back slightly at this. His eyes bold with shock.

"Maybe Adaire figured something out that got her killed. I think she found evidence that could prove Ellis was kin. Did you bring the package?"

Davis nods. From his EMT bag, he pulls out the brown paper package Adaire hid for him before she died. The birthday gift he believes was meant for him to find months ago.

Both of us stare at the unopened package like it's a ghost.

"Open it." It's a gentle request, really. In my heart of hearts, if I believed this was some private gift for Davis, I wouldn't be asking him this. But I think Adaire hid it in his toolbox, knowing she was going to die and preserving the evidence for when she did, because she knew he'd believe me, knew he would help. And she couldn't risk Grandmama finding it somewhere at our house.

Davis's throat bobs with a single swallow, and he pulls the ribbon off the package, unfolding the brown paper and revealing a stack of papers. We each take one off the top and begin to read. They're letters, written in the same handwriting as the one I saw Adaire with in that dream as she stood in Stone Rutledge's office. Beautiful, soulful writings, each signed by or addressed to the same two people.

Love letters between my mother and Stone Rutledge. If I was a betting man, I'd guess Adaire found them at that farmhouse in that old button tin. There's fifteen or so letters. We sit in silence, reading each one.

They had loved each other for a time. Both acknowledged they lived worlds apart; her a simple country girl, him with a family fortune off studying law. He seemed torn about which life to live, but leaving his family would mean cutting ties financially. My mother worried that would make him bitter in time.

"She was nine when they first kissed." I smile at the thought and hand Davis the letter so he can read it. "A graveyard kiss."

Remember our first kiss? I was nine. Your grandfather had died and Bone Layer took me with him to dig the grave. It rained that day, just like it should at a funeral. A slow drizzle that guaranteed you'd feel the sadness all the way down in your bones.

There was something mesmerizing about your green eyes. Cool crisp color that shivered me plum through.

At the close of the service, I watched your father nudge you. It was a tough nudge like he was saying enough was enough with your crying. It felt wrong the way he yanked on your arm before you were done saying your goodbyes. Like he was embarrassed by your grief.

I don't know what made me do it.

I suppose love, though I didn't know I loved you yet.

But something bit me, like a horsefly in the heat of summer, and I popped off Bone Layer's truck bed, and plucked one of those perfect white long stem roses from a flower spread and ran it over to you.

Your mama looked at me like a leper with my muddy bare feet and scraggly jean overalls. Her smile, lemon-puckered and strained at the sight of me. There I was looking like a feral child and all y'all were dressed in your best black clothes. I was flooded with embarrassment, ready to hightail it out of there, tuck and run. Then you kissed me. Quick as lightning. Lips to lips. You stole my heart that day.

I stood there, feet sinking into the graveyard mud and watched as your shiny black Studebaker drove away. You looked back at me through the window. The white rose tight in your fist.

I knew right then I was going to love you for the rest of my life. But I think it's time I let you go.

As the letter goes on, my mother tells him a long-distance relationship probably isn't the best, since Stone was a few years older, already in college. So she breaks it off with him. I wonder if my mama was just trying to beat him to the punch, fearing he'd choose wealth over her in the end.

Months later, Mama found out she was pregnant, around the same time Stone got engaged to Rebecca. Happened quick—like he was trying to heal his broken heart.

"Stone told your mother Rebecca fit his family's lifestyle better than her. Ouch," Davis says. "He told her it was too late to go backward and he had already moved on." He's not wrong, but I can see—there's hurt in his words, too.

Davis finishes reading the last letter. "Do you really think Stone is your father?"

I shrug. "It sure looks like it."

"Okay." Davis nods, digesting this. "You're Stone's 'illegitimate' child. Who cares? Why kill Adaire for figuring that out? Rich people always have skeletons in their closets. The Rutledges are so established and in deep with this town, would it even scathe their reputation?"

"I don't think it's about preserving their reputation," I say with the shake of my head. "Those letters prove my mother and Stone had an intimate relationship. What if it's more than the letters? What if Stone had wanted to take care of my mother, give her some money or something?"

"Or," Davis began slowly, the thought forming as he spoke, "what if he left some money for you?"

"Me?"

"Look, it seems like your mom and Stone couldn't be together, not in the way they wanted, right? He was engaged already, clearly this was something they kept hidden. And if he knew about you, but couldn't be there for you in any concrete way, maybe he wanted to be there for you in the only way he could—with some money."

"Well then, where is it? I certainly haven't seen any Rutledge money come my way."

He gives this some thought.

"Maybe that's what Adaire found out about? Money for you—I can't imagine Lorelei is the sharing kind of person. That family has never been generous. Doubtful she'd want you to have any of it. Maybe she didn't want you to know who you really were."

Greed will make folks do all kinds of wrong, Papaw used to say. I nod, letting the idea take root.

"You think Lorelei faked her father's suicide?" Davis asks.

*Our father—my father—*skips through my mind. I try the words on for size, and they just don't fit. It feels like a truth for someone else.

I shake my head. "I don't think so. Stone knew she killed Adaire, and he covered it up for her. And when Ellis found out, I think Lorelei killed him. Or at least she tried to stop him from telling, and he died in the process. I don't even know if she cared. And I believe that's what pushed Stone over the edge, knowing she had killed a second time. A daughter he could not control. One he could not save. Sheriff said there wasn't a suicide note. What if there was, but Lorelei found it first and destroyed it?" Probably something we'll never find out. "It's gotta be her who's trying to make me look guilty with that Sin Eater Oil—though I haven't figured out how she got ahold of it yet. But Ellis knew her secret. So did Stone. Ellis wasn't going to let Lorelei get away with it. And you know what?" I lean into Davis, all my gumption revving itself up. "I'm not going to let her get away with any of it, either. Give me your keys."

I open my palm to Davis.

If I want justice for Adaire, I'm going to have to take it myself.

Davis steps back, wary, as if I've just asked him to rob a bank. "Why? So you can do something stupid?"

"No. So I can finally give Adaire the closure her soul deserves." This softens him. I can see it in the way his posture wilts and how he ponders the idea that maybe Adaire—or at least her spirit—is not at rest.

I jab my open hand at him again. "Can I borrow your truck or not?"

If I have to, I'll get Aunt Violet's car. She'd probably drive me to Sugar Hill herself. I've just about decided that's a better option when Davis hands over the keys to the Boneyard's wrecker.

Determination and fight rise up in me as I make my way across the hospital's parking lot. I'm not leaving that mansion until Lorelei owns up to what she did.

After I jump in the truck, I'm about to crank the ignition when something sitting in the front seat catches my eye.

The little red suitcase.

Davis must have rescued it from our truck when he towed it to the junkyard.

In light of everything that's happened the last twenty-four hours, it honestly slipped my mind.

But there the suitcase is, ready and waiting.

TWENTY-TWO

Death Be on Your Tongue

Insects swarm a lamppost in the parking lot. It casts down a harsh beam on Davis's tow truck. I lightly smile at one of the nurses who's on her way inside. From the seat next to me, I slide the little red suitcase into my lap.

My thumbs poise over the metal clasps. The latches spring open with a bounced *thung*.

I don't know what I was hoping for, really. A treasure trove of something; not sure of what, though.

There's only one item inside.

A single manila envelope with an official law office logo printed in the return-address portion. My mother's name typed in the center with our home address. I tilt the postage stamp in the dim light. The postmark is dated two weeks after my birth.

Inside, legal documents my mother signed, promising to keep my father's identity a secret in exchange for a huge chunk of money.

"Holy shit." I sit back against the truck seat and give my mind a second to digest the number. "What in the world would I do with a million dollars?" I huff a laugh. I continue reading the paperwork.

The money is supposed to sit in a trust fund, earning interest, until I turn twenty-five—just one year away. Every year thereafter, an additional fifty-thousand dollar bonus to stay quiet.

"Wow."

There, at the bottom of the page, two signatures.

Darbee May Wilder.

Stone Ellison Rutledge.

I don't know what hits me harder—that both my parents gave me up as easily as trash or learning for certain who my father is and knowing he's dead.

I tell myself I don't give a damn. Two people who loved each other enough to make a child but didn't leave enough behind when the child came.

But then maybe I'm looking at this wrong.

If this was about money for my mother, why set up a trust fund solely for me? Why not get a chunk for herself, too? My mom doesn't have two nickels to rub together. This couldn't have been about money for her. My father signed this document because *he* chose money and the power of his family's status over her.

Over us.

She had some wild oats to sow—heartache will do that to you. That's what Aunt Violet told me when I asked about my father.

So it was too painful for her to stay. I can't imagine how I would feel, looking at my baby every day and being reminded of the love I could never have. Somehow, this sliver of a thought cracks the surface of this grudge I've been holding on to ever since she left, and I can almost understand it.

But Stone—even if he loved my mama once, he chose money. I want to hate him, I do. He cared about me enough to set up this trust fund, just not enough to be my father. My heart just can't square how I should feel.

But that family, especially how they've behaved these last few months, leaves a foul taste in my mouth. I wonder if Rebecca forced my father to have nothing to do with me. She forced her own sister to abort those babies, why not make Stone disown me? Hell, I bet she knows exactly what Lorelei did and doesn't even give a shit. It's impossible to believe I share the same blood as these monsters. They snatched Adaire from me. For what? Money? Money that was coming my way, anyway?

These people.

My sister.

She killed my cousin. Murdered my best friend.

The more I churn this over, the angrier I get. It lights a fire in me. A white-hot heat that eats up every last ounce of my humanity. I want to make Lorelei Rutledge pay.

The engine revs.

Gear thrown into Drive.

I peel out of the parking lot.

There's no staff in the kitchen when I slip in the mansion's back door, but I hear two murmuring voices as they close down the house for the evening. The only cars out front are Stone's red Corvette and a beat-up sedan that's probably one of the staff's. It's awfully late for Mrs. Rutledge to not be home, but I bet she's dealing with Gabby, now that she's been taken away to a mental hospital. Which means there's only one Rutledge upstairs.

I dip into the shadows of the hall and wait for the last of the staff to lock up the house and leave for the night. Once they're gone, I sneak up the private stairs, taking them two at a time, to the third floor. My blood rising with each step.

Lorelei took my cousin.

She took a brother I never knew I had.

She's the reason my father killed himself.

The house key Becky gave me still works, and I let myself in. Moonlight barely sweeps across the receiving room. Opposite of Gabby's tearoom, a thin light bleeds from underneath a door down the hallway.

"Hello, Lorelei," I say as I open the door.

She flinches in her father's desk chair. She eyes me up and down, assessing. Then she relaxes once she decides I'm probably not a threat. "Victoria," she casually calls out as if I'm some nuisance she needs the staff to remove.

I smirk. "Oh, honey, they're gone. It's just you and me now."

Panic flits her eyes back to the door.

"You're not going anywhere." I step into the room and close the door behind me.

She lunges for the telephone on the desk. I yank the cord from the wall before she can reach it. I toss the cord to the floor, and she leans back into her seat.

It feels strange being in Stone's office. I've never physically been here, only seen the room during that Sin Eater Oil haze. How incredibly accurate it was.

Oak paneling stretches along the walls all the way to the ceiling. Those monstrous law books and shelves still lord over the room. Even the maroon leather chair is a beast to contend with. Right there between Lorelei and me, the very desk where Stone Rutledge signed away his parental rights. It confirms all the sins the dead showed me were true.

Lorelei glares, jaw clenched tight, scathing. "What do you want?"

"The truth." I plop down in the receiving chair in front of the desk and kick my feet on top of it. "So," I start, never feeling more alive than right now. "Tell me exactly why you ran my cousin over?"

"I didn't. My father—"

"Liar!" I jam my foot against the desk so hard the green Tiffany lamp wobbles, threatening to topple over.

"Let's try this again. *Why* did you run my cousin over?"

Lorelei watches me a long calculated minute, contemplating exactly how she's going to respond. There's only two years between her and I, but somehow I feel so much older. Maybe that's the difference between hard living and being pampered all your life.

She slinks back into that desk chair; her glare dripping with hate. "What is it you think you know?"

I lean on the edge of the desk and square her with a look. "I know Stone lied to the police and covered up your little hit-and-run. I know Gabby was with you when you did it." From my pocket, I pull out the slinky gold chain and lazily coil it onto the desk. "I know you killed your brother."

That bob in her throat is my sweet reward.

I let her sit on that egg a bit, but it doesn't take long before she's grinding her teeth.

"Ellis was weak. Second from the womb always are. He was too soft to live up to the Rutledge name. He didn't have the stomach to do what it takes to protect this family."

It's shocking to hear how callous she is. She doesn't even deny killing him. "The hardest part," I say, "is for the life of me I could not figure out where you got that poison to pour down your father's throat to make me look guilty. But wait a minute." I pause, mocking contemplation. "What I should have been asking myself is how would you even know that poison existed, much less know that it could be tied to me?"

The worried look in her eyes says I'm on the right track.

"Rebecca." I drop her mother's name like the final ace of spades to win the poker game. "Those black veins of poison still sprawl across Gabby's belly like a spiderweb. Curious kids ask questions. Questions I'm sure your mother answered. Who would have guessed she had some of that poison left over after all these years.

"Asking you why you killed my cousin is more of a rhetorical question. Because we both already know the answer. But there's a little something you didn't know." I pull the folded papers out of my back pocket. "What sucks for you, little sister, is our father already made sure I get a piece of the pie." I drop the legal documents on the desk in front of her. It doesn't take her eyes more than a few seconds to gobble up the shocking truth she had no idea about.

I'm about half a second away from doing a victory lap when Lorelei smirks.

Somehow, this sets me at unease. Like maybe all my assumptions and conclusions from everything I uncovered are somehow wrong.

"Go ahead." She calmly slides the papers back to me. "By all means, take these documents and go running to the police. Tell them I killed your cousin to keep the fortune. That I poured *your* poison down my father's throat to set you up for murder. You have my blessing. Please, tell the sheriff everything." Lorelei fans her hands open wide.

I'm a bit stunned, not sure why she's making such a show or what she's trying to get at. Of course, I'm going to tell the sheriff everything I know.

"Are you sure you want to do that, though? Because it looks to me like you didn't read the fine print. If you or anyone in your family reveal who your father is, then you don't inherit a *dime*." She punctuates the last word as if that little fact matters to me.

I don't give a fuck about the money. I'm about to open my mouth to say just that, and she keeps going.

"Look, here's the thing," Lorelei continues. "Stone was a bastard of a man who couldn't give two shits about Ellis or me, and apparently not about you, either." She says this rather nonchalantly. "Sure, he did his fatherly duty and covered up my little…blunder." A wry smile slips onto that smug-ass face of hers. "Then he found out my blunder was just a little bit on purpose and he freaked out. Couldn't believe I would do such a thing, and over something as trivial as money. But you try going without once you've had a taste, seen what life can be. I wasn't about to let any more than necessary slip away, not if we didn't have to. You know how fast money can go? When your brother, the artist, is setting himself up to be nothing more than a drain on family resources, your aunt needs special round-the-clock care, and the tours of the mansion barely bring in enough to cover the electric bill. I was doing him a favor. Did you a favor, too!" She throws her hands up as if she's given me a gift. "Both of us would be out a lot more money. This way you get a little, and I get a little more, it's a win-win." She leans forward. "So you're not going to tell a damn soul what I did," she says through gritted teeth.

My nails bite into palms as I stew in a pit of my own anger. She sits back, confident she's bought my silence.

"So why not buy Adaire off? Why not throw her a little bit, too, keep her quiet. You didn't have to kill her."

"I didn't plan to, but she came in here one day with *proof*. That letter that spoke to how much they loved each other, how she was carrying his child, how she planned to keep you. Adaire knew too much, enough to tell the whole town who you really were. Father tried to reason with her, told her she'd be hurting you and your future. But she wouldn't hear it, left here in a rush and was on her way to tell you everything. And I couldn't have that, couldn't have her ruining our name and reputation.

"Father would have never won a reelection once everyone found out. My mother would have divorced him and we wouldn't survive a disgraced mayor and a nasty divorce. We already have a crazy lady in the family. Who's going to pay money to tour the once-esteemed Sugar Hill? Plantations are already falling out of favor with folks. If the tour buses stop coming, and more and more of our money is being leeched out to dirty little beggars like you, where would that leave me? You've no idea what it takes to keep this family together, what it takes to keep our heads above water. Father just smiled through it all, through the bills that piled up and the debts, through my mother's drinking binges when she'd disappear for weeks, locked away in her room—imagine that, yet they called her sister crazy, said she was the one with a problem. I did what I had to do for my family, what do you know about that?"

I fall back in my chair in disbelief. "So it really was just about the money—that was enough of a reason to kill my cousin? Your own brother."

"That was an accident. He wouldn't listen to me, just like Adaire. He planned to tell the cops everything. He'd have given all our money to you if it were up to him, he didn't care a lick for it. Imagine that—Ellis, the weak link from day one, thinking he knows how to take care of our family better than me! He couldn't see the bigger picture the way I could. And Adaire as good as sealed her own fate, running off like she did. I only wanted to talk. Barely nudged her tire to get her attention, but we were going too fast—"

My blood begins to boil, I know what's coming next.

Lorelei huffs a laugh. "You should have seen the way the bike twisted around her broken legs."

Anger jolts through my body.

"It was wrong to let her suffer like that. So I put her out of her misery and ran over her properly the second time—"

I don't even understand how it happens.

One minute, I'm on this side of the desk. The next my hand is gripped around Lorelei's throat.

"Shut your fucking mouth." My words spit in her face. She scrabbles at my hand, trying to loosen my grip.

The murderous death stain of Adaire seeps from Lorelei's pores. It grows deep inside her like a black fern, uncoiling itself.

I taste it now, the sweet lick of anger. Like a blue flame, I feed on it. Except it isn't anger that burns inside me. Or rage.

It's death.

Death that has rotted away in my bones from years of death-talking.

It lives there in the marrow and blood. Patiently waiting. I draw upon it, the power of my death-talking, and let it find the evil that resides in Lorelei Rutledge. I never considered that if I could talk the death out of someone, maybe I could talk the death into them.

So I listen.

I listen for that exact sound I heard when her twin brother Ellis died. That sweet violin of sadness from his soul-song. Except Lorelei's violin is sharp and shrill. The winding grind of the Devil's fiddle, playing a tune for the demons that live inside her. I know the second I find it because the glass in the chandelier begins to rattle. The objects around the room vibrate as I tune into her soul-song.

I glare at Lorelei under hooded eyes. She gasps as I hook my deathly finger into her black soul. Open and vulnerable, ready for me to fill it with death.

Then something soft touches my shoulder. *Don't.*

A gentle, ghostly hand that draws out all the anger from me. It tells me everything is going to be okay. That I can let it go now. Nothing more needs to be done. No one else needs to be hurt. It's finished.

I release Lorelei from my grasp.

She coughs and sputters, trying to catch her breath. I leave her there on the floor. I need to get away from her, this house, and anything to do with these vile people. It doesn't matter what those papers say; these people aren't my family. Never were. Never will be. I'm down the stairs and making my way through the kitchen when I hear Lorelei raging behind me. Something about how lawyers and judges won't believe trash like me.

A hard whack clips the back of my head, and I stumble forward. A blue floral vase crashes against the floor.

What the hell?

I look back just long enough to see her lunge for the butcher knife. I bolt out the back door and crash into Davis.

"You're here? But how?"

Blue lights from Oscar's Bronco flicker, as he steps out of the driver's side.

"Please tell me you didn't murder her," Davis mumbles to me.

Lorelei rushes out the door behind me, knife gripped tight, screaming profanities, then she stops cold when she sees Oscar.

"Arrest her!" Lorelei points to me. "She assaulted me and broke the restraining order."

Both her claims are true. I press a hand to the knot rising on the back of my head, grateful it's not bleeding at least.

Oscar walks over. I sigh, holding out my hands for him to take me in because I'm done with all this. Ready for it be over.

Then Lorelei is shoved up against the wall, her face pushed into the brick building as her hands are yanked painfully behind her.

"You won't get a dime!" she screams as Oscar locks the cuffs on her.

"Lorelei Rutledge," Oscar boastfully calls out. "You have the right to remain silent…" He slips me a smug grin.

TWENTY-THREE

Feel It in My Bones

Grandmama's people came from Appalachia a long way back. Taking care of the dead was the way of things.

Aunt Violet and I tie her body down to the heirloom laying board with the twine Bone Layer gives us, so her body doesn't sit upright when the bone cracking starts. Her body is still cold after being in the hospital morgue these last few days.

I lick the tips of my fingers to thread the needle, then I dip the fine string in dove's blood. Carefully, I stitch her frail, thin eyelids shut. Zigzagged across twice, so she can't see her way through the otherworld or this again.

Three things I stuff inside her mouth. Cocklebur seeds, so their prickly spines bring her uncomfortable suffering for all eternity. A crumpled strip of paper cut from her Bible; Galatians 6:8. Most fitting.

"Those who live only to satisfy their own sinful nature will harvest decay and death from that sinful nature..."

The last item—the heart of a freed chicken—so the Devil can welcome her home.

Four safety pins, blackened by my Sin Eater Oil, pin Grandmama's mouth shut. When it's time to remove her innards, we fill her with ash so her body knows exactly where her soul should stay at rest, in the fiery pit of hell. Aunt Violet stands off to the side, chain-smoking, refusing to watch as her mother heads for the afterlife.

Davis helps us move her and the heirloom laying board to the pine box Bone Layer built, something he forged many a year ago, waiting for this day.

"You ready?" Bone stands in the doorway, shovel in his hand, sweat across his brow.

The three of us manage down the short porch steps with the small pine box, Grandmama not even weighing a whole buck. The coffin itself made from thin cheap pine. On purpose, so that it won't last past a year. That's the way we want it, the earth to gobble her up as soon as possible.

We stand over the hole in the ground.

Deep enough to cover, not enough for forever.

It's a patch of worthless land you couldn't grow a garden on even if you wanted to. An unmarked grave that will eventually be consumed by vegetation and the forest, and the existence of Agnes Wilder will simply disappear.

Grave dirt scatters across the lid as I make a small prayer to the Lord that he treat her as she treated those in her life. Then I ask him to give her what the Bible promises, that ye shall reap what you sow. I'm certain my prayers will be heard. I can feel it in my bones.

From the driveway, gravel *crackles* under tires. Bone Layer and I both turn to see Oscar's Bronco pull up.

"Give me a minute," I say as Bone finishes covering her grave while Aunt Violet stands there still staring—just staring.

We meet halfway, Oscar and me, under the guarding limbs

of the oak tree. There's a measure of silence as he scans the house and yard.

"Place looks good," he says, though I know he can't quite put his finger on why. It looks pretty much the same but feels so different without Grandmama.

The energy lighter, calmer. Freer.

"Did you find Lorelei's car?"

He nods. "Yeah, we did. I had the local law enforcement up there in Ohio document it into evidence. Hair and blood were found under the carriage. We're getting it tested for human or animal. Good chance they'll follow through with charges, once the lab work comes back. Just so you know, it was the sheriff who pushed for me—and only me—to handle Lorelei's car. Looks like Deputy Rankin's report after Adaire's accident wasn't exactly accurate."

I truly couldn't imagine Sheriff Johns would allow such corruption under his watch. But I also believe people with as little integrity as Deputy Rankin can be bought—bought by the likes of Lorelei Rutledge, from the sound of it.

"You said you wanted to give me something?" he asks. I wave for him to follow me inside.

"I was going through Grandmama's closet to find something to bury her in."

Oscar waits in the living room while I disappear into Grandmama's bedroom.

It was weird being in her space, pilfering through her things; something I would have never dared to do while she was living. I didn't even realize how many of Papaw's clothes she still kept in the back of her closet. It's amazing how something as simple as clothing could bring back such vivid memories. Like his favorite blue dress shirt he wore to church that brought out the sapphire in his eyes. Or a brown-plaid coat he used in winter when he worked on the tractor.

Small things I'd forgotten over time that came rushing back at the sight of them.

I probably wouldn't have noticed it, had it not been for the folded piece of paper sticking out of the front coat pocket. Picture of a boy tugging at my curiosity.

A black corduroy jacket, something a young boy would wear. The bumpy ridged texture like brail underneath my fingertips. My thumb rubs over the lapel's copper button. A missing patch of fabric ripped from the cuff sleeve tells a tragic story. One I know well.

Stuffed in the pocket a funeral service brochure for a William Robert Rivers, from Blackbeak Falls, Tennessee. Called "Will" by his family and friends. He was the beloved and only son of Jesse and Lola Rivers. Taken from this world at the age of nine after drowning in the Cumberland River.

Right there, smack-dab on the front of the brochure, Rook's big happy grin. His third-grade photo—or rather Will's. It was the proof I needed to know that Rook was more than something in my head.

A boy did drown.

A family did bury him.

And a girl brought him back to life in her imagination.

Between him being from Blackbeak Falls and that crow feather I wished on, no wonder my mind made Rook into this spectacular creature.

R for Rook.

R for Rivers.

I pull the initial R ring off my pinky finger and hold it up to the funeral brochure. It's the same one nine-year-old Will is wearing in the photo.

My young mind told me a crow brought this little trinket to me, but I must have taken it off his finger—like a dirty thief. It's not mine. It never was. It's something that belongs to his family.

"In the back of her closet, I found this," I say to Oscar who stands near the doorway. His deputy Stetson hat politely in his hands, abiding by the Southern gentleman rule of no hats indoors. "I found this coat with this brochure and ring in the pocket," I lie. But how I found the ring doesn't matter. I hand him the brochure; he stiffens lightly as he reads it. Then he eyes me, trying to read what I know. I don't let on that I saw his *Unknown drowning victim???* note on my file.

"I think Papaw found a boy a long time ago? It was right around the time he died. I bet he meant to get this back to the family, but it probably got tucked away in the closet to address after his funeral but was forgotten." I can't attest to that for certain, but that's what I believe to be true. My heart still stings from the realization there never was a Rook. Only a Will.

"Maybe you could get it back to his family somehow?" I ask, handing him the ring as well.

"Yeah, sure." He nods, seeming as somber as anyone might feel when discussing a drowned child.

"I believe this was his coat." I hold it out for him to take.

Oscar holds the boy's funeral service brochure and ring in his hand. "You know," he says somewhat pensive, "this boy's file came across my desk recently." When he looks up at me, I keep my face thoughtful and interested, not letting on that I know he was actually looking into the case. "The family never found the boy's body."

Something about hearing these words sends my heart into my throat.

"They looked and looked for weeks, never found the kid. They just ended up burying an empty casket." He holds up the coat with a grateful gesture. "I think this coat and the boy's ring might give them a bit of closure. Thank you for this."

I nod, agreeing with him. But inside my head, I'm stumbling over the fact that they never found a body and what that could mean. My imagination, something I tried to let go of, flutters back to life.

"Where ya headed?" Oscar nods toward my packed bags sitting by the door, disrupting my thoughts.

A bear of a suitcase—full of my clothes and some of Adaire's vivid creations. Then that tiny red suitcase, now filled with all the memories I hold dear: the witching coins my papaw gave me, Adaire's conjuring cards, a few of the fantasy books she loved. And my wind chime, trinkets the crow brought me, even if only in my imagination.

And my asphidity bag, full of medicinal herbs, a very old recipe box, and two bone-tooth keys.

"I'm going to see the ocean," I tell him.

"Which one?" Oscar asks. I sigh, thinking about Adaire and my pledge to drive one coast to the other.

"Both," I answer. "I've always wanted to see the ocean."

From the front door, Davis clears his throat. We both turn to him. "You want to do this?" He taps his watch; his second shift is starting soon.

More casual pleasantries as I thank Oscar again for coming by and him wishing me safe travels.

"I've gotta get to work, sweetie," Aunt Violet says after Oscar leaves. She pulls me into a long hug. "I expect a postcard from every city you stop in, okay? Go out there and have a little fun for me, too. Don't worry about things around here, I'll watch over our girl while you're gone." We both look over to Adaire's grave.

Davis stands by it with a bouquet of daisies in his hand. Adaire's buried right next to our Papaw, who's properly back in the ground where he belongs.

It's strange to think I've lost four family members in a span of two months. Sure, I didn't know Ellis or Stone were kin at the time. It might have been nice to have a little brother, though. I'd like to think him and I would have gotten along alright. I thought about going to his graveside; maybe it would ease that ache of never knowing him. But he's buried next to a father I'm not ready to forgive just yet.

Aunt Violet kisses my forehead as she leaves. I turn to Davis. "I need to grab something first," I say as I head off into the woods. "I promise I'll be fast!" I add, after he grumbles about the time.

You can't properly say goodbye to your best friend without leaving her with something from your childhood. It feels fitting to give Adaire some extra love seeing as Davis is moving down to Texas soon. And me leaving Black Fern with no plans to return.

The old chain-link camper ladder clatters against the kudzu vine wall as I climb the rungs to our old cave. A little bit of Dolly and Patsy will do just the trick.

TWENTY-FOUR

Tuggin' at Your Heartstrings

The gathering of birds begins as dusk rolls in. A black waterfall dribbles from the sky as hundreds of them settle in the trees.

The hour of crows.

When the day is no longer and the night is not yet.

Davis and I stand over Adaire's grave. The mounded soil already settled. Tiny violets carpet the top. I wedge the two records in front of her headstone. It's nothing too flashy, just a rectangle with her name and the dates framing her short life. I tuck a small crow feather in between.

Davis lays the daisies on the ground. "Give 'em hell, baby." He kisses his fingers, then presses his palm to the earth. "I'll let you say your goodbyes." Davis barely gets these words out before he excuses himself, somberly walking over to the edge of the woods. His shoulders shake as he tries to gather himself.

"I wouldn't insult you by bringing you roses." I hold up the thistle I found in the woods. "An homage to our Scottish roots." I lay the purple prickly flower at the head of her grave and sit crossed-legged on the grass.

"He looks good in a uniform, I have to admit," I say slyly to Adaire, looking over my shoulder at Davis. "He's moving to Galveston, it's way more metro than Black Fern. Mrs. Yancey sold the junkyard, and they have family down there. That's why they chose it. Don't be mad at him. It hurts, you know, staying here. Because everywhere we turn, we see you. He's gotta move on. We all do.

"I don't want to leave you," I whisper into my palm, the words rattling in my chest. "I can't say goodbye. Not to you. Never. But there's nothing keeping me here anymore." The house I've lived in my entire life looks tiny and frail now, empty. It's a reminder of all that happened—good and bad—to me in Black Fern, and that's not something I need anymore.

"Bone's sticking around, though, to make sure you and Papaw are never alone. I know, I know, he's not a prize to be won, but he's a good man…deep, deep, *deep* down under all that stoic silence. Plus, you have Papaw, right?

"I won't forget you. I can never forget you. Jesus, who could forget those freckles on your face, like dirt they were. I swear to God if my kids inherit that chicken-scratched hair of yours—" I laugh. "Oh, Aunt Violet cleared out your closet— a part of her *get-sober-clean-up-my-life* commitment. I think she means it this time. I might have rescued a piece or two for myself. Felt sorry for the church's free-clothes bin. Who knows, maybe I'll start a flannel plaid miniskirt trend down in Florida." I pull the little seashell out of my pocket and fiddle with it between my fingers.

"I'm going to the beach, like we always planned. I hear warm sand feels amazing under your bare feet. With nothing but water to see for miles." I set the seashell my mama gave me on the granite of her headstone. "It won't be the same without you." I let the weight of those words seep into the earth. "But I think you'll be pissed if I don't go—or that's the story I'm going to tell myself."

"Good lord," Raelean hollers from the car. "Are you saying goodbye or reciting the Declaration of Independence over there?"

"Oh, yeah." I wince at the grave. "I'm kind of taking Raelean with me. We've grown closer, but…" More words get clogged in my throat. "We all have a journey and ours just happens to be headed the same direction. She has a marine down in Destin she's been talking to," I say from the side of my mouth.

Davis begins to walk over, his fingers shuffling the rim of his new EMT hat, needing to get to work.

"Don't get yourself kicked out, okay?" I kiss the tips of my fingers and blow Adaire a kiss goodbye.

Davis dips his head to make contact with my glassy eyes. "Wherever we go, she will always be with us," he says. The soft sounds of the grass crunch under our feet as we walk toward the house.

"I know." A piece of her is within us all. Those she truly loved. A tear slips from my eye, but it has nothing to do with saying goodbye to Adaire.

"We'll be alright." Davis slips his arm around my shoulder, giving me a side hug.

We will.

I turn and grab both of his hands and squeeze them tight. "I need you to do something for me."

"Of course. Anything." But his expression goes wary as he realizes this isn't going to be a *can-you-water-the-plants-while-I'm-away* type of request.

"I feel like you're about to deliver some bad news," he says.

"I hope you don't think it's bad." A few more tears slip free. I feel silly for even letting myself be emotional, because I've never been more sure of anything in all my life. I think these tears are relief, relief of the burden I'm about to be free of.

"I want to give you something."

Davis's throat bobs as he swallows. The gravity of this moment dawning on him.

"I want to give you my gift."

"Oh, hey, wait up." He steps back a little unsure.

"Only if you want it," I reassure him.

"Well, yeah, who wouldn't? What you can do is incredible. Miraculous."

"Yes." I nod. "But I'm exhausted. There's a burden of duty that comes with it, I'm not going to lie." I explain to him how it eventually took Papaw and that he must pass it on to someone else before it does. This gift is truly just a gift now, without Grandmama manipulating people with my Sin Eater Oil. I gather up his hands in mine. "But with you becoming an EMT, you could save so many more lives than I ever could. You have such a passion for helping others. Think of all the good you could do."

The idea of what I'm saying to him slowly sinks in. His face lights up, marveling over the possibilities of it. He straightens a little taller, rising to the task. His eyes meet with mine. He looks at me, truly looks at me. I see the dead certainty of a yes before he even says it.

I don't tell him there's another reason for me wanting to give away my gift. I truly believe in my heart of hearts, that somewhere out there, Rook could exist as simply a human again. Free from the burden of the crow, no longer the walker of souls. But only if I were to pass on my gift. Even if he's just a figment of my imagination, at the very least it will help me let him go.

Davis releases a heavy breath. "Okay." He smarts a nod.

If it wasn't for how firm he says it, a declaration to do right by the miracle, I would press him to be sure. But I can see it in the way Davis pulls back his shoulders and grips my hands a little firmer, readying himself.

"Okay, then." I lightly smile at him. "There are a few rules…"

If you tell someone the secret scriptures, your gift is gone. You can only pass it to someone of the opposite sex. If you die with your gift, it disappears forever. You can't talk the death out of someone twice.

"And you can't save your kin."

Then I tell him what I can do. And how to use the secret Bible verses to do it.

The gift jumps out of me and into him.

"It's hotter than shit in this car!" Damn if Raelean doesn't get an A in timing. She sits on the passenger door, elbows propped on the roof. Her red bra glows under her white tank top. "You sure you fixed the AC, Davis? Because if we get down in Alabama and suffocate, I'll hold you personally responsible."

He chuckles. "AC is good…for at least a few hundred miles."

Raelean frowns. He winks at me.

He grabs my hand, his dark skin against my pale. We stand there quiet, the emotion too thick to speak. "We would have been family. You know that, right?" he says and I look up into his glassy eyes, a tear slivering down his cheek.

"We already are family." I throw my arms around his neck and squeeze.

I know we will call and write and visit when we can. But I'm scared time and life will dull our shared loss. He'll find another to love eventually. She'll never compare to Adaire; not many could. Maybe our kids will know each other. Or maybe time will fade our bond. But right here, right now in our goodbye, he is a brother. The one I never had and don't plan to let go of.

"You take care of yourself, you here?" I say as I pull away, wiping away the teardrops I left on his uniform.

"You, too, Weatherly." Davis steps back and opens the car door for me. He replaced the battery, fixed the starter and the clutch. *A going-away gift*, he said. I am ever grateful.

I glance over to the only house I've ever known to say goodbye. Sitting there on the one-room smokehouse porch, Bone Layer rocks slowly in that old rocking chair of his, standing guard over Papaw and Adaire. How many years has he done this? How many more does he have left to keep doing it? The toil of the last few months has aged him more than the years and time.

I lean into the car to tell Raelean to give me a minute, but before I can speak, she says, "Go on. I'll wait."

I run over to Bone Layer and throw my arms around his neck. Nothing is really said, just thoughts of love and regret for never understanding this silent dutiful man. Grandmama wasn't the kindest, but she always made a home for Bone. I never considered what losing her meant to him. I want to say I'll be back soon, but it's a I promise I can't guarantee. Something tells me he may not even be here when I return.

Bone Layer's large hand cups around mine, dwarfing it to a child's size. "He will cover you with his feathers, and under his wings you will find refuge; his faithfulness will be your shield and rampart."

A loving expression warms my face. Psalms, one of the sacred Bible verses that only a Death Talker knows. I give him one more bear hug before heading back to the car.

As I walk over, a black crow feather quivers on the ground in the light breeze.

A wish on a crow feather.

"Hurry up and turn the AC on," Raelean says as I get in the car. "I'm going to have sweat rings under my titties if you don't."

I laugh. She digs the big atlas out from the back seat and cracks it open. "Where to first?"

I flip my visor down to tuck the feather underneath the rubber band and the Polaroid photo I found on the cave floor. The image is pretty dark. My hair and shoulder make up the majority of it. The camera captured a smattering of glowing blue speckles of light, like dust particles. But there's something more behind the tiny out-of-focus points of light. Right past my shoulder, a fanned blur, like the spreading of a wing.

And a ghostly face of a man floating behind it.

"We're going to Florida," I say to Raelean. "But first, I want to swing by Tennessee."

She watches me eyeing the photo. "Tennessee it is!"

I adjust my rearview mirror before setting the gear in Drive. I swear I can almost see ten-year-old Adaire there, standing next to my old pink pedal bike in the yard.

The faint sound of that bike's little bell *chings* goodbye.

EPILOGUE

Stone's Throw, Florida
Waffle House, Hwy 19

"Johnny?" Janice, the waitress, calls my name—a name I borrowed from a stolen lunch box.

From the rear of the diner, Janice holds her hand high to block the early-morning sun, shocked to see me asleep on the picnic table behind the diner I recently got a job at.

I close my eyes, savoring the last remnants of the dream I was having. She was there again, the green-eyed beauty that haunts my sleep. She's so real I swear I've touched her skin. Tasted her lips. Felt her body firm against mine.

"Are you going to lay there all morning or what?" Janice says as she stubs out her cigarette.

The back of the diner is reminiscent of every other truck stop I've ever worked. Discarded metal fixtures huddle desperately together along the dingy back wall. Cigarette butts scatter across on the crumbling pavement like a dead army. And that ever-present foul perfume of a dumpster hangs in the air.

I get up from my makeshift bed, no real answer to give her.

"I told Gordon your aunt was sick and you had to check on her," Janice says, following me in the rear kitchen door.

"Okay." I slip the busboy apron over my head.

"Okay? That's it? That's the second time this month I've caught you sleeping out back, late for your shift."

"Okay," I say again, because there's nothing more to say. I scoop up the gray tub and press my back against the kitchen's swinging door.

"Dude," Janice's harsh whisper causes me to pause. "How about a thank-you for covering for your ass?"

"Thanks." I push into the diner.

The chatter of patrons and the clank and scrapes on dishes swallows me in.

"Cool tattoo!" The little boy's squeaky voice an exclamation point among the diner's low rumbling chatter and the percussion of silverware scraping against plates.

His eyes hunger over the image inked on my forearm. My thanks is a half-grunt sound.

His mother turns her attention to my arm and frowns as her eyes pass over the bloody nails punctured through the crow's feet, disapproving of the artwork. From the hollow of the crow's body, I see the sorrowful beautiful eyes of the girl from my dreams.

"Hurry up and finish your milk," the mom snaps at the boy, and she quickly downs the last of her coffee.

I clear their table in appreciated silence. Disappearing as quickly as I appeared.

It's been a week or so of this now. Of simply being here; no more gaps of lost time, no more unexplained absences. When

I'm not looking for a place to sleep, I'm trying to figure out what happened and why's it's stopped.

Darkness falls upon the diner, the summer now fading into fall. I wait in the parking lot next to Janice. The half cigarette hanging from the side of her mouth burns my nose. She counts out a percentage of her tips for me.

"So, do you actually have a place to stay?" Janice asks after getting into her car. Eyes aglimmer as a sly smile pulls at her lips. Hope waits in the air. She could be my age, whatever that is, or a few years older. There's nothing unappealing about Janice, but nothing remarkable, either. Her offer and intentions clear, though. I'm uninterested in either.

I fold the bills and stow them in my back pocket, then douse her hope. "Yeah. Friend's couch. See ya tomorrow." I tuck my hands into the jacket I lifted from the diner's lost and found and walk away.

I don't get all the way across the parking lot before I hear a loud swear.

"Shit, shit, shit!"

I lightly glance over my shoulder toward the streetlamp. The silhouette of a young woman swatting at the smoke plumes steaming from underneath her hood. A few more swears fly when she burns her hand popping open the hood.

I duck my head and mind my business when an "Excuse me!" calls from near the car.

I close my eyes, mumbling my own swear. Just wanting to put my tired head on a lumpy pillow at the motel I found a room at after calling around this afternoon.

"Do you know anything about cars?" she asks me. As much as I'd like to pretend she's not talking to me, I am the only person left in the parking lot.

Reluctantly, I turn back around. I've never owned a car, but I've worked at enough truck stops to pick up a few helpful tricks or two.

"Thank you so much," she says as I get closer. "I swear this car is more trouble than it's worth."

"It might be overheated." I step under the streetlight to get a closer look.

My heart stutters at the sight of her. There, standing before me, is the girl who's haunted my dreams ever since I was a child.

"Rook?"

★ ★ ★ ★ ★

ACKNOWLEDGMENTS

To my agent, Jill Marr, thank you for falling in love with this book, for your enthusiasm, for believing in me and my writing. You expected great things and delivered big-time. I am ever grateful. And I could not be more thrilled to work with you on the many more books to come.

To my editor, Meredith Clark, thank you for your sharp editing eye, for loving this book and seeing it's potential, for just wanting more of the story. *Damn if* you didn't have a lot of pesky word repeats and weird phrase repetitions to weed out. From the *pit of my stomach*, I want to thank you with all my *hammering heart*. ;)

And to the entire Mira team, thank you for loving this story and helping it make its way into the world.

To CJ Redwine, for reaching out a hand and lifting me up in one of the hardest moments of my career. For showing me kindness and love. And giving me the courage to keep going. For that I am forever grateful.

To Valerie Cole, for reading those early drafts and cheering me on, for supporting me through my hardest times. Your friendship and loyalty have meant the world to me. Be the boat.

To my Tennessee girls: Jackie, Lisa, Cat, Emily, Belinda, and Michelle. You did absolutely nothing to help me write this book, but you wanted your name in my book, so here you go. "It ain't rude if it's true." Our epic girl trips have given me all the joy and laughter I needed between writing. Love you bitches!

To Heather Demetrios, my writer's coach, my friend, this book would not exist without your keen insight. You saw my potential to write something special even before I could. You taught me how to dig deep and find the words only I could write. I am ever grateful for the work we did together. Thank you for teaching me how to trust myself, so I could take my writing to the next level.

To my daddy, your love and support my entire life has meant the world to me. Nothing brings me more happiness than porch sitting with you. I love you, Daddy.

To my dearest friend Evelyn Skye, I cherish every ounce of our friendship. You have stood by my side through the thickest of it. Thank you for reading those early drafts and helping me find the story.

To my boys Luke and Jackson, who have never read one of my books, I love you with all my soul. Now what do you want Momma to cook you?

To my husband, Chris, for always supporting me and believing I could do it. I love you.